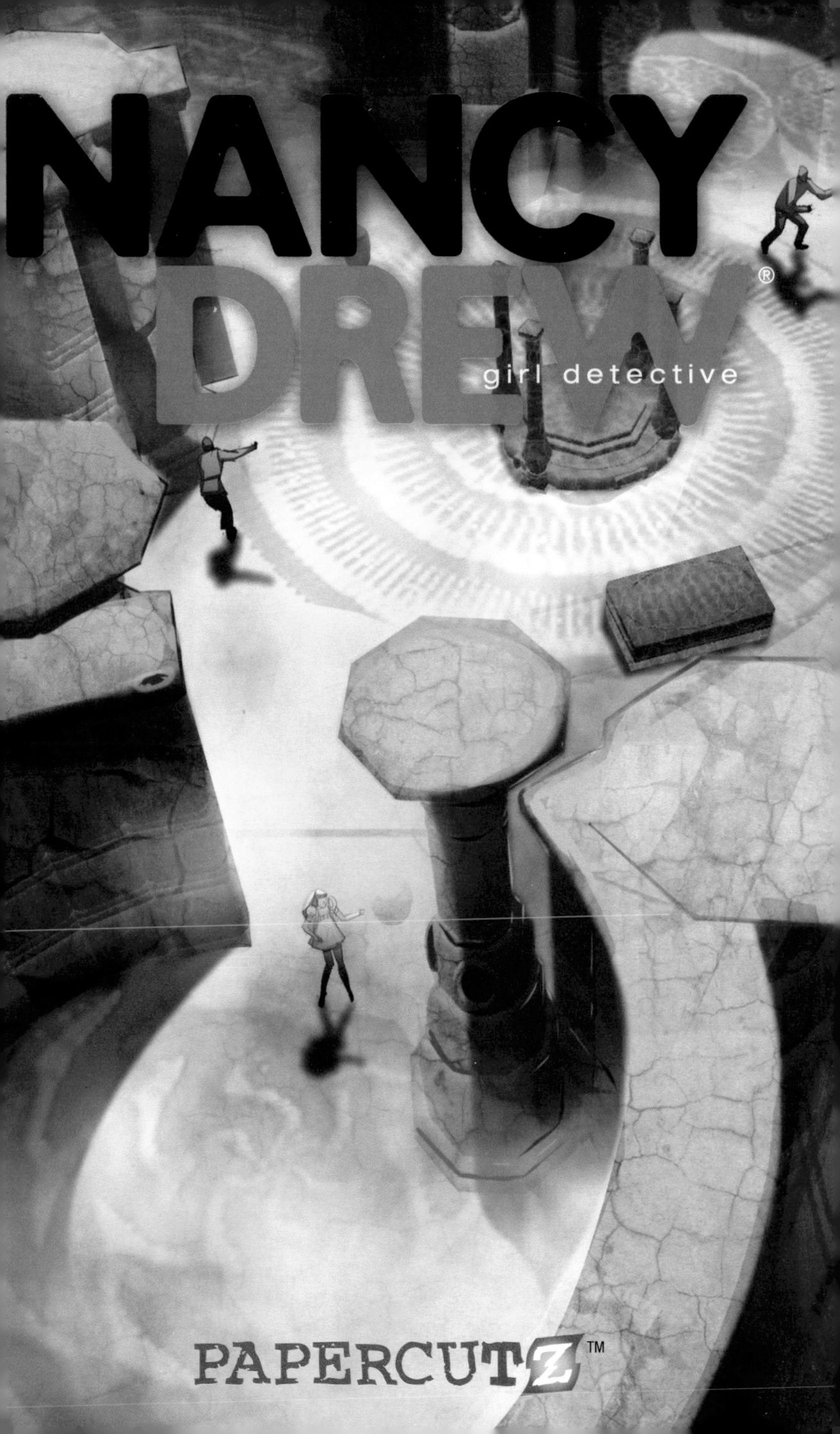
NANCY DREW®
girl detective
PAPERCUTZ™

NANCY DREW GRAPHIC NOVELS AVAILABLE FROM PAPERCUTZ

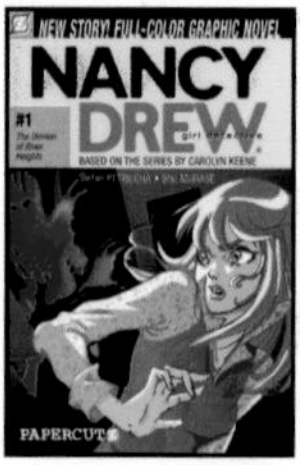
NEW STORY! FULL-COLOR GRAPHIC NOVEL
NANCY DREW
BASED ON THE SERIES BY CAROLYN KEENE
PAPERCUTZ

#1 “The Demon of River Heights”

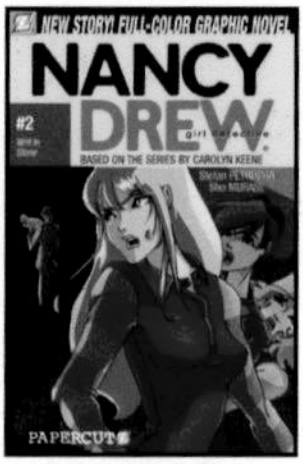
NEW STORY! FULL-COLOR GRAPHIC NOVEL
NANCY DREW
BASED ON THE SERIES BY CAROLYN KEENE
PAPERCUTZ

#2 “Writ In Stone”

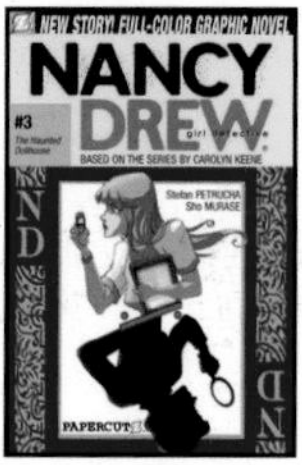
NEW STORY! FULL-COLOR GRAPHIC NOVEL
NANCY DREW
BASED ON THE SERIES BY CAROLYN KEENE
PAPERCUTZ

#3 “The Haunted Dollhouse"

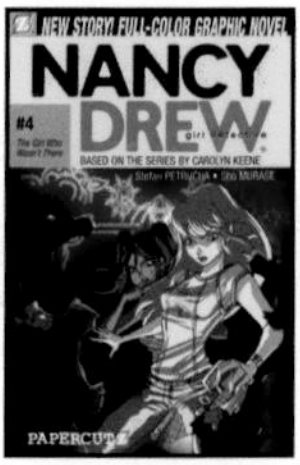
NEW STORY! FULL-COLOR GRAPHIC NOVEL
NANCY DREW
BASED ON THE SERIES BY CAROLYN KEENE
PAPERCUTZ

#4 “The Girl Who Wasn't There"

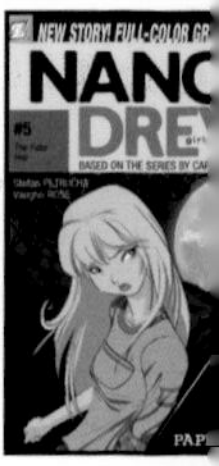

#5 “Th Fake He.

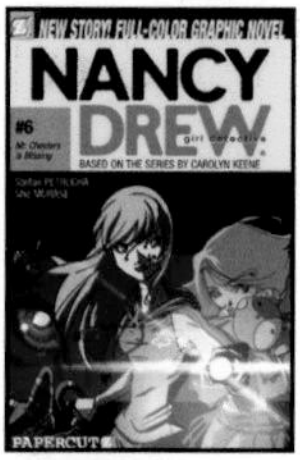
NEW STORY! FULL-COLOR GRAPHIC NOVEL
NANCY DREW
BASED ON THE SERIES BY CAROLYN KEENE
PAPERCUTZ

#6 “Mr. Cheeters Is Missing”

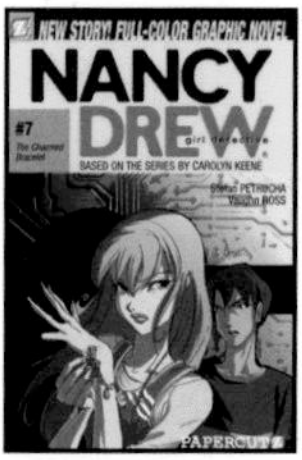
NEW STORY! FULL-COLOR GRAPHIC NOVEL
NANCY DREW
BASED ON THE SERIES BY CAROLYN KEENE
PAPERCUTZ

#7 “The Charmed Bracelet"

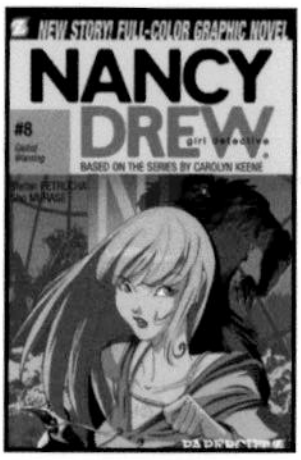
NEW STORY! FULL-COLOR GRAPHIC NOVEL
NANCY DREW
BASED ON THE SERIES BY CAROLYN KEENE

#8 “Global Warning"

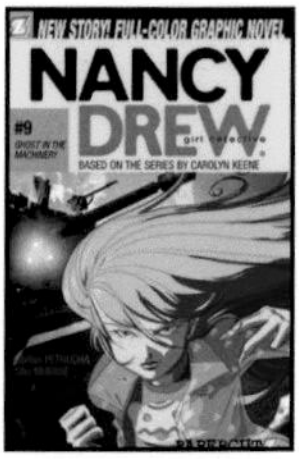
NEW STORY! FULL-COLOR GRAPHIC NOVEL
NANCY DREW
BASED ON THE SERIES BY CAROLYN KEENE

#9 “Ghost In The Machinery"

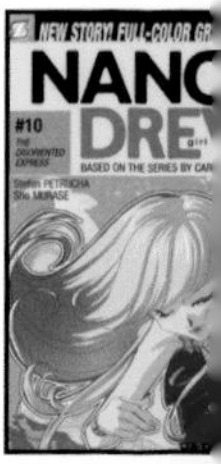

#10 “The Disc ed Expres

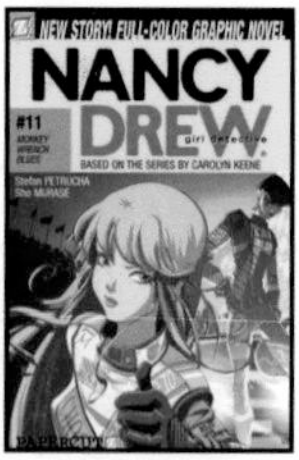
NEW STORY! FULL-COLOR GRAPHIC NOVEL
NANCY DREW
BASED ON THE SERIES BY CAROLYN KEENE
PAPERCUTZ

#11 “Monkey Wrench Blues"

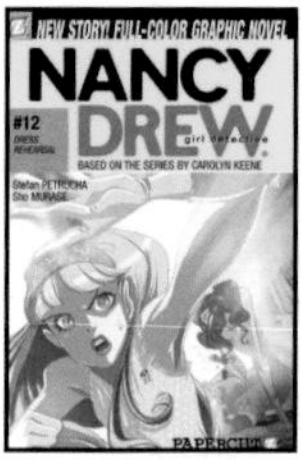
NEW STORY! FULL-COLOR GRAPHIC NOVEL
NANCY DREW
BASED ON THE SERIES BY CAROLYN KEENE
PAPERCUTZ

#12 “Dress Reversal"

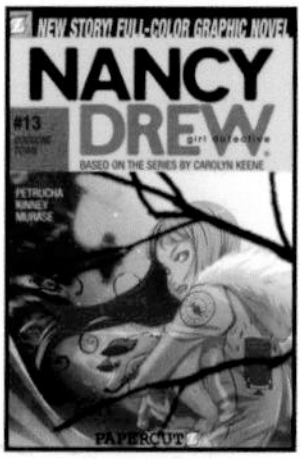
NEW STORY! FULL-COLOR GRAPHIC NOVEL
NANCY DREW
BASED ON THE SERIES BY CAROLYN KEENE
PAPERCUTZ

#13 “Doggone Town”

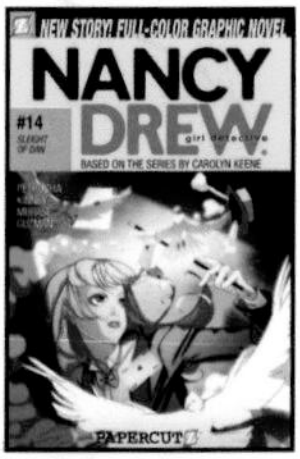
NEW STORY! FULL-COLOR GRAPHIC NOVEL
NANCY DREW
BASED ON THE SERIES BY CAROLYN KEENE
PAPERCUTZ

#14 “Sleight of Dan”

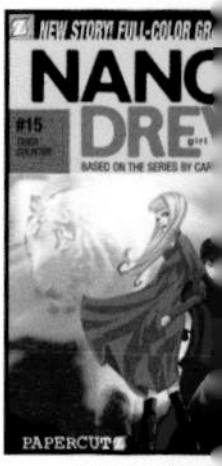
PAPERCUTZ

#15 “Tige Counter”

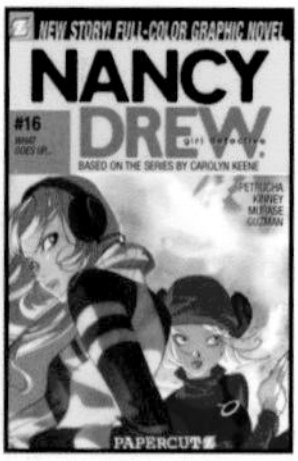
NEW STORY! FULL-COLOR GRAPHIC NOVEL
NANCY DREW
BASED ON THE SERIES BY CAROLYN KEENE
PAPERCUTZ

#16 “What Goes Up...”

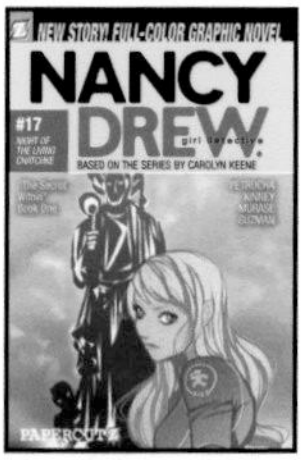
NEW STORY! FULL-COLOR GRAPHIC NOVEL
NANCY DREW
BASED ON THE SERIES BY CAROLYN KEENE
PAPERCUTZ

#17 “Night of the Living Chatchke”

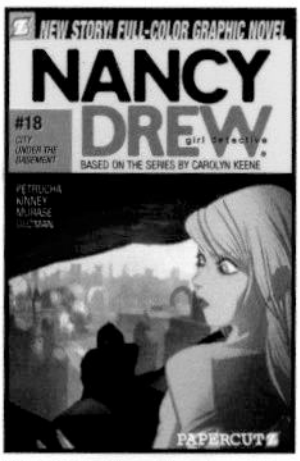
NEW STORY! FULL-COLOR GRAPHIC NOVEL
NANCY DREW
BASED ON THE SERIES BY CAROLYN KEENE
PAPERCUTZ

#18 “City Under the Basement”

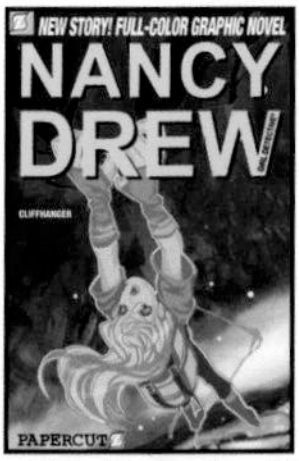
NEW STORY! FULL-COLOR GRAPHIC NOVEL
NANCY DREW
CLIFFHANGER
PAPERCUTZ

Coming November '09
#19 “Cliffhanger”

$7.95 each in paperback, $12.95 each in hardcover. Please add $4.00 for postage and handling for the book, add $1.00 for each additional book. Please make check payable to NBM Publishing. Send to:

Papercutz, 40 Exchange Place, Suite 1308, New York, NY 10005, 1-800-886-1223

www.papercutz.com

NANCY DREW

#18

DREW

girl detective ®

City Under the Basement

STEFAN PETRUCHA & SARAH KINNEY • Writers
SHO MURASE • Artist
with 3D CG elements and color by CARLOS JOSE GUZMAN
Based on the series by
CAROLYN KEENE

PAPERCUT Z™

New York

City Under the Basement
STEFAN PETRUCHA & SARAH KINNEY – Writers
SHO MURASE – Artist
with 3D CG elements and color by CARLOS JOSE GUZMAN
BRYAN SENKA – Letterer
MIKHAELA REID and MASHEKA WOOD – Production
MICHAEL PETRANEK - Editorial Assistant
JIM SALICRUP
Editor-in-Chief

ISBN 10: 1-59707-154-4 paperback edition
ISBN 13: 978-1-59707-154-3 paperback edition
ISBN 10: 1-59707-155-2 hardcover edition
ISBN 13: 978-1-59707-155-0 hardcover edition

Printed in China.
April 2009 by WKT Co. LTD.
3/F Phase I Leader Industrial Centre
188 Texaco Road, Tseun Wan, N.T.
Hong Kong

Distributed by Macmillan.

10   9   8   7   6   5   4   3   2   1

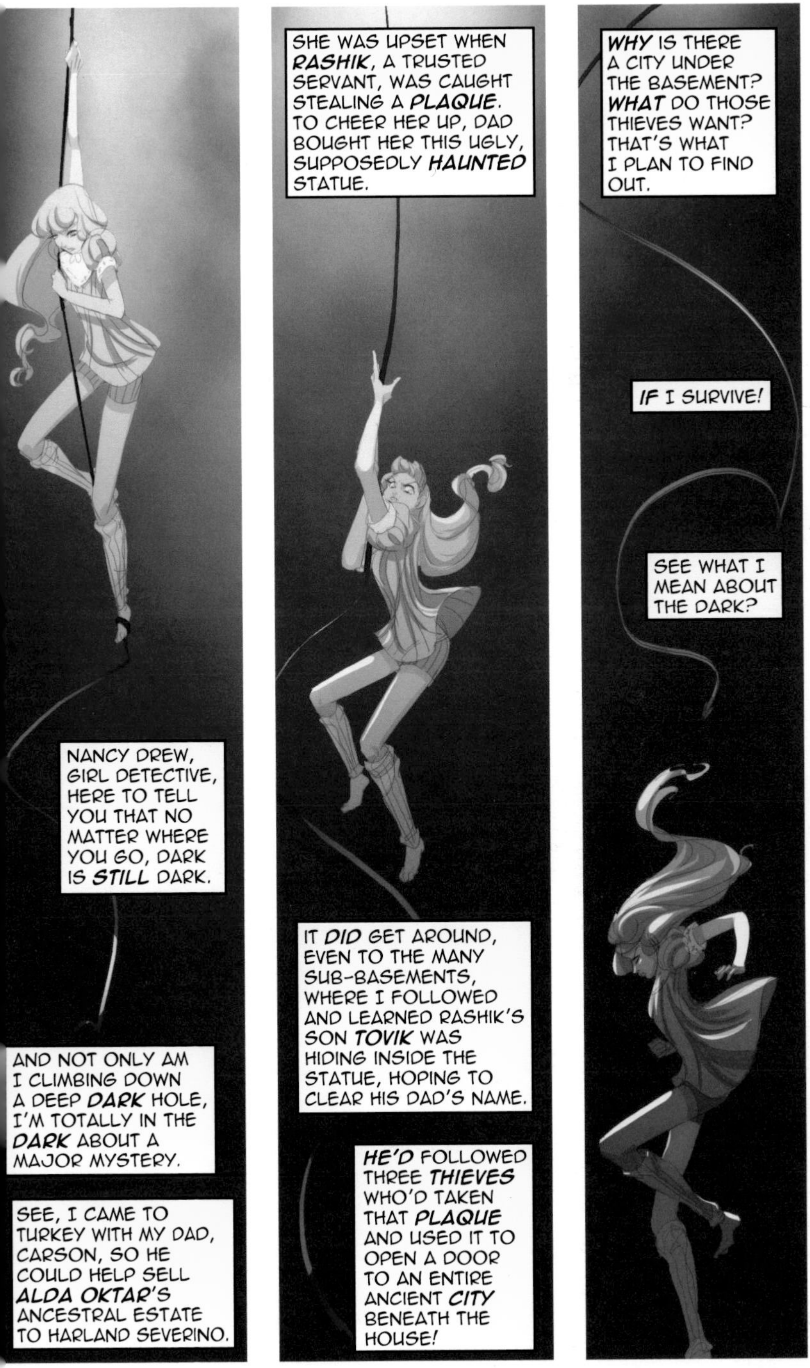
NANCY DREW, GIRL DETECTIVE, HERE TO TELL YOU THAT NO MATTER WHERE YOU GO, DARK IS *STILL* DARK.
AND NOT ONLY AM I CLIMBING DOWN A DEEP *DARK* HOLE, I'M TOTALLY IN THE *DARK* ABOUT A MAJOR MYSTERY.
SEE, I CAME TO TURKEY WITH MY DAD, CARSON, SO HE COULD HELP SELL *ALDA OKTAR*'S ANCESTRAL ESTATE TO HARLAND SEVERINO.
SHE WAS UPSET WHEN *RASHIK*, A TRUSTED SERVANT, WAS CAUGHT STEALING A *PLAQUE*. TO CHEER HER UP, DAD BOUGHT HER THIS UGLY, SUPPOSEDLY *HAUNTED* STATUE.
IT *DID* GET AROUND, EVEN TO THE MANY SUB-BASEMENTS, WHERE I FOLLOWED AND LEARNED RASHIK'S SON *TOVIK* WAS HIDING INSIDE THE STATUE, HOPING TO CLEAR HIS DAD'S NAME.
HE'D FOLLOWED THREE *THIEVES* WHO'D TAKEN THAT *PLAQUE* AND USED IT TO OPEN A DOOR TO AN ENTIRE ANCIENT *CITY* BENEATH THE HOUSE!
WHY IS THERE A CITY UNDER THE BASEMENT? *WHAT* DO THOSE THIEVES WANT? THAT'S WHAT I PLAN TO FIND OUT.
IF I SURVIVE!
SEE WHAT I MEAN ABOUT THE DARK?

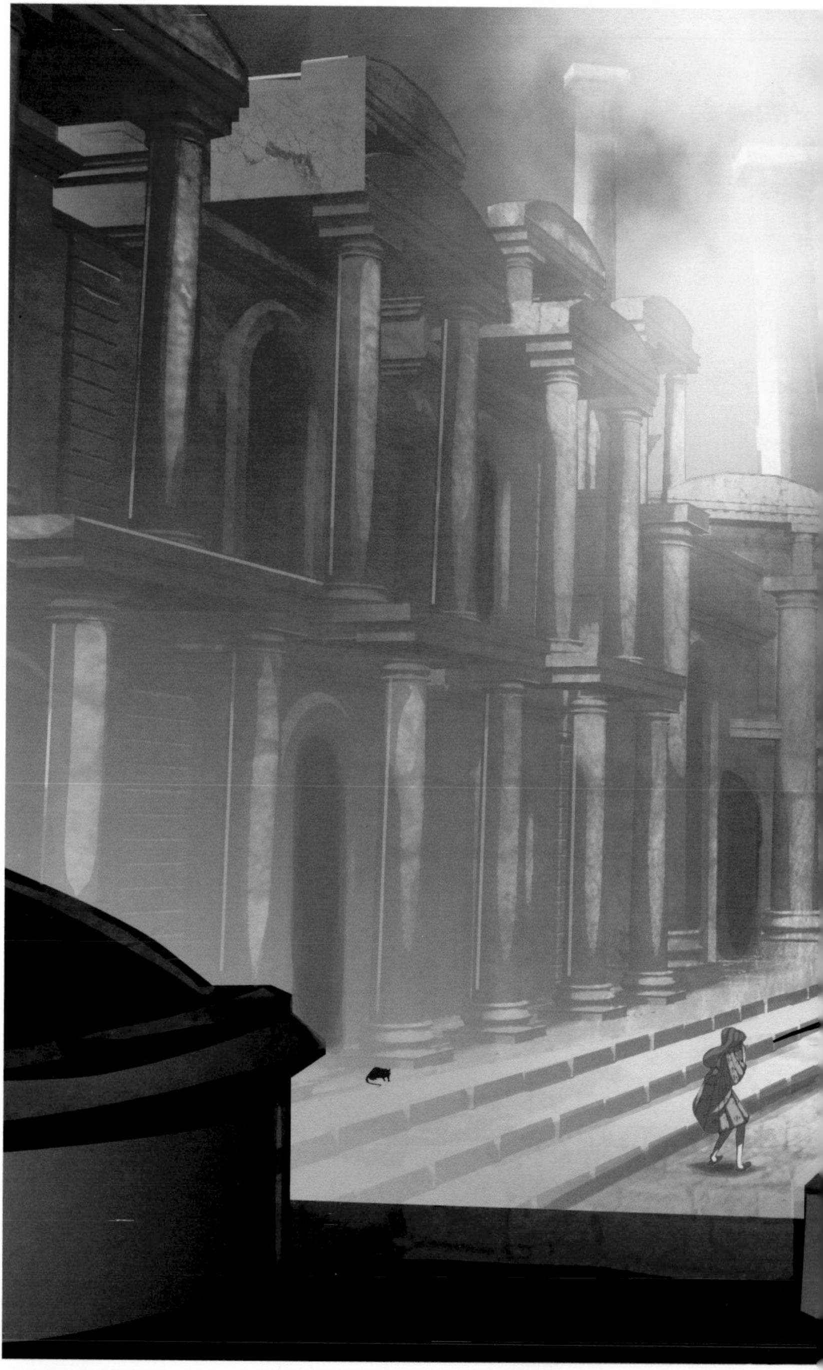

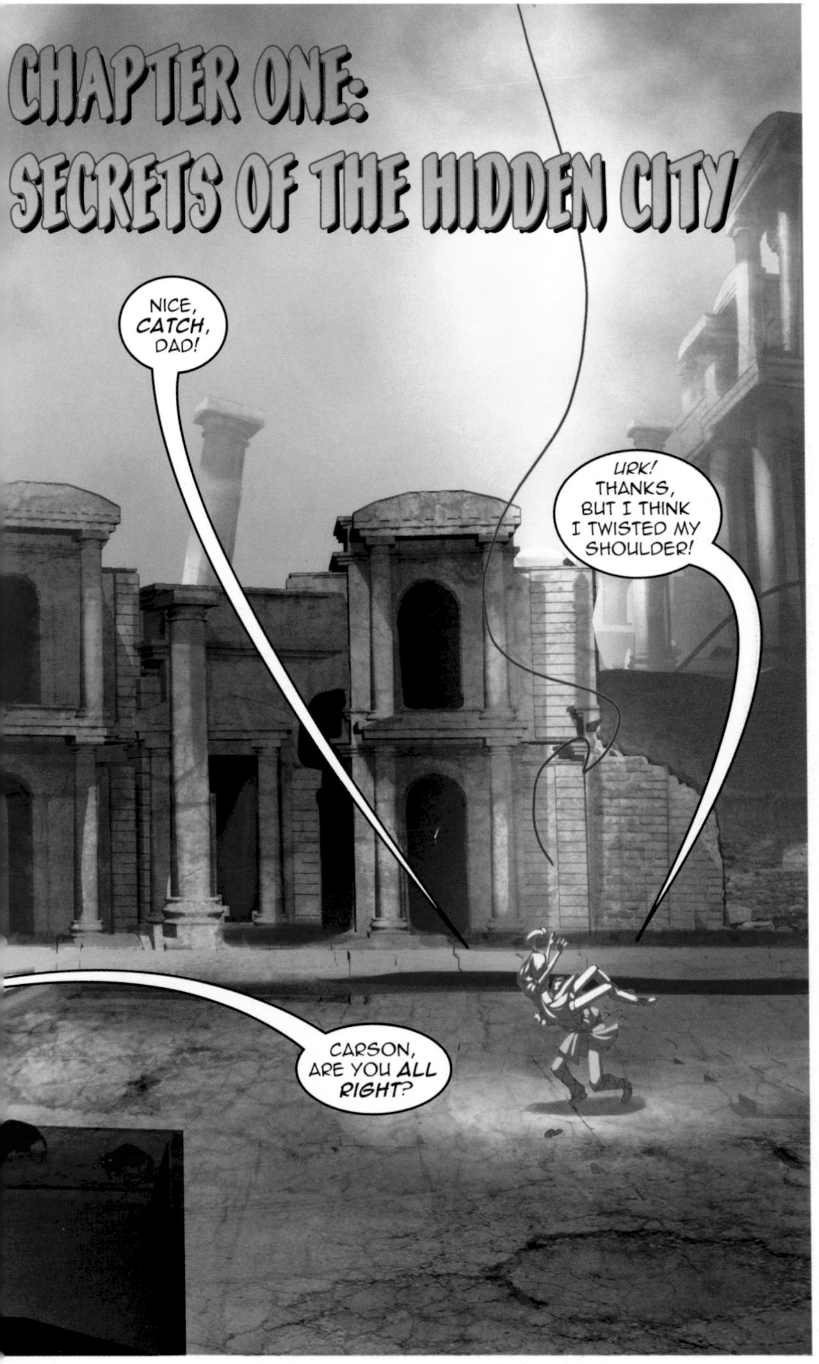
CHAPTER ONE:
SECRETS OF THE HIDDEN CITY
NICE, CATCH, DAD!
URK! THANKS, BUT I THINK I TWISTED MY SHOULDER!
CARSON, ARE YOU ALL RIGHT?

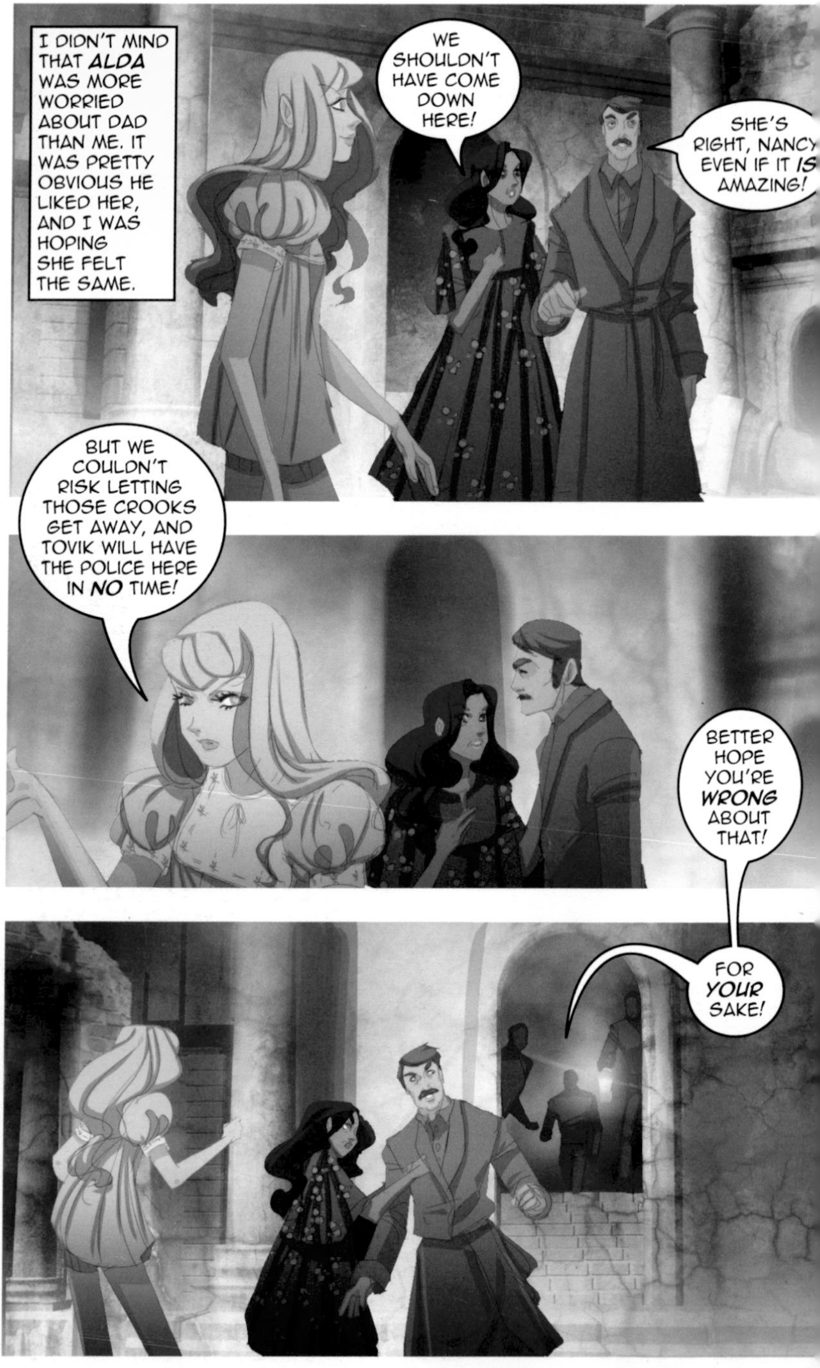
I DIDN'T MIND THAT ALDA WAS MORE WORRIED ABOUT DAD THAN ME. IT WAS PRETTY OBVIOUS HE LIKED HER, AND I WAS HOPING SHE FELT THE SAME.
WE SHOULDN'T HAVE COME DOWN HERE!
SHE'S RIGHT, NANCY EVEN IF IT IS AMAZING!
BUT WE COULDN'T RISK LETTING THOSE CROOKS GET AWAY, AND TOVIK WILL HAVE THE POLICE HERE IN NO TIME!
BETTER HOPE YOU'RE WRONG ABOUT THAT!
FOR YOUR SAKE!

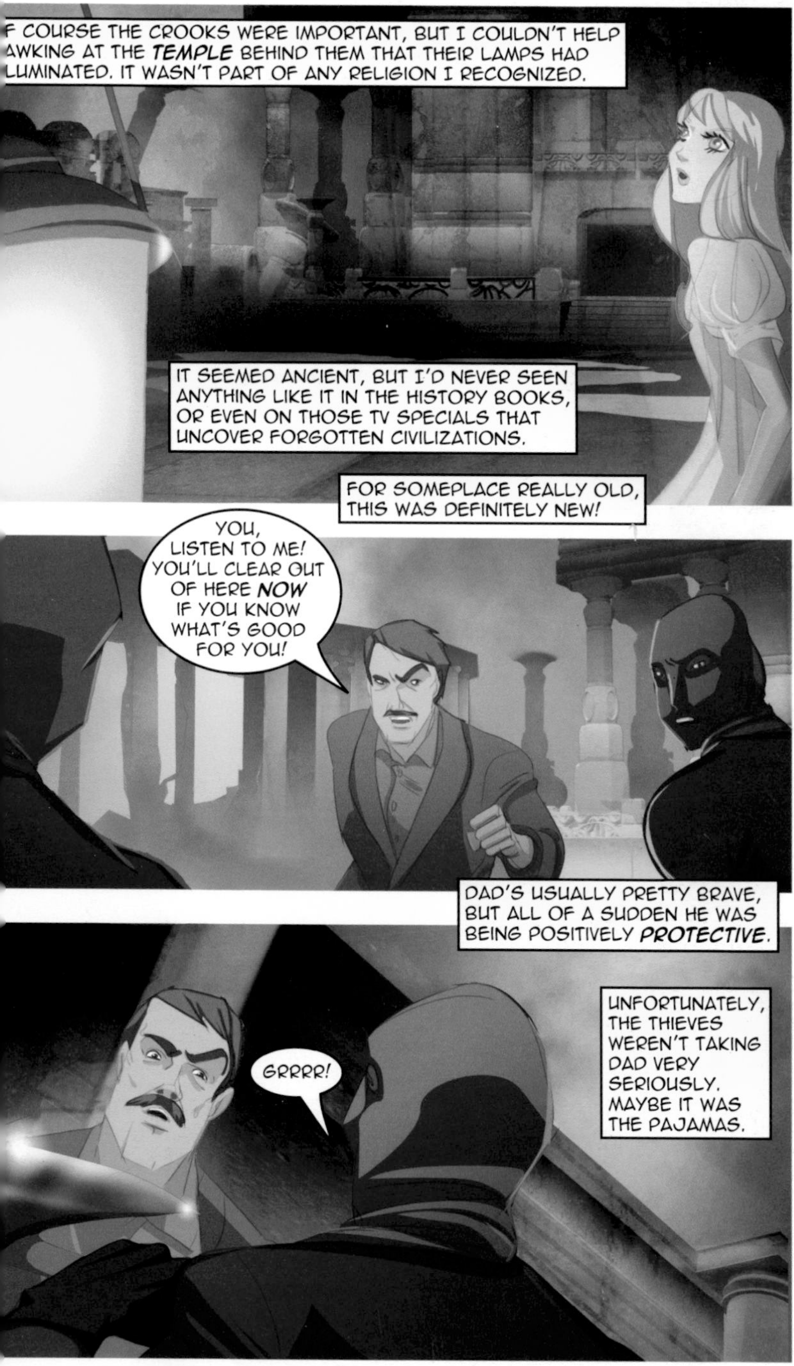
F COURSE THE CROOKS WERE IMPORTANT, BUT I COULDN'T HELP AWKING AT THE *TEMPLE* BEHIND THEM THAT THEIR LAMPS HAD LUMINATED. IT WASN'T PART OF ANY RELIGION I RECOGNIZED.
IT SEEMED ANCIENT, BUT I'D NEVER SEEN ANYTHING LIKE IT IN THE HISTORY BOOKS, OR EVEN ON THOSE TV SPECIALS THAT UNCOVER FORGOTTEN CIVILIZATIONS.
FOR SOMEPLACE REALLY OLD, THIS WAS DEFINITELY NEW!
YOU, LISTEN TO ME! YOU'LL CLEAR OUT OF HERE *NOW* IF YOU KNOW WHAT'S GOOD FOR YOU!
DAD'S USUALLY PRETTY BRAVE, BUT ALL OF A SUDDEN HE WAS BEING POSITIVELY *PROTECTIVE*.
UNFORTUNATELY, THE THIEVES WEREN'T TAKING DAD VERY SERIOUSLY. MAYBE IT WAS THE PAJAMAS.
GRRRR!

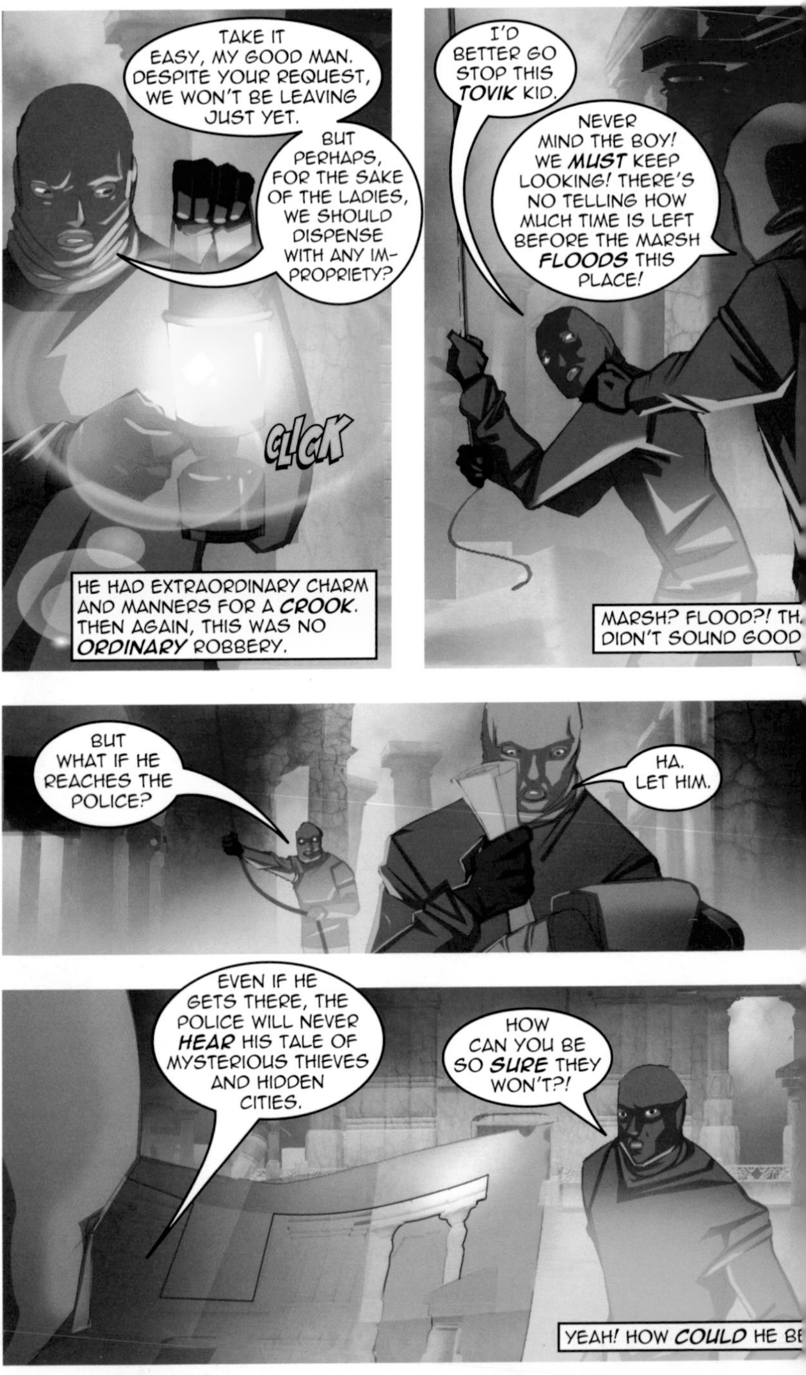
TAKE IT EASY, MY GOOD MAN. DESPITE YOUR REQUEST, WE WON'T BE LEAVING JUST YET.
BUT PERHAPS, FOR THE SAKE OF THE LADIES, WE SHOULD DISPENSE WITH ANY IM-PROPRIETY?
CLICK
HE HAD EXTRAORDINARY CHARM AND MANNERS FOR A CROOK. THEN AGAIN, THIS WAS NO ORDINARY ROBBERY.
I'D BETTER GO STOP THIS TOVIK KID.
NEVER MIND THE BOY! WE MUST KEEP LOOKING! THERE'S NO TELLING HOW MUCH TIME IS LEFT BEFORE THE MARSH FLOODS THIS PLACE!
MARSH? FLOOD?! TH
DIDN'T SOUND GOOD
BUT WHAT IF HE REACHES THE POLICE?
HA. LET HIM.
EVEN IF HE GETS THERE, THE POLICE WILL NEVER HEAR HIS TALE OF MYSTERIOUS THIEVES AND HIDDEN CITIES.
HOW CAN YOU BE SO SURE THEY WON'T?!
YEAH! HOW COULD HE BE

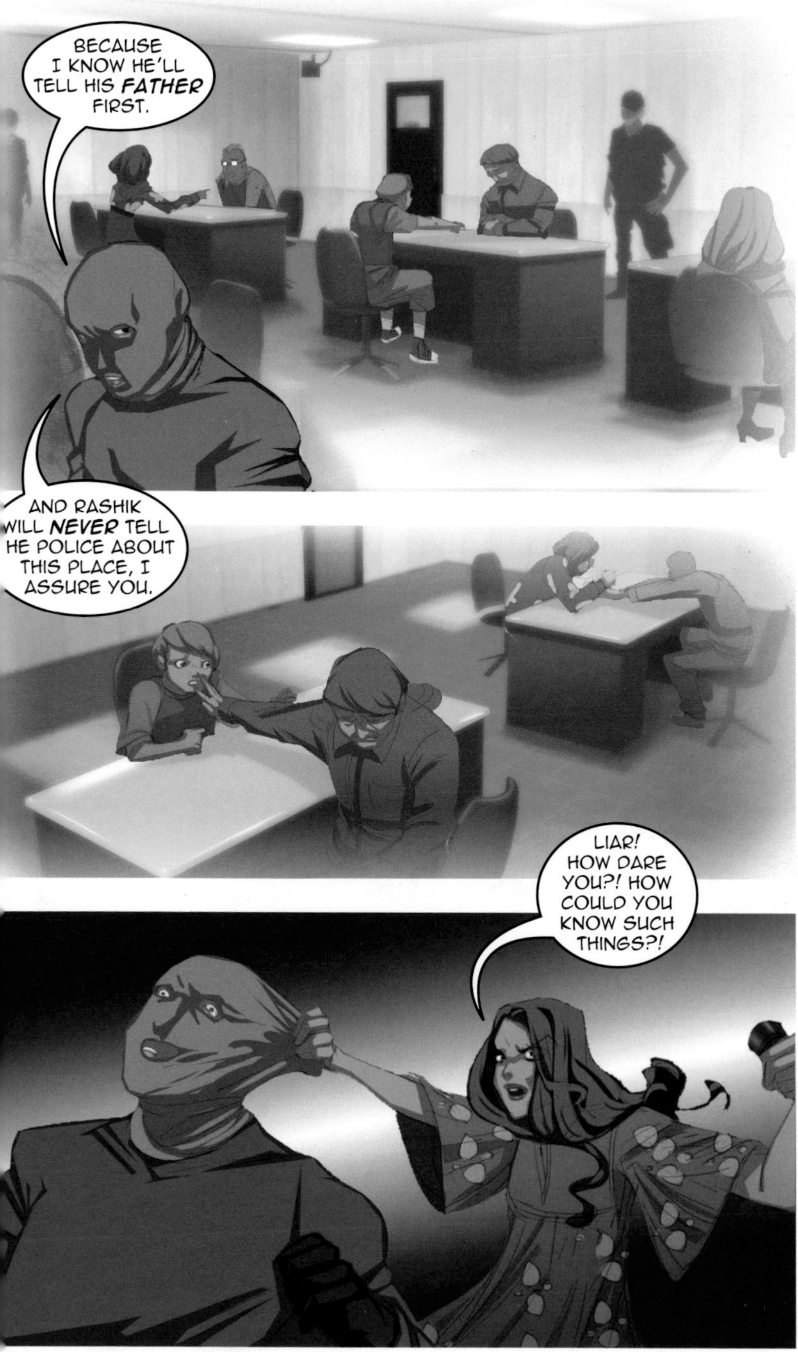

BECAUSE I KNOW HE'LL TELL HIS FATHER FIRST.
AND RASHIK WILL NEVER TELL HE POLICE ABOUT THIS PLACE, I ASSURE YOU.
LIAR! HOW DARE YOU?! HOW COULD YOU KNOW SUCH THINGS?!

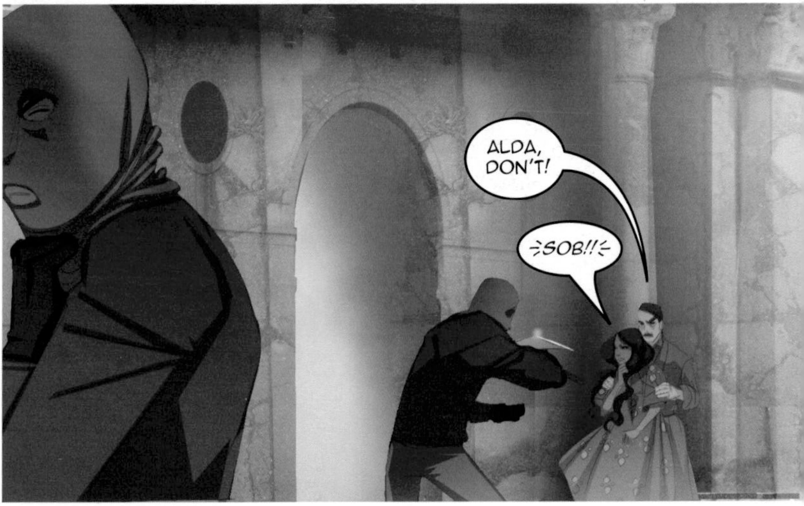
ALDA, DON'T!
≈SOB!!≈

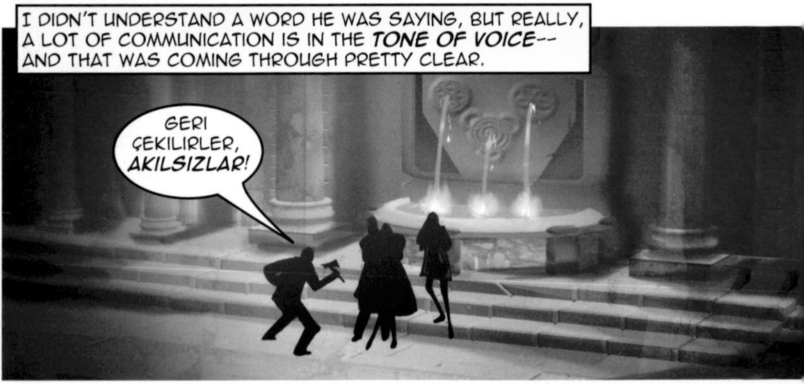
I DIDN'T UNDERSTAND A WORD HE WAS SAYING, BUT REALLY, A LOT OF COMMUNICATION IS IN THE *TONE OF VOICE*-- AND THAT WAS COMING THROUGH PRETTY CLEAR.
GERI ÇEKILIRLER, *AKILSIZLAR*!

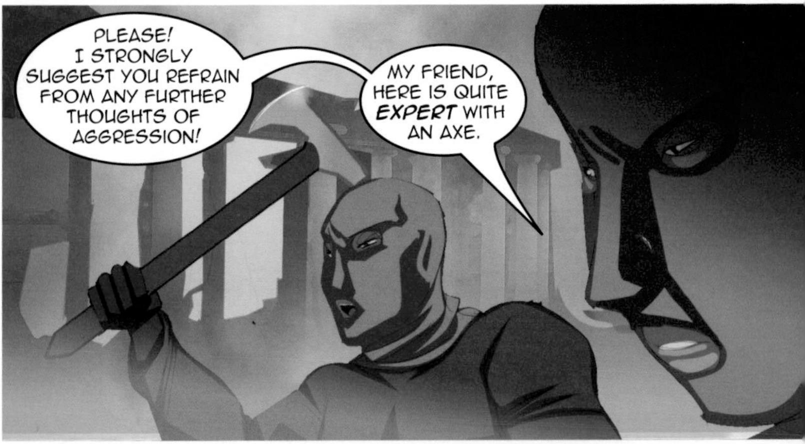
PLEASE! I STRONGLY SUGGEST YOU REFRAIN FROM ANY FURTHER THOUGHTS OF AGGRESSION!
MY FRIEND, HERE IS QUITE *EXPERT* WITH AN AXE.

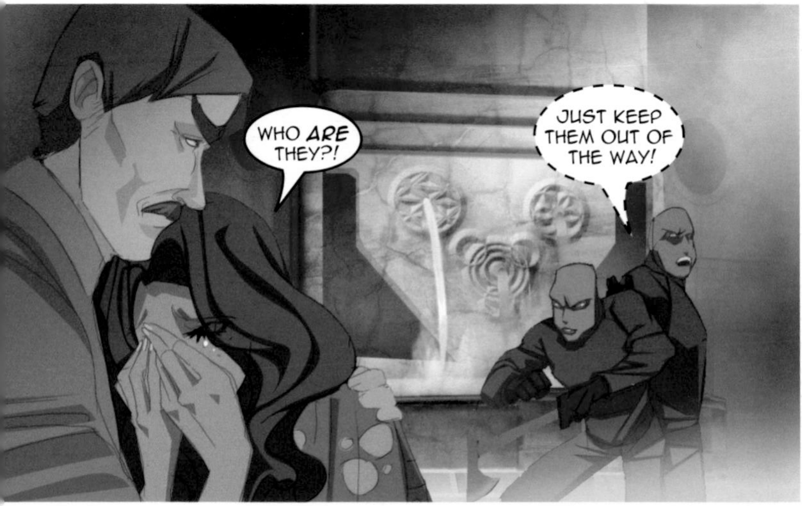
WHO ARE THEY?!
JUST KEEP THEM OUT OF THE WAY!

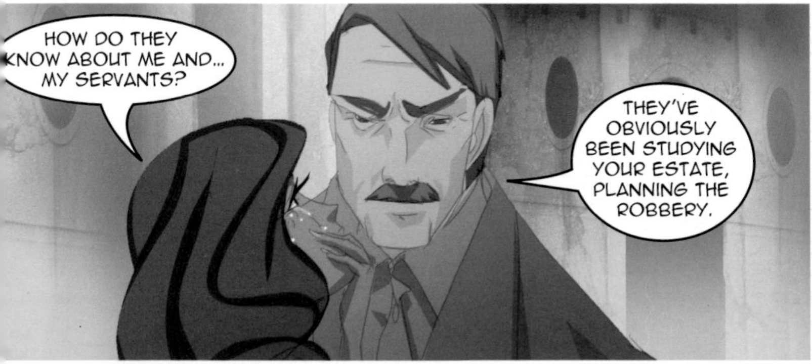
HOW DO THEY KNOW ABOUT ME AND... MY SERVANTS?
THEY'VE OBVIOUSLY BEEN STUDYING YOUR ESTATE, PLANNING THE ROBBERY.

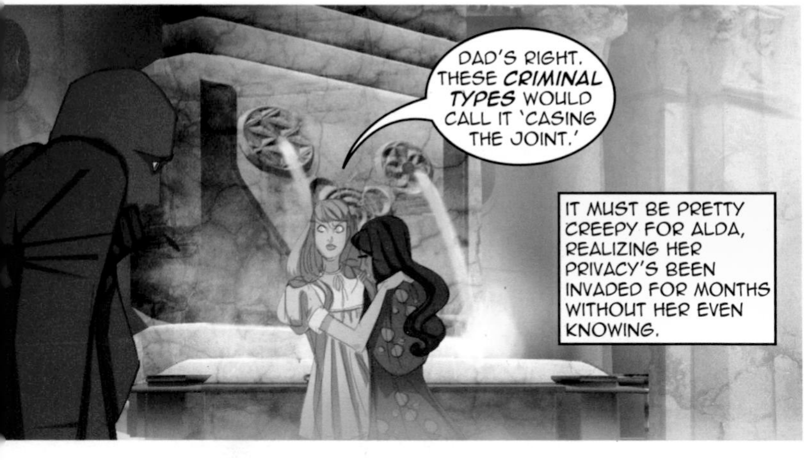
DAD'S RIGHT. THESE CRIMINAL TYPES WOULD CALL IT 'CASING THE JOINT.'
IT MUST BE PRETTY CREEPY FOR ALDA, REALIZING HER PRIVACY'S BEEN INVADED FOR MONTHS WITHOUT HER EVEN KNOWING.

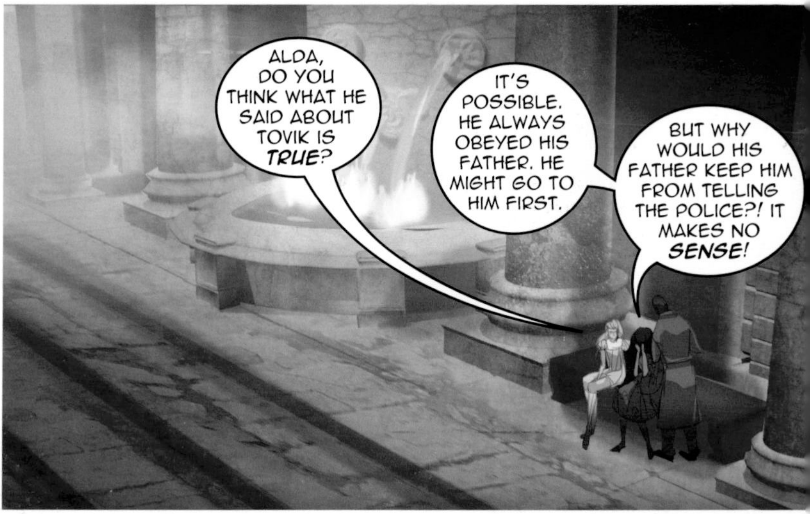
ALDA, DO YOU THINK WHAT HE SAID ABOUT TOVIK IS TRUE?
IT'S POSSIBLE. HE ALWAYS OBEYED HIS FATHER. HE MIGHT GO TO HIM FIRST.
BUT WHY WOULD HIS FATHER KEEP HIM FROM TELLING THE POLICE?! IT MAKES NO SENSE!

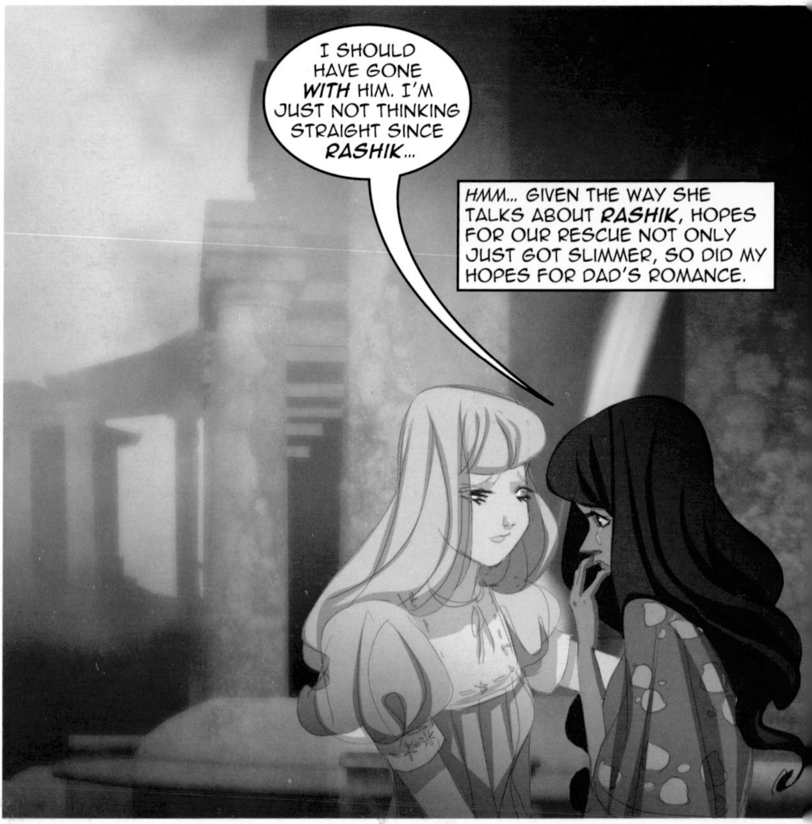
I SHOULD HAVE GONE WITH HIM. I'M JUST NOT THINKING STRAIGHT SINCE RASHIK...
HMM... GIVEN THE WAY SHE TALKS ABOUT RASHIK, HOPES FOR OUR RESCUE NOT ONLY JUST GOT SLIMMER, SO DID MY HOPES FOR DAD'S ROMANCE.

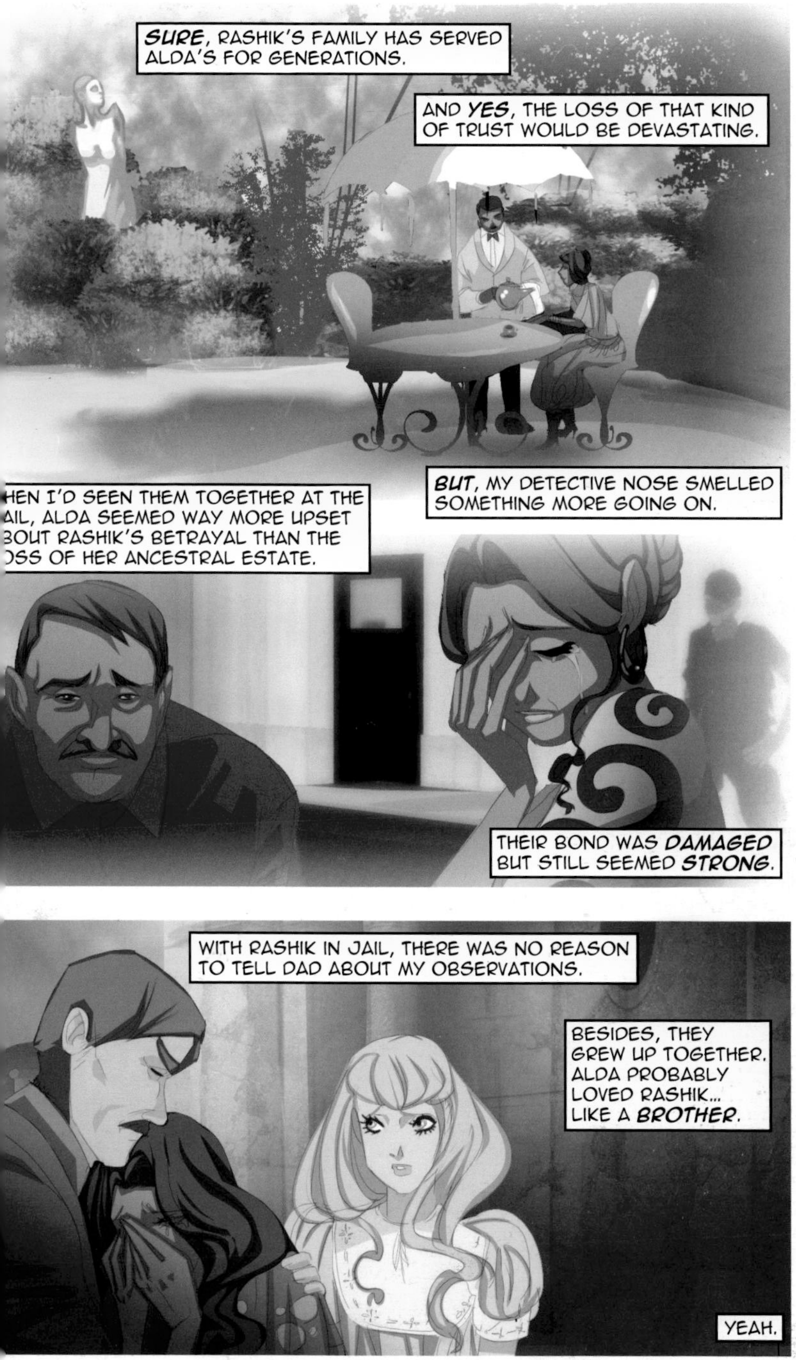
SURE, RASHIK'S FAMILY HAS SERVED ALDA'S FOR GENERATIONS.
AND YES, THE LOSS OF THAT KIND OF TRUST WOULD BE DEVASTATING.
BUT, MY DETECTIVE NOSE SMELLED SOMETHING MORE GOING ON.
HEN I'D SEEN THEM TOGETHER AT THE AIL, ALDA SEEMED WAY MORE UPSET BOUT RASHIK'S BETRAYAL THAN THE OSS OF HER ANCESTRAL ESTATE.
THEIR BOND WAS DAMAGED BUT STILL SEEMED STRONG.
WITH RASHIK IN JAIL, THERE WAS NO REASON TO TELL DAD ABOUT MY OBSERVATIONS.
BESIDES, THEY GREW UP TOGETHER. ALDA PROBABLY LOVED RASHIK... LIKE A BROTHER.
YEAH.

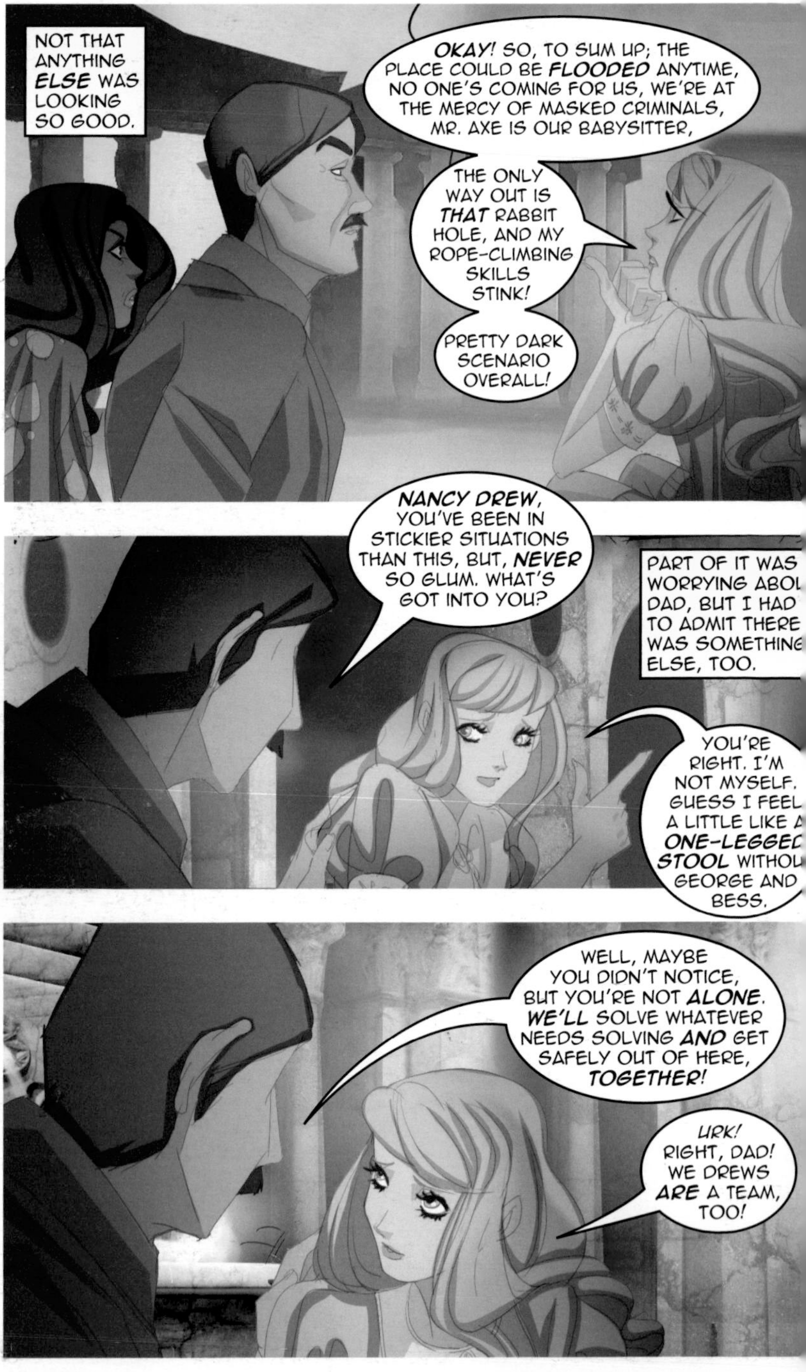

NOT THAT ANYTHING *ELSE* WAS LOOKING SO GOOD.
OKAY! SO, TO SUM UP; THE PLACE COULD BE *FLOODED* ANYTIME, NO ONE'S COMING FOR US, WE'RE AT THE MERCY OF MASKED CRIMINALS, MR. AXE IS OUR BABYSITTER,
THE ONLY WAY OUT IS *THAT* RABBIT HOLE, AND MY ROPE-CLIMBING SKILLS STINK!
PRETTY DARK SCENARIO OVERALL!
NANCY DREW, YOU'VE BEEN IN STICKIER SITUATIONS THAN THIS, BUT, *NEVER* SO GLUM. WHAT'S GOT INTO YOU?
PART OF IT WAS WORRYING ABO DAD, BUT I HAD TO ADMIT THERE WAS SOMETHING ELSE, TOO.
YOU'RE RIGHT. I'M NOT MYSELF. GUESS I FEEL A LITTLE LIKE A *ONE-LEGGED STOOL* WITHOU GEORGE AND BESS.
WELL, MAYBE YOU DIDN'T NOTICE, BUT YOU'RE NOT *ALONE*. *WE'LL* SOLVE WHATEVER NEEDS SOLVING *AND* GET SAFELY OUT OF HERE, *TOGETHER!*
URK! RIGHT, DAD! WE DREWS *ARE* A TEAM, TOO!

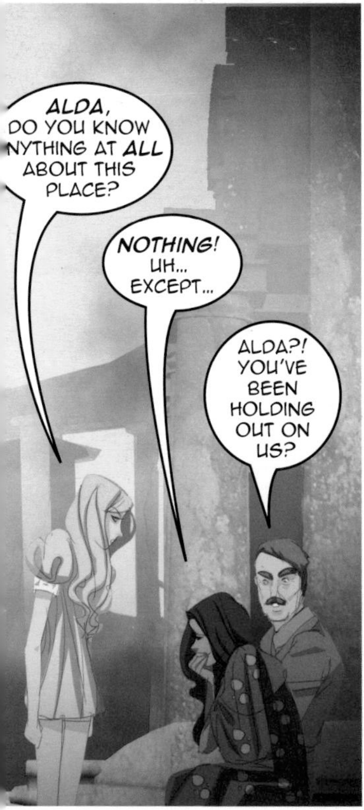
ALDA, DO YOU KNOW NYTHING AT ALL ABOUT THIS PLACE?
NOTHING! UH... EXCEPT...
ALDA?! YOU'VE BEEN HOLDING OUT ON US?

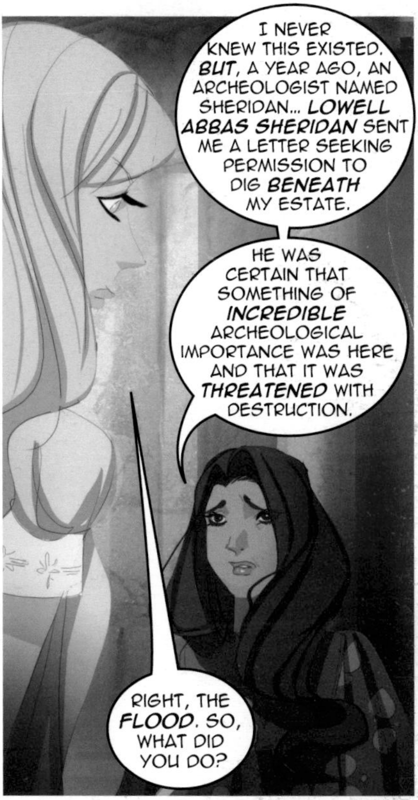
I NEVER KNEW THIS EXISTED. BUT, A YEAR AGO, AN ARCHEOLOGIST NAMED SHERIDAN... LOWELL ABBAS SHERIDAN SENT ME A LETTER SEEKING PERMISSION TO DIG BENEATH MY ESTATE.
HE WAS CERTAIN THAT SOMETHING OF INCREDIBLE ARCHEOLOGICAL IMPORTANCE WAS HERE AND THAT IT WAS THREATENED WITH DESTRUCTION.
RIGHT, THE FLOOD. SO, WHAT DID YOU DO?

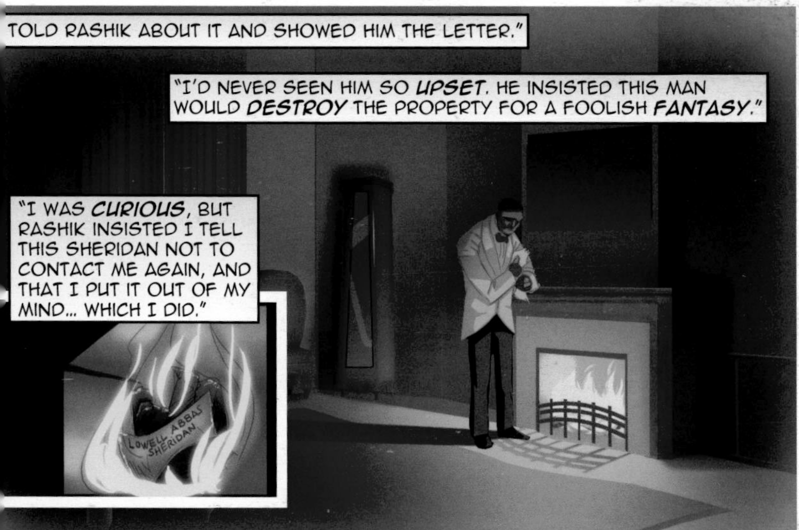
TOLD RASHIK ABOUT IT AND SHOWED HIM THE LETTER."
"I'D NEVER SEEN HIM SO UPSET. HE INSISTED THIS MAN WOULD DESTROY THE PROPERTY FOR A FOOLISH FANTASY."
"I WAS CURIOUS, BUT RASHIK INSISTED I TELL THIS SHERIDAN NOT TO CONTACT ME AGAIN, AND THAT I PUT IT OUT OF MY MIND... WHICH I DID."
LOWELL ABBAS SHERIDAN

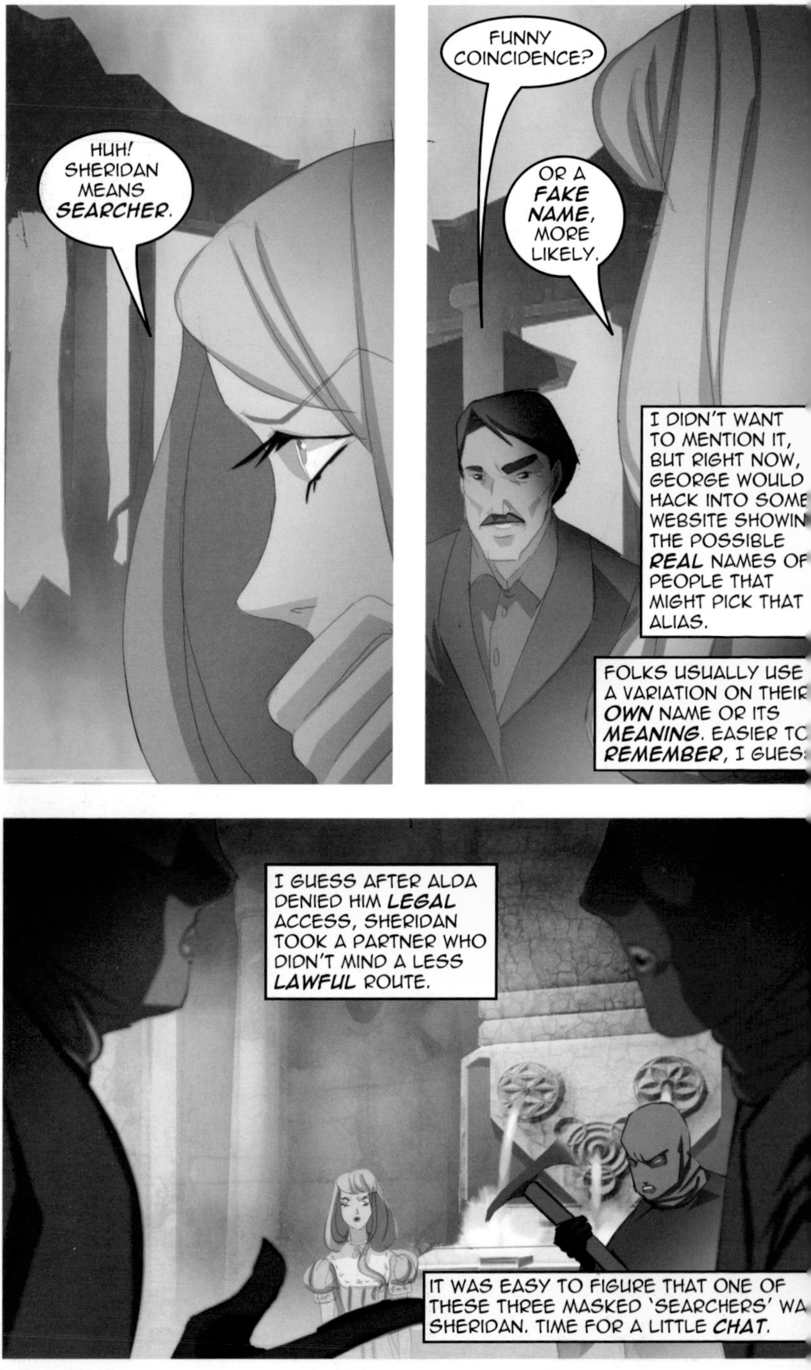
HUH! SHERIDAN MEANS SEARCHER.
FUNNY COINCIDENCE?
OR A FAKE NAME, MORE LIKELY.
I DIDN'T WANT TO MENTION IT, BUT RIGHT NOW, GEORGE WOULD HACK INTO SOME WEBSITE SHOWIN THE POSSIBLE REAL NAMES OF PEOPLE THAT MIGHT PICK THAT ALIAS.
FOLKS USUALLY USE A VARIATION ON THEIR OWN NAME OR ITS MEANING. EASIER TO REMEMBER, I GUES
I GUESS AFTER ALDA DENIED HIM LEGAL ACCESS, SHERIDAN TOOK A PARTNER WHO DIDN'T MIND A LESS LAWFUL ROUTE.
IT WAS EASY TO FIGURE THAT ONE OF THESE THREE MASKED 'SEARCHERS' WA SHERIDAN. TIME FOR A LITTLE CHAT.

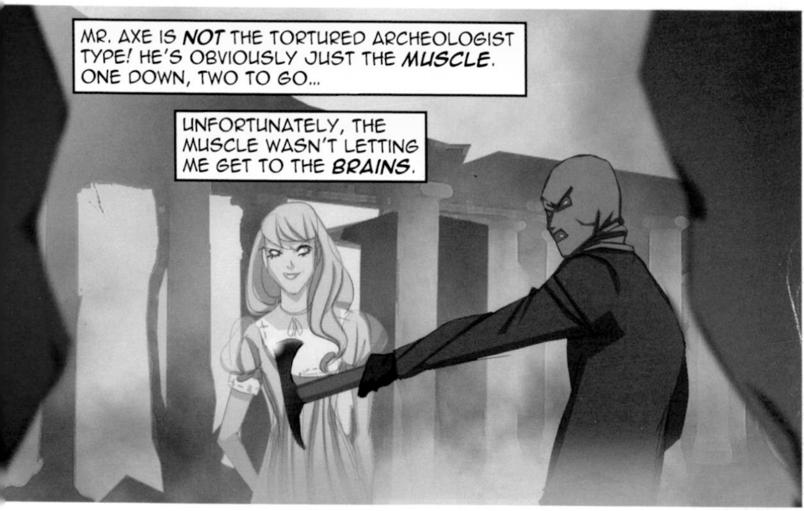
MR. AXE IS NOT THE TORTURED ARCHEOLOGIST TYPE! HE'S OBVIOUSLY JUST THE MUSCLE. ONE DOWN, TWO TO GO...
UNFORTUNATELY, THE MUSCLE WASN'T LETTING ME GET TO THE BRAINS.

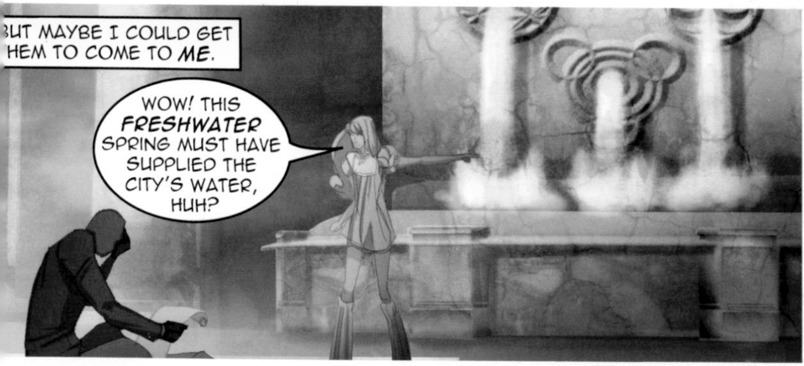
UT MAYBE I COULD GET HEM TO COME TO ME.
WOW! THIS FRESHWATER SPRING MUST HAVE SUPPLIED THE CITY'S WATER, HUH?

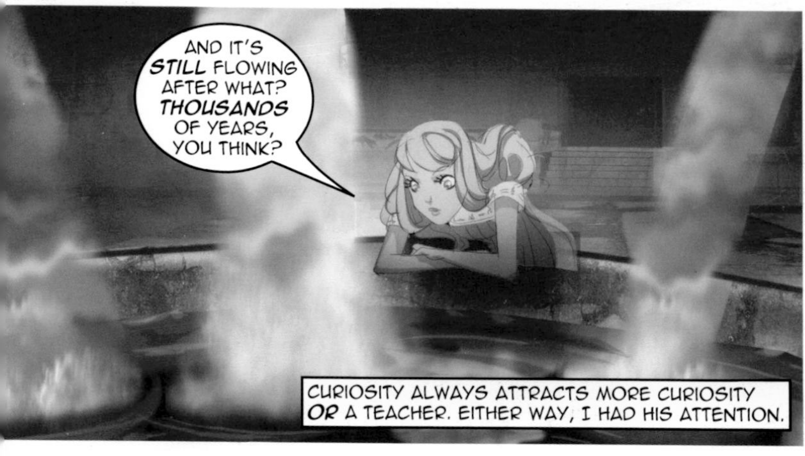
AND IT'S STILL FLOWING AFTER WHAT? THOUSANDS OF YEARS, YOU THINK?
CURIOSITY ALWAYS ATTRACTS MORE CURIOSITY OR A TEACHER. EITHER WAY, I HAD HIS ATTENTION.

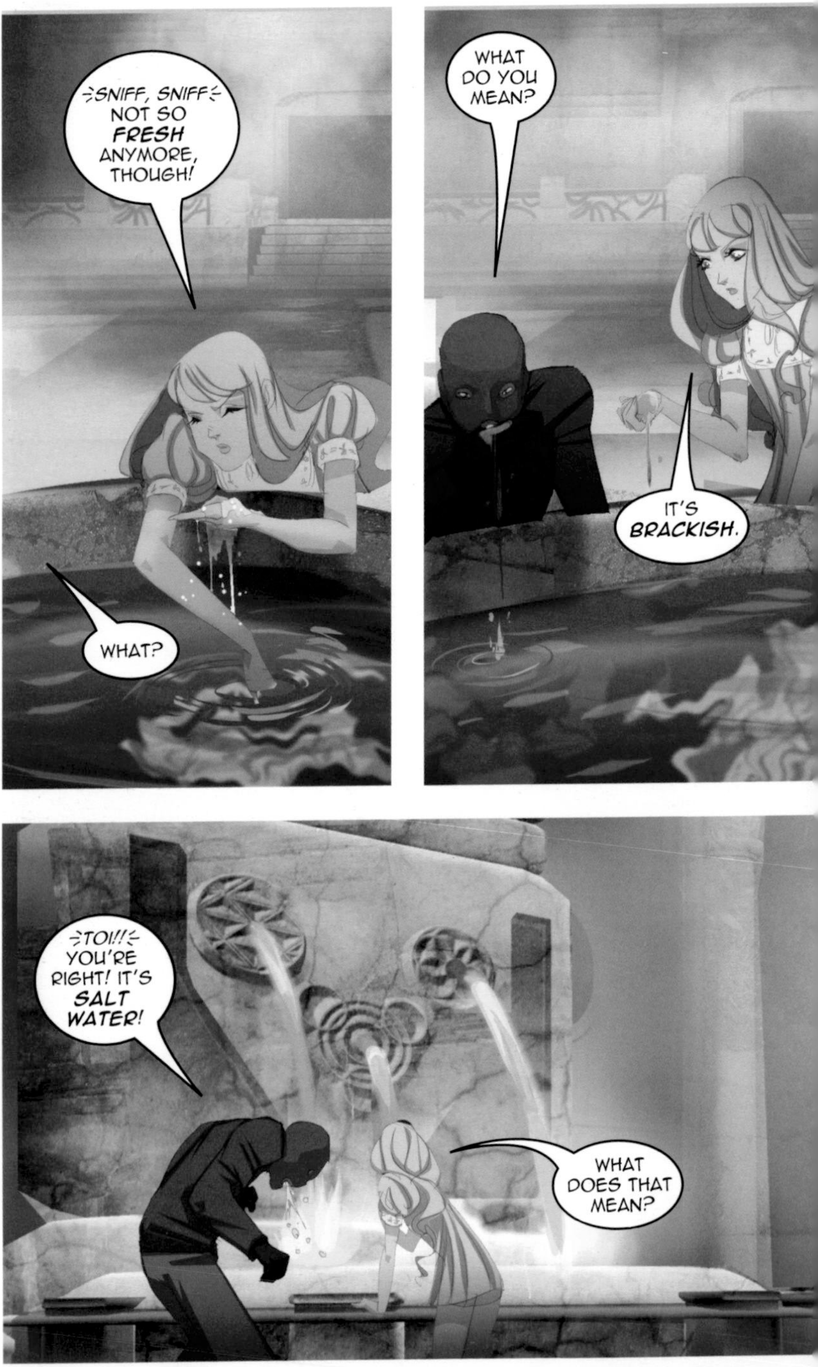
⇆SNIFF, SNIFF⇆ NOT SO FRESH ANYMORE, THOUGH!
WHAT?
WHAT DO YOU MEAN?
IT'S BRACKISH.
⇆TOI!!⇆ YOU'RE RIGHT! IT'S SALT WATER!
WHAT DOES THAT MEAN?

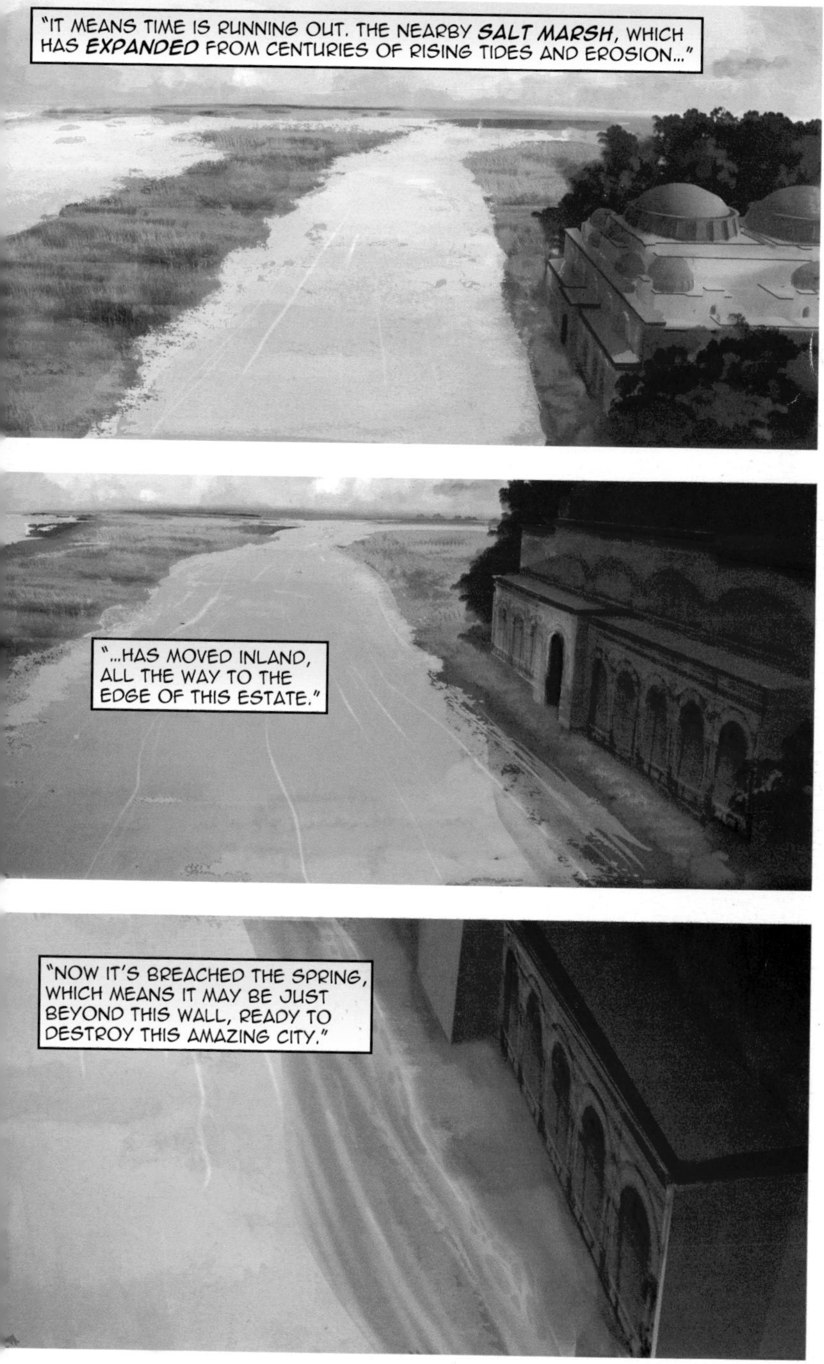
"IT MEANS TIME IS RUNNING OUT. THE NEARBY SALT MARSH, WHICH HAS EXPANDED FROM CENTURIES OF RISING TIDES AND EROSION..."
"...HAS MOVED INLAND, ALL THE WAY TO THE EDGE OF THIS ESTATE."
"NOW IT'S BREACHED THE SPRING, WHICH MEANS IT MAY BE JUST BEYOND THIS WALL, READY TO DESTROY THIS AMAZING CITY."

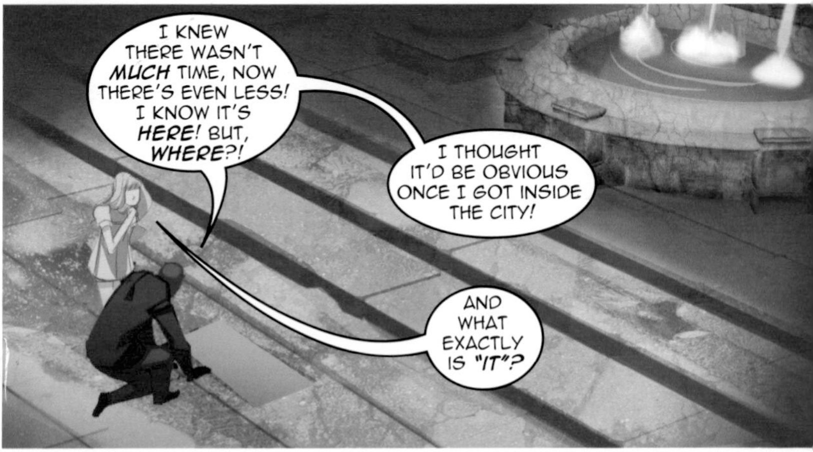
I KNEW THERE WASN'T MUCH TIME, NOW THERE'S EVEN LESS! I KNOW IT'S HERE! BUT, WHERE?!
I THOUGHT IT'D BE OBVIOUS ONCE I GOT INSIDE THE CITY!
AND WHAT EXACTLY IS "IT"?

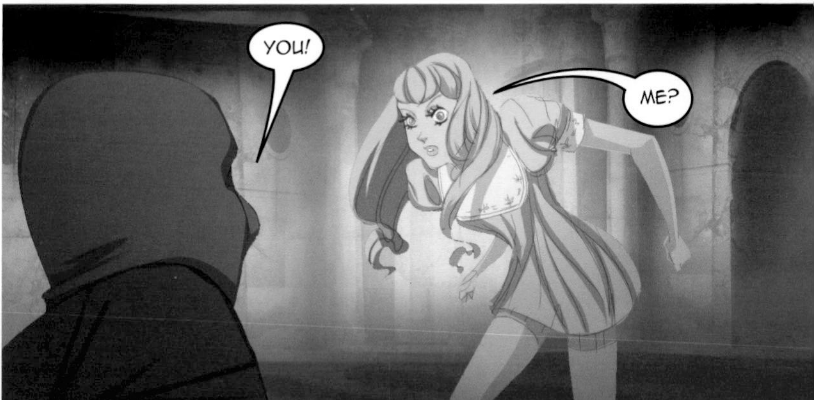
YOU!
ME?

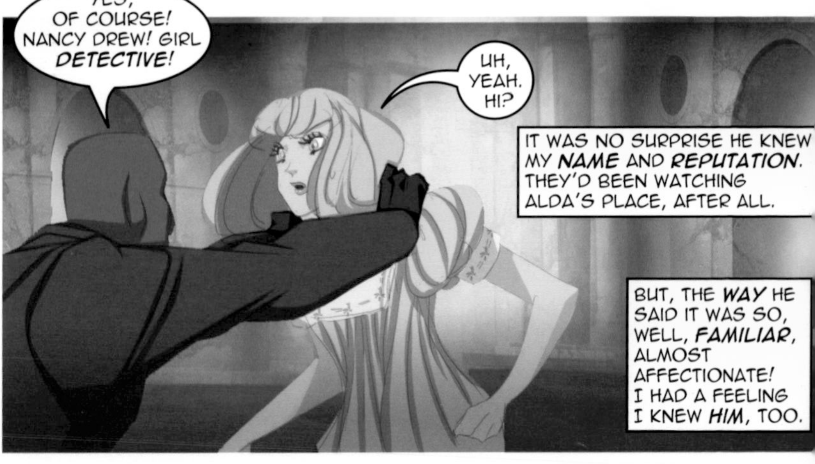
YES, OF COURSE! NANCY DREW! GIRL DETECTIVE!
UH, YEAH. HI?
IT WAS NO SURPRISE HE KNEW MY NAME AND REPUTATION. THEY'D BEEN WATCHING ALDA'S PLACE, AFTER ALL.
BUT, THE WAY HE SAID IT WAS SO, WELL, FAMILIAR, ALMOST AFFECTIONATE! I HAD A FEELING I KNEW HIM, TOO.

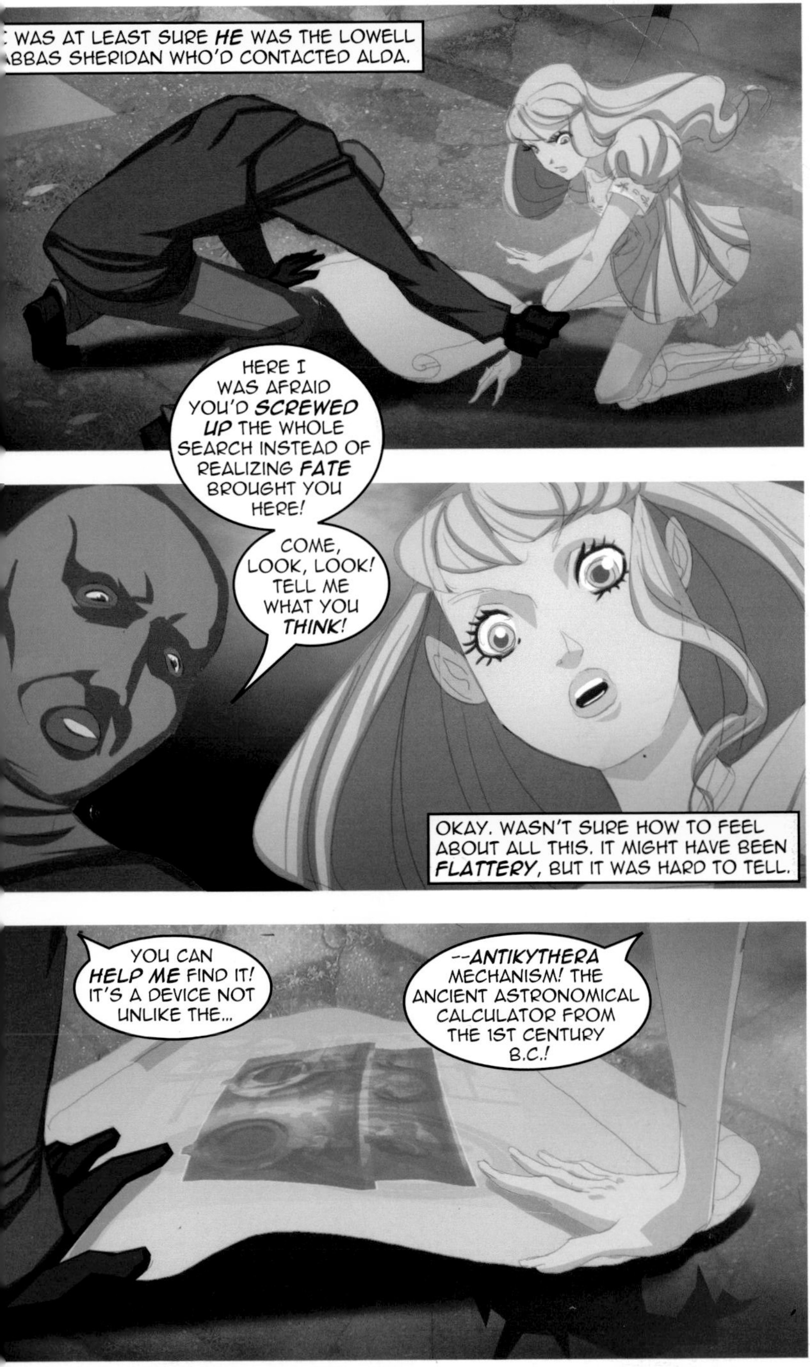

I WAS AT LEAST SURE *HE* WAS THE LOWELL ABBAS SHERIDAN WHO'D CONTACTED ALDA.
HERE I WAS AFRAID YOU'D *SCREWED UP* THE WHOLE SEARCH INSTEAD OF REALIZING *FATE* BROUGHT YOU HERE!
COME, LOOK, LOOK! TELL ME WHAT YOU *THINK*!
OKAY. WASN'T SURE HOW TO FEEL ABOUT ALL THIS. IT MIGHT HAVE BEEN *FLATTERY*, BUT IT WAS HARD TO TELL.
YOU CAN *HELP ME* FIND IT! IT'S A DEVICE NOT UNLIKE THE...
--*ANTIKYTHERA* MECHANISM! THE ANCIENT ASTRONOMICAL CALCULATOR FROM THE 1ST CENTURY B.C.!

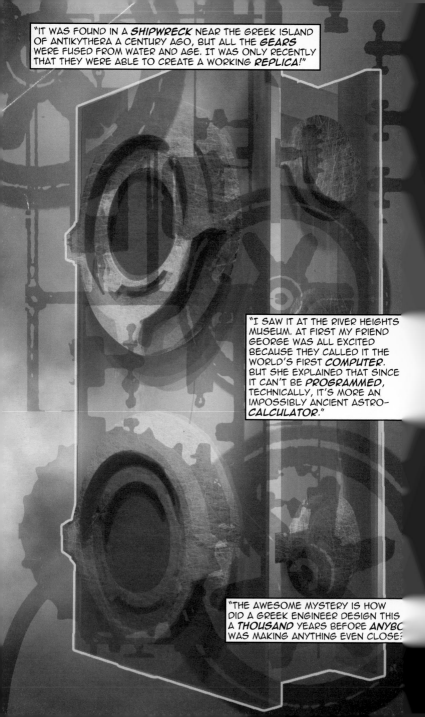

"IT WAS FOUND IN A *SHIPWRECK* NEAR THE GREEK ISLAND OF ANTIKYTHERA A CENTURY AGO, BUT ALL THE *GEARS* WERE FUSED FROM WATER AND AGE. IT WAS ONLY RECENTLY THAT THEY WERE ABLE TO CREATE A WORKING *REPLICA!*"

"I SAW IT AT THE RIVER HEIGHTS MUSEUM. AT FIRST MY FRIEND GEORGE WAS ALL EXCITED BECAUSE THEY CALLED IT THE WORLD'S FIRST *COMPUTER.* BUT SHE EXPLAINED THAT SINCE IT CAN'T BE *PROGRAMMED,* TECHNICALLY, IT'S MORE AN IMPOSSIBLY ANCIENT ASTRO-*CALCULATOR.*"

"THE AWESOME MYSTERY IS HOW DID A GREEK ENGINEER DESIGN THIS A *THOUSAND* YEARS BEFORE *ANYBO* WAS MAKING ANYTHING EVEN CLOSE?

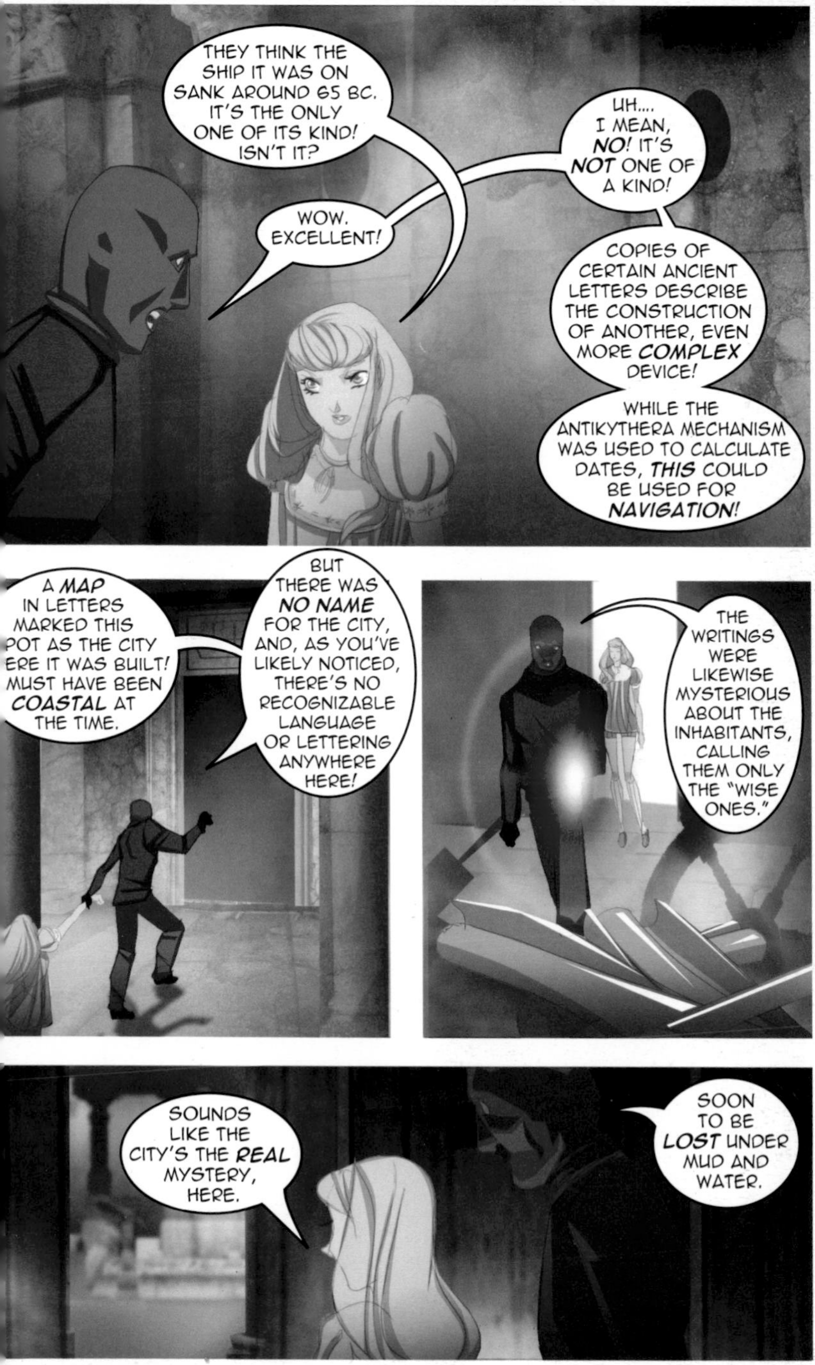
THEY THINK THE SHIP IT WAS ON SANK AROUND 65 BC. IT'S THE ONLY ONE OF ITS KIND! ISN'T IT?
WOW. EXCELLENT!
UH.... I MEAN, NO! IT'S NOT ONE OF A KIND!
COPIES OF CERTAIN ANCIENT LETTERS DESCRIBE THE CONSTRUCTION OF ANOTHER, EVEN MORE COMPLEX DEVICE!
WHILE THE ANTIKYTHERA MECHANISM WAS USED TO CALCULATE DATES, THIS COULD BE USED FOR NAVIGATION!
A MAP IN LETTERS MARKED THIS POT AS THE CITY ERE IT WAS BUILT! MUST HAVE BEEN COASTAL AT THE TIME.
BUT THERE WAS NO NAME FOR THE CITY, AND, AS YOU'VE LIKELY NOTICED, THERE'S NO RECOGNIZABLE LANGUAGE OR LETTERING ANYWHERE HERE!
THE WRITINGS WERE LIKEWISE MYSTERIOUS ABOUT THE INHABITANTS, CALLING THEM ONLY THE "WISE ONES."
SOUNDS LIKE THE CITY'S THE REAL MYSTERY, HERE.
SOON TO BE LOST UNDER MUD AND WATER.

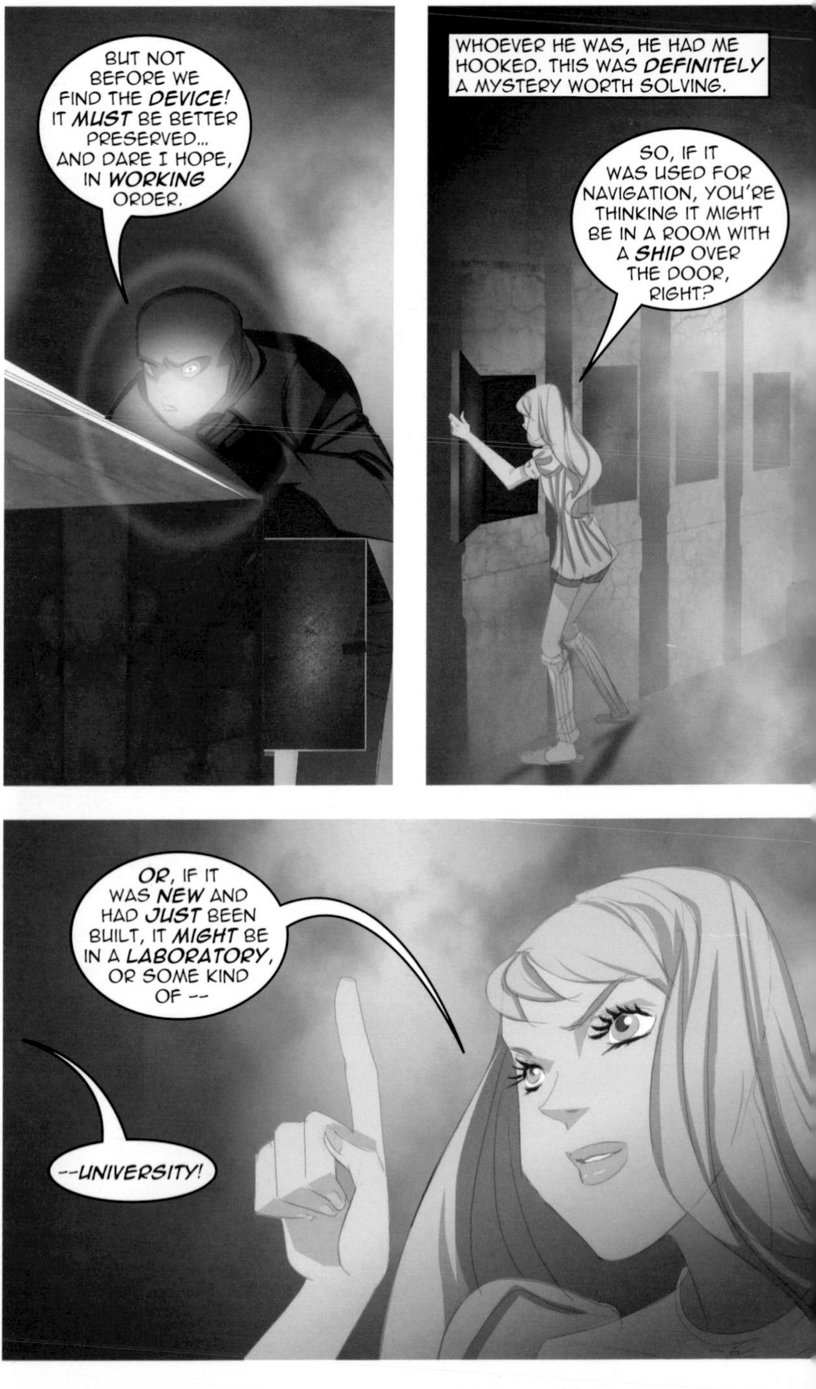
BUT NOT BEFORE WE FIND THE DEVICE! IT MUST BE BETTER PRESERVED... AND DARE I HOPE, IN WORKING ORDER.
WHOEVER HE WAS, HE HAD ME HOOKED. THIS WAS DEFINITELY A MYSTERY WORTH SOLVING.
SO, IF IT WAS USED FOR NAVIGATION, YOU'RE THINKING IT MIGHT BE IN A ROOM WITH A SHIP OVER THE DOOR, RIGHT?
OR, IF IT WAS NEW AND HAD JUST BEEN BUILT, IT MIGHT BE IN A LABORATORY, OR SOME KIND OF --
--UNIVERSITY!

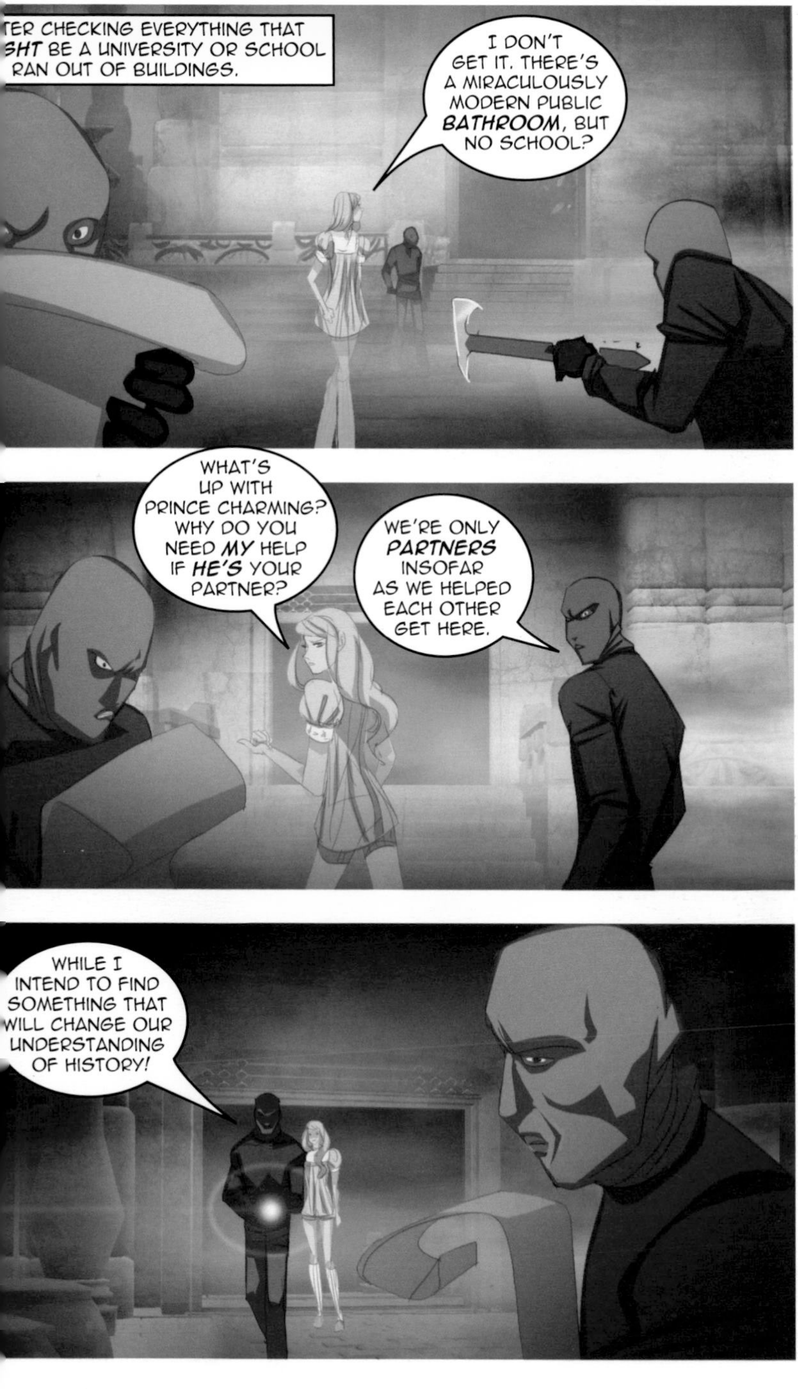
TER CHECKING EVERYTHING THAT
GHT BE A UNIVERSITY OR SCHOOL
RAN OUT OF BUILDINGS.
I DON'T GET IT. THERE'S A MIRACULOUSLY MODERN PUBLIC BATHROOM, BUT NO SCHOOL?
WHAT'S UP WITH PRINCE CHARMING? WHY DO YOU NEED MY HELP IF HE'S YOUR PARTNER?
WE'RE ONLY PARTNERS INSOFAR AS WE HELPED EACH OTHER GET HERE.
WHILE I INTEND TO FIND SOMETHING THAT WILL CHANGE OUR UNDERSTANDING OF HISTORY!

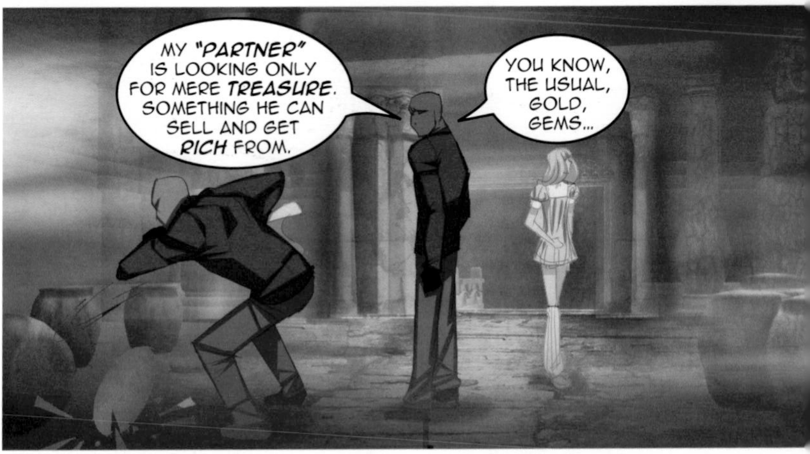
MY "PARTNER" IS LOOKING ONLY FOR MERE TREASURE. SOMETHING HE CAN SELL AND GET RICH FROM.
YOU KNOW, THE USUAL, GOLD, GEMS...

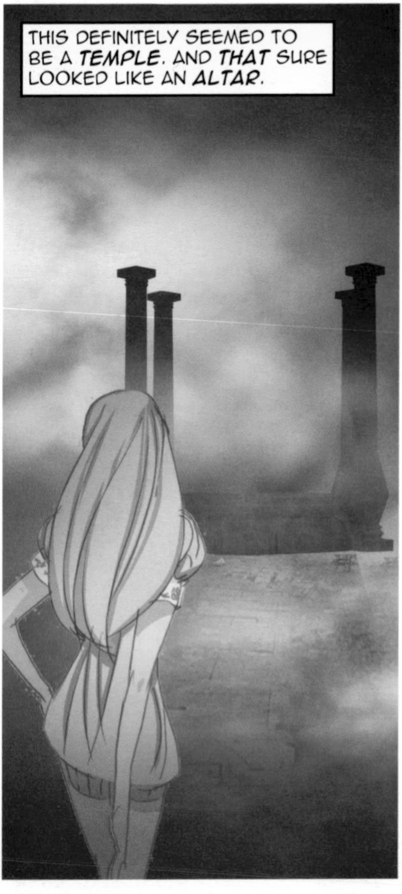
THIS DEFINITELY SEEMED TO BE A TEMPLE. AND THAT SURE LOOKED LIKE AN ALTAR.

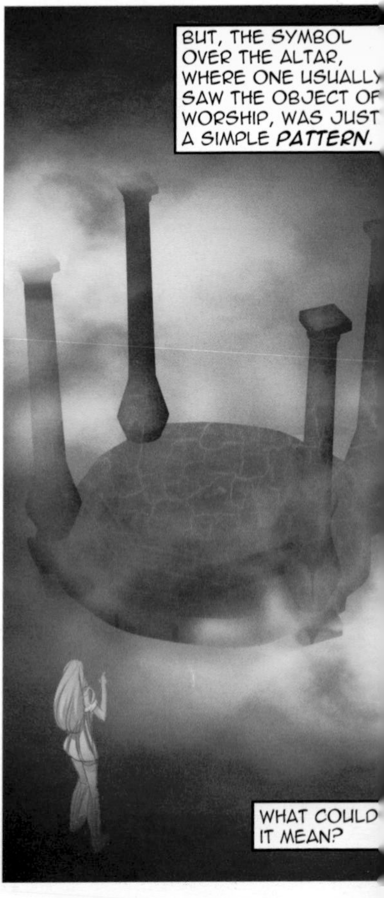
BUT, THE SYMBOL OVER THE ALTAR, WHERE ONE USUALLY SAW THE OBJECT OF WORSHIP, WAS JUST A SIMPLE PATTERN.
WHAT COULD IT MEAN?

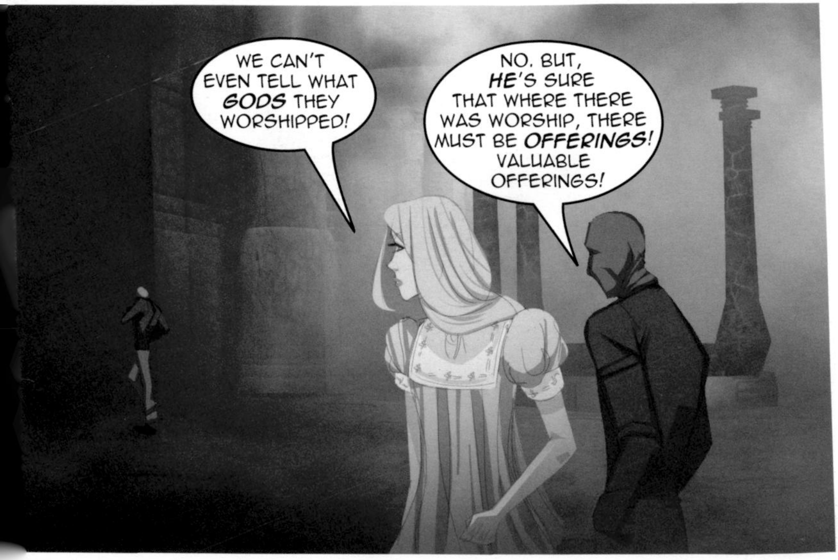
WE CAN'T EVEN TELL WHAT GODS THEY WORSHIPPED!
NO. BUT, HE'S SURE THAT WHERE THERE WAS WORSHIP, THERE MUST BE OFFERINGS! VALUABLE OFFERINGS!

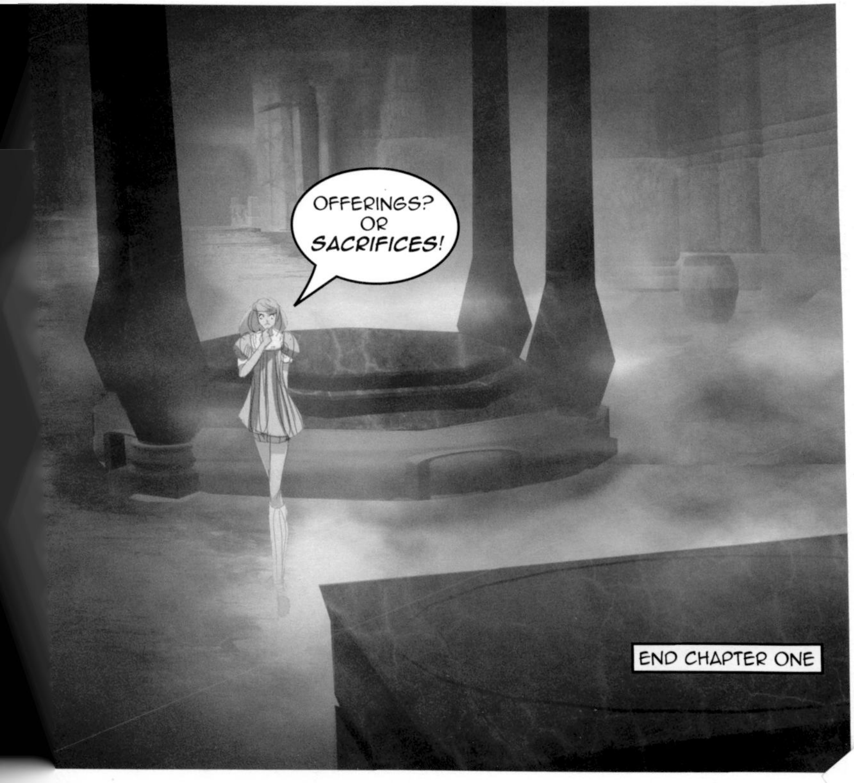
OFFERINGS? OR SACRIFICES!
END CHAPTER ONE

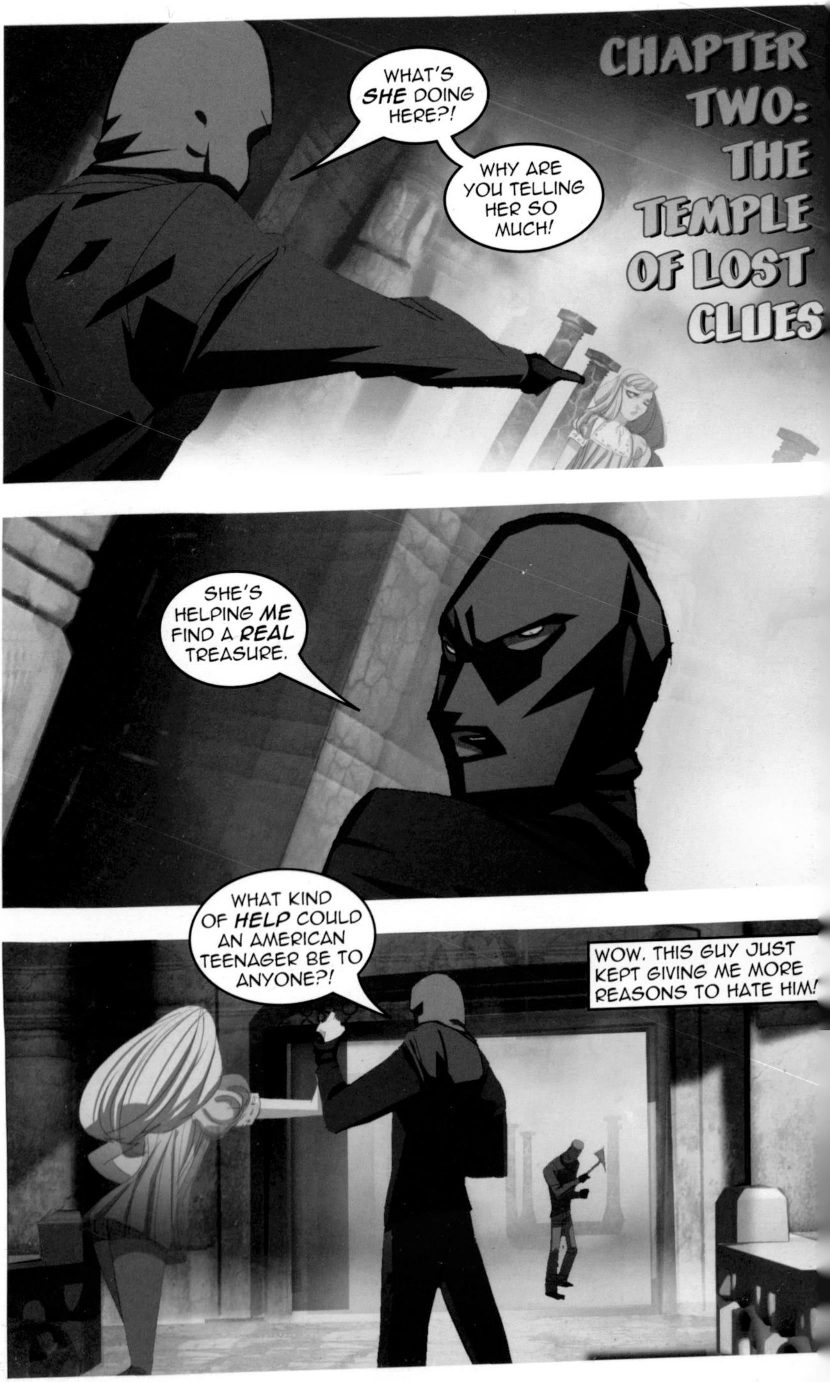
CHAPTER TWO: THE TEMPLE OF LOST CLUES
WHAT'S SHE DOING HERE?!
WHY ARE YOU TELLING HER SO MUCH!
SHE'S HELPING ME FIND A REAL TREASURE.
WHAT KIND OF HELP COULD AN AMERICAN TEENAGER BE TO ANYONE?!
WOW. THIS GUY JUST KEPT GIVING ME MORE REASONS TO HATE HIM!

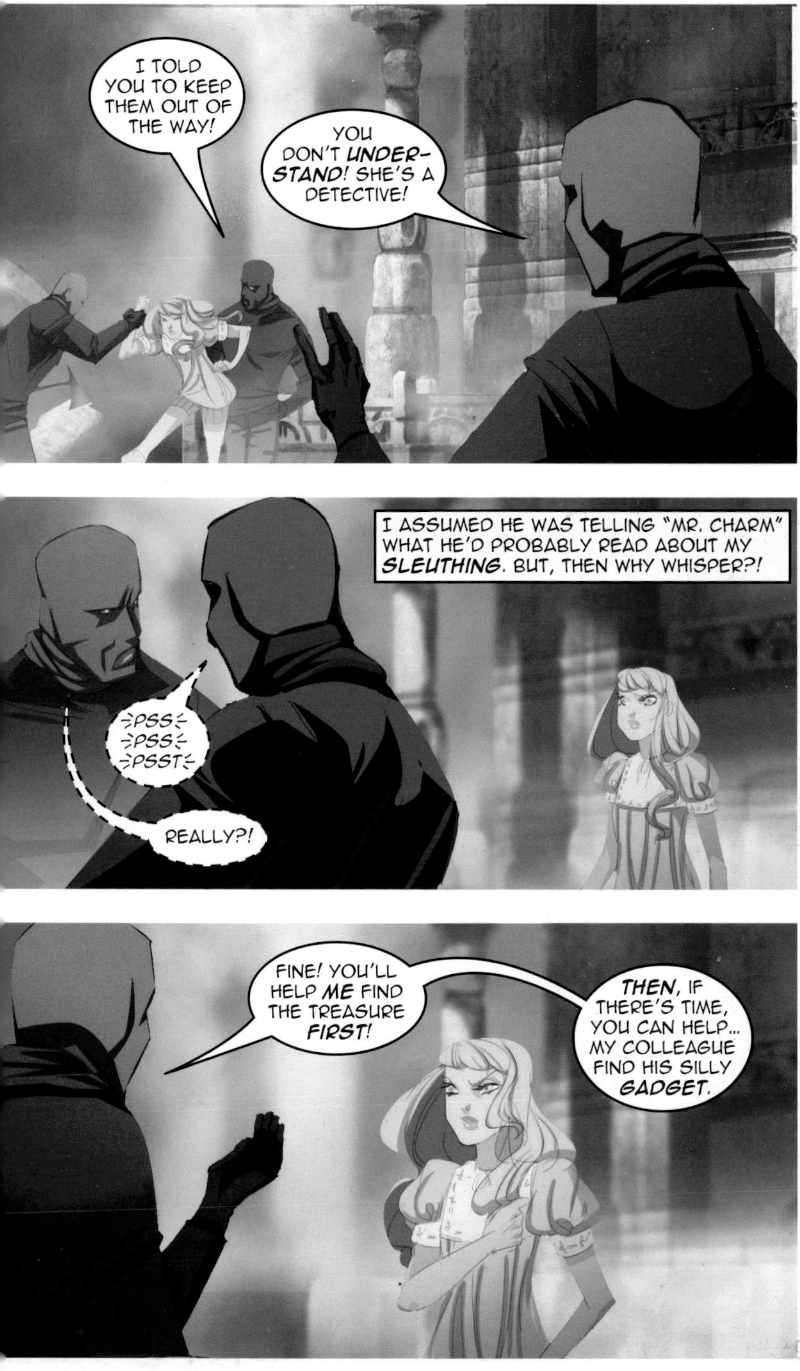

I TOLD YOU TO KEEP THEM OUT OF THE WAY!
YOU DON'T UNDER-STAND! SHE'S A DETECTIVE!
I ASSUMED HE WAS TELLING "MR. CHARM" WHAT HE'D PROBABLY READ ABOUT MY SLEUTHING. BUT, THEN WHY WHISPER?!
PSS PSS PSST
REALLY?!
FINE! YOU'LL HELP ME FIND THE TREASURE FIRST!
THEN, IF THERE'S TIME, YOU CAN HELP... MY COLLEAGUE FIND HIS SILLY GADGET.

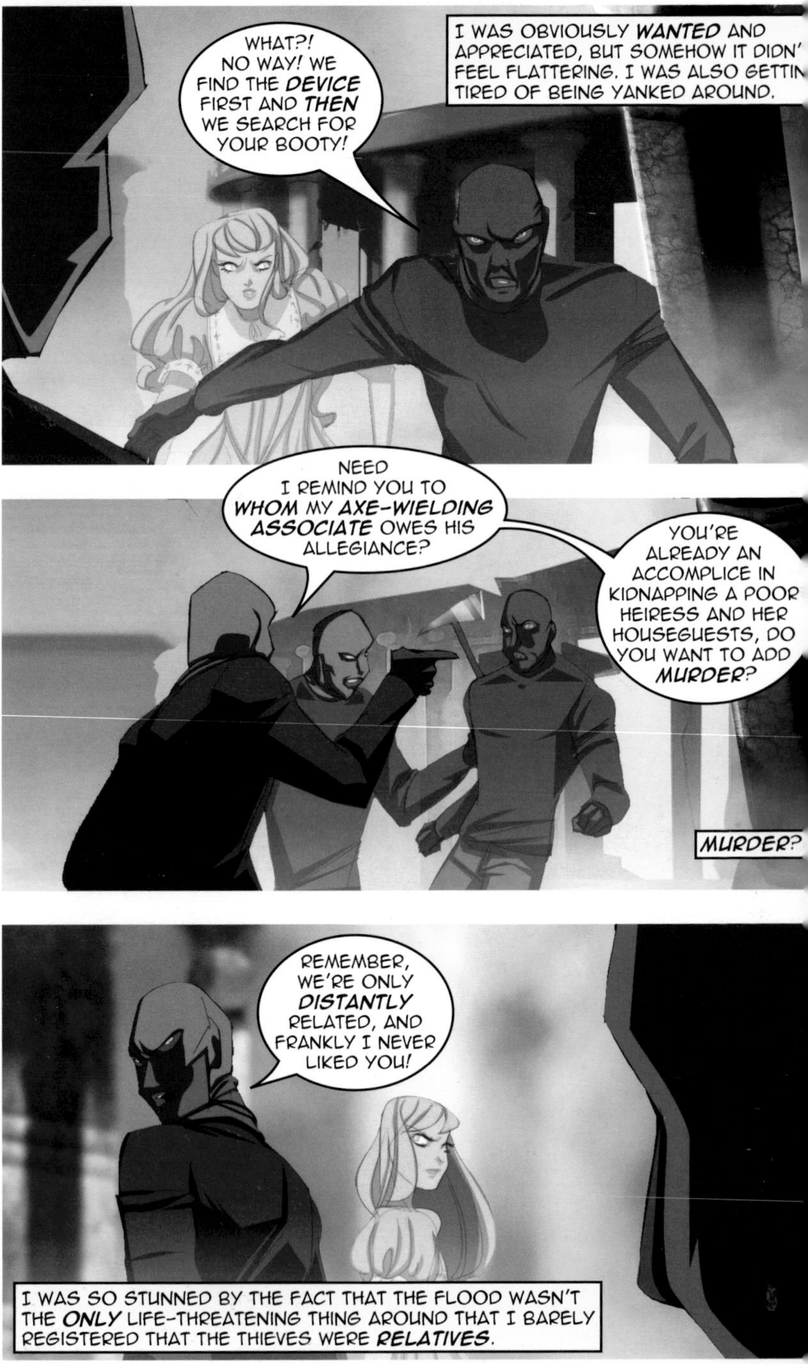
I WAS OBVIOUSLY WANTED AND APPRECIATED, BUT SOMEHOW IT DIDN' FEEL FLATTERING. I WAS ALSO GETTIN TIRED OF BEING YANKED AROUND.
WHAT?! NO WAY! WE FIND THE DEVICE FIRST AND THEN WE SEARCH FOR YOUR BOOTY!
NEED I REMIND YOU TO WHOM MY AXE-WIELDING ASSOCIATE OWES HIS ALLEGIANCE?
YOU'RE ALREADY AN ACCOMPLICE IN KIDNAPPING A POOR HEIRESS AND HER HOUSEGUESTS, DO YOU WANT TO ADD MURDER?
MURDER?
REMEMBER, WE'RE ONLY DISTANTLY RELATED, AND FRANKLY I NEVER LIKED YOU!
I WAS SO STUNNED BY THE FACT THAT THE FLOOD WASN'T THE ONLY LIFE-THREATENING THING AROUND THAT I BARELY REGISTERED THAT THE THIEVES WERE RELATIVES.

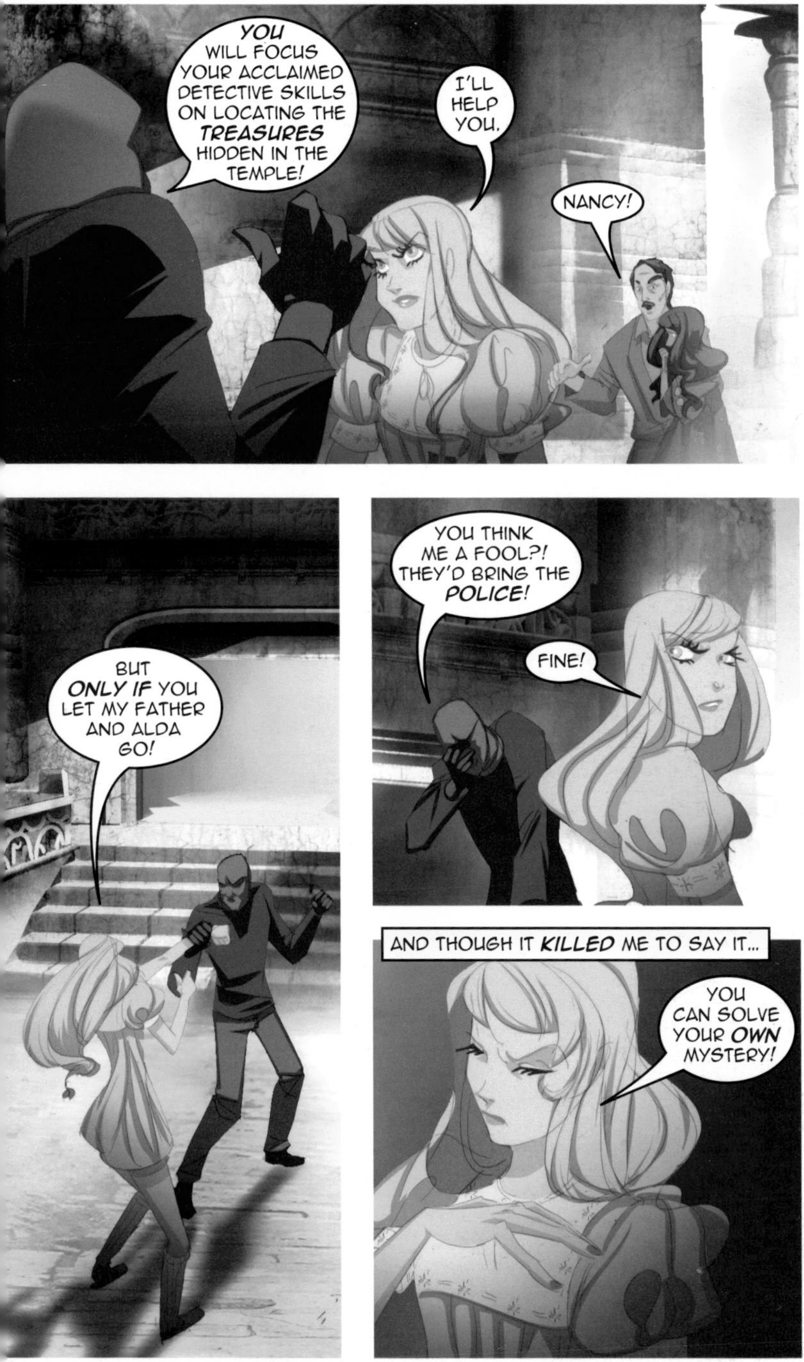
YOU WILL FOCUS YOUR ACCLAIMED DETECTIVE SKILLS ON LOCATING THE TREASURES HIDDEN IN THE TEMPLE!
I'LL HELP YOU.
NANCY!
BUT ONLY IF YOU LET MY FATHER AND ALDA GO!
YOU THINK ME A FOOL?! THEY'D BRING THE POLICE!
FINE!
AND THOUGH IT KILLED ME TO SAY IT...
YOU CAN SOLVE YOUR OWN MYSTERY!

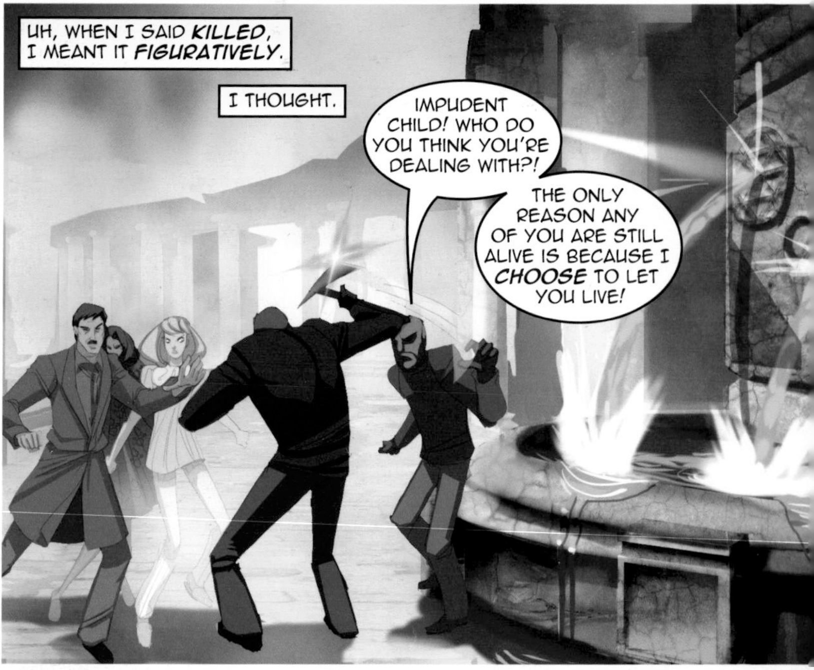
UH, WHEN I SAID KILLED, I MEANT IT FIGURATIVELY.
I THOUGHT.
IMPUDENT CHILD! WHO DO YOU THINK YOU'RE DEALING WITH?!
THE ONLY REASON ANY OF YOU ARE STILL ALIVE IS BECAUSE I CHOOSE TO LET YOU LIVE!

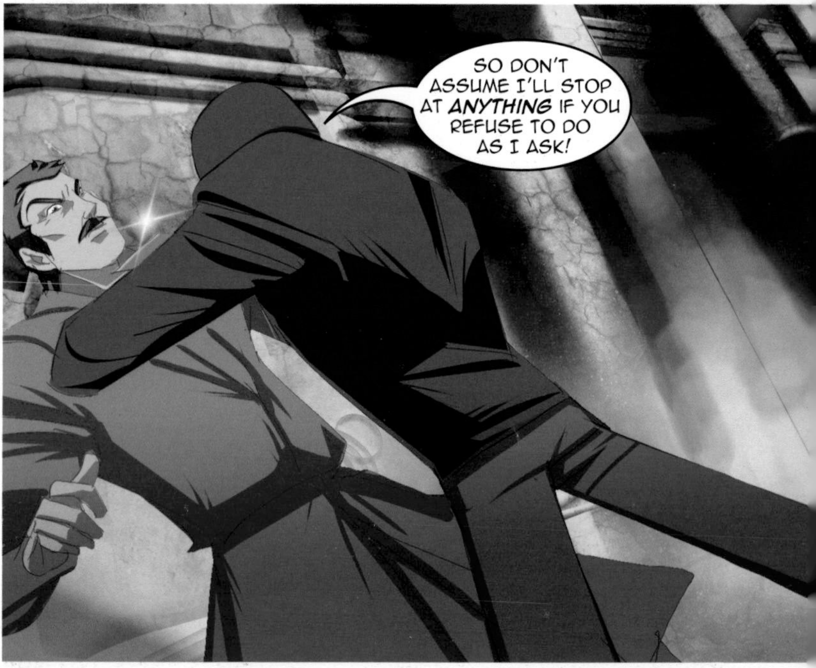
SO DON'T ASSUME I'LL STOP AT ANYTHING IF YOU REFUSE TO DO AS I ASK!

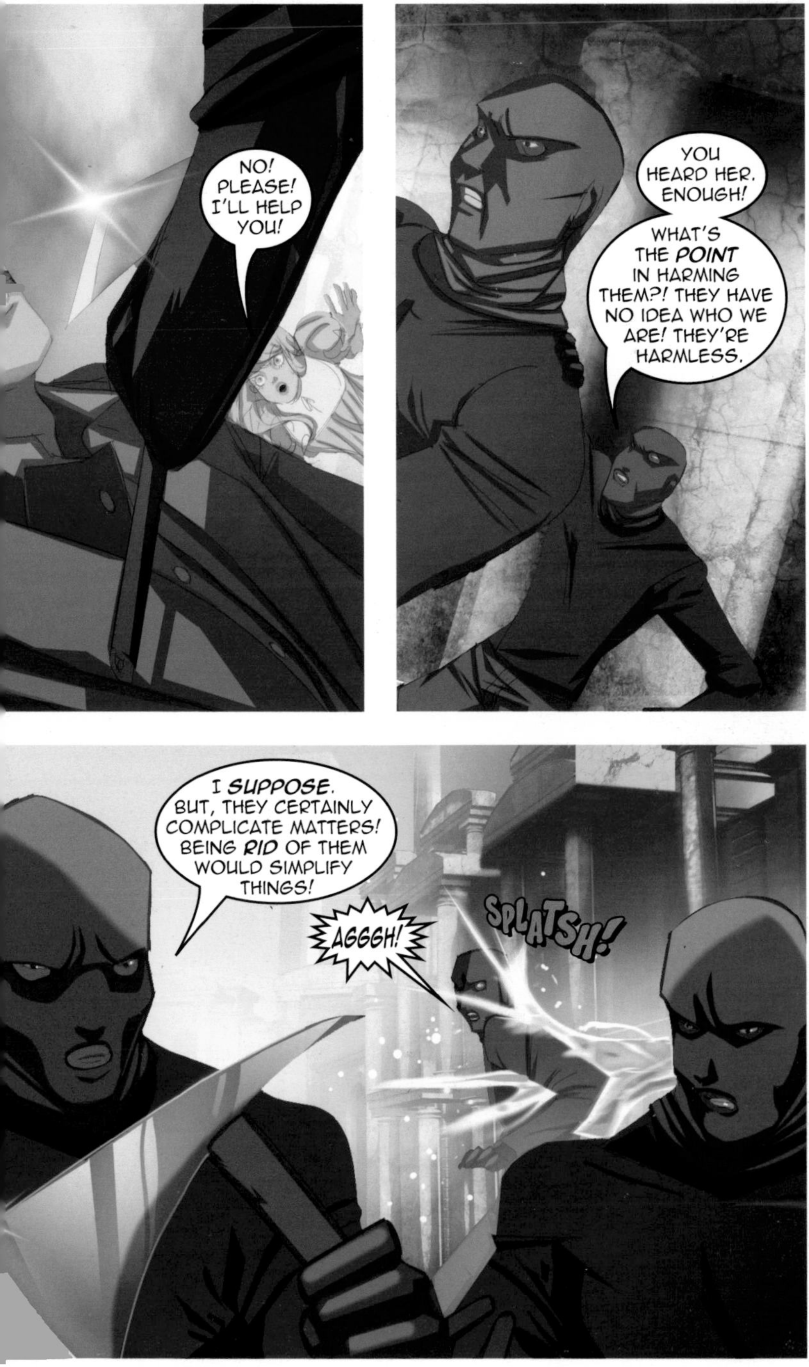
NO! PLEASE! I'LL HELP YOU!
YOU HEARD HER. ENOUGH!
WHAT'S THE POINT IN HARMING THEM?! THEY HAVE NO IDEA WHO WE ARE! THEY'RE HARMLESS.
I SUPPOSE. BUT, THEY CERTAINLY COMPLICATE MATTERS! BEING RID OF THEM WOULD SIMPLIFY THINGS!
AGGGH!
SPLATSH!

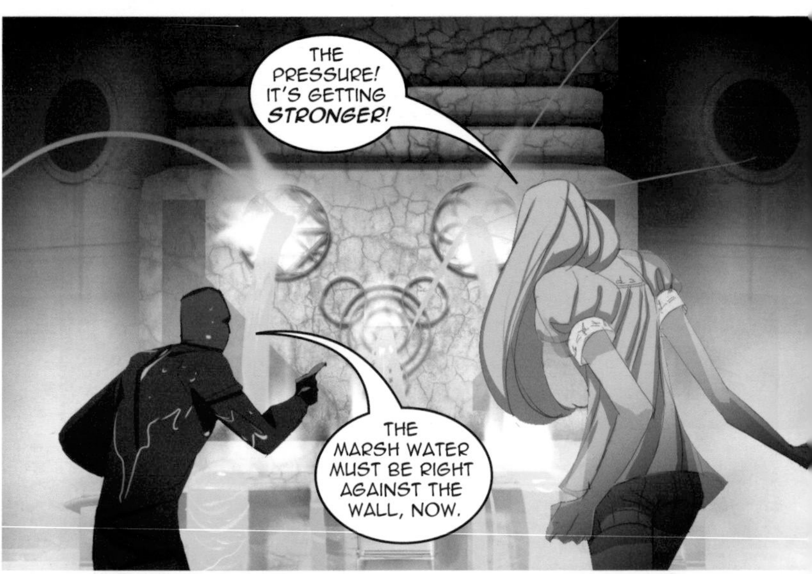
THE PRESSURE! IT'S GETTING STRONGER!
THE MARSH WATER MUST BE RIGHT AGAINST THE WALL, NOW.

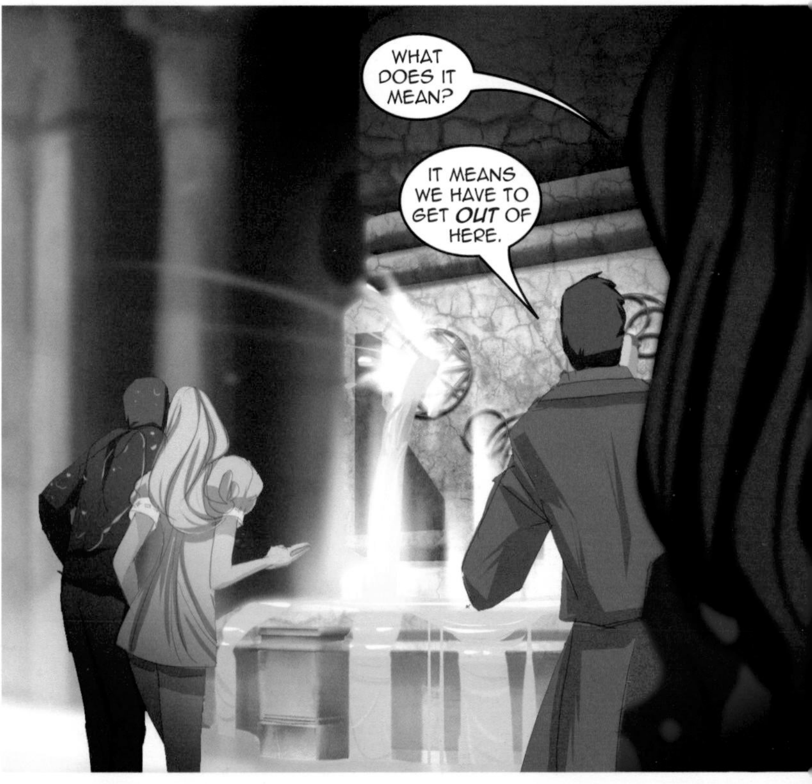
WHAT DOES IT MEAN?
IT MEANS WE HAVE TO GET OUT OF HERE.

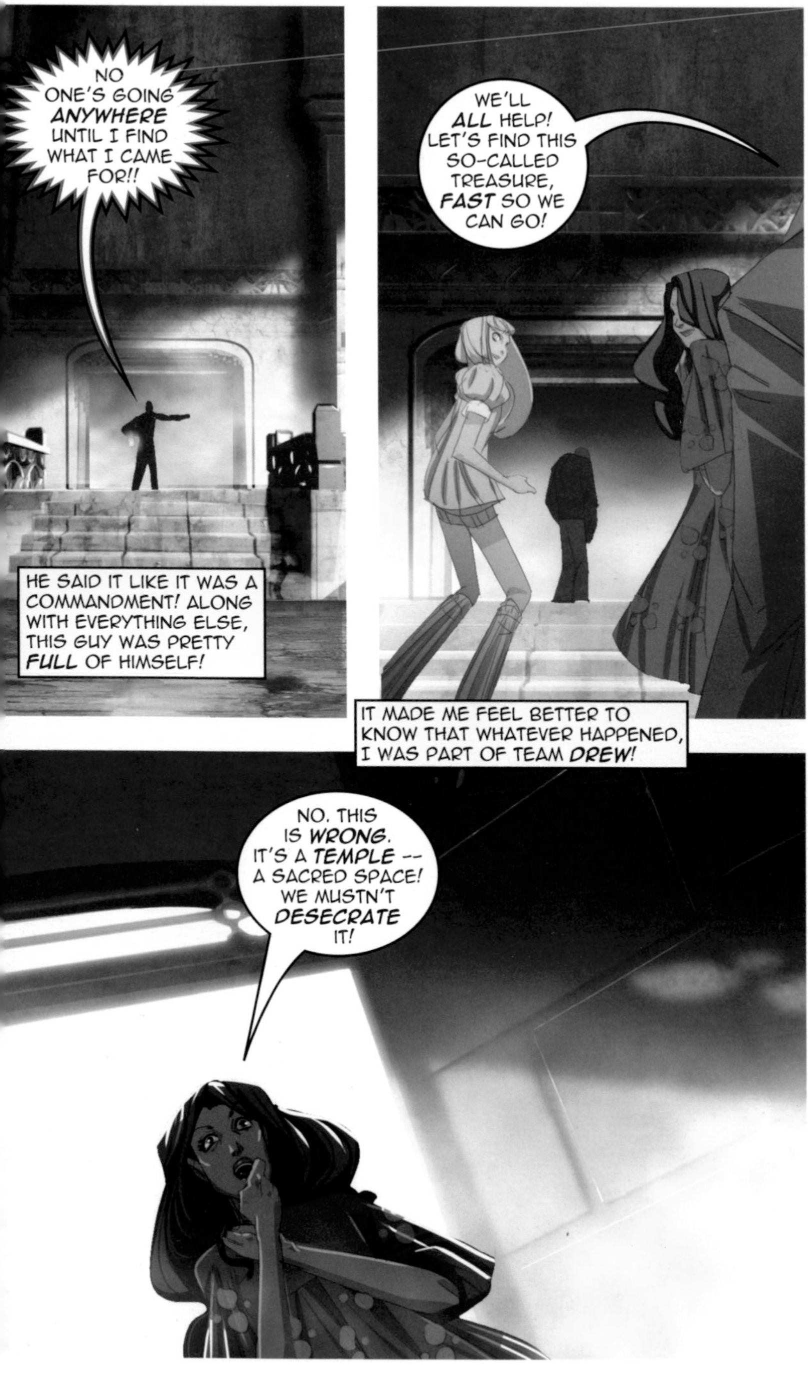
NO ONE'S GOING ANYWHERE UNTIL I FIND WHAT I CAME FOR!!
HE SAID IT LIKE IT WAS A COMMANDMENT! ALONG WITH EVERYTHING ELSE, THIS GUY WAS PRETTY FULL OF HIMSELF!
WE'LL ALL HELP! LET'S FIND THIS SO-CALLED TREASURE, FAST SO WE CAN GO!
IT MADE ME FEEL BETTER TO KNOW THAT WHATEVER HAPPENED, I WAS PART OF TEAM DREW!
NO. THIS IS WRONG. IT'S A TEMPLE -- A SACRED SPACE! WE MUSTN'T DESECRATE IT!

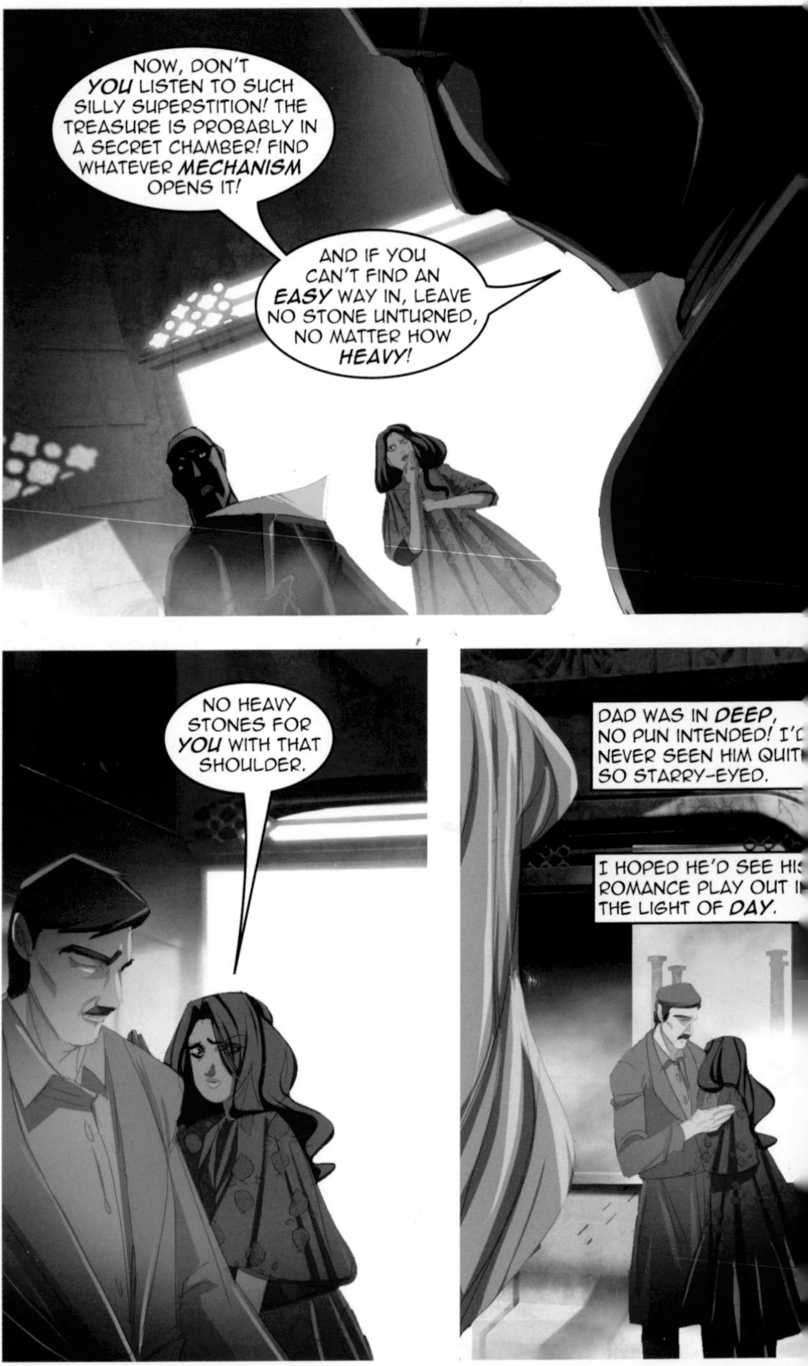
NOW, DON'T YOU LISTEN TO SUCH SILLY SUPERSTITION! THE TREASURE IS PROBABLY IN A SECRET CHAMBER! FIND WHATEVER MECHANISM OPENS IT!
AND IF YOU CAN'T FIND AN EASY WAY IN, LEAVE NO STONE UNTURNED, NO MATTER HOW HEAVY!
NO HEAVY STONES FOR YOU WITH THAT SHOULDER.
DAD WAS IN DEEP, NO PUN INTENDED! I'D NEVER SEEN HIM QUITE SO STARRY-EYED.
I HOPED HE'D SEE HIS ROMANCE PLAY OUT IN THE LIGHT OF DAY.

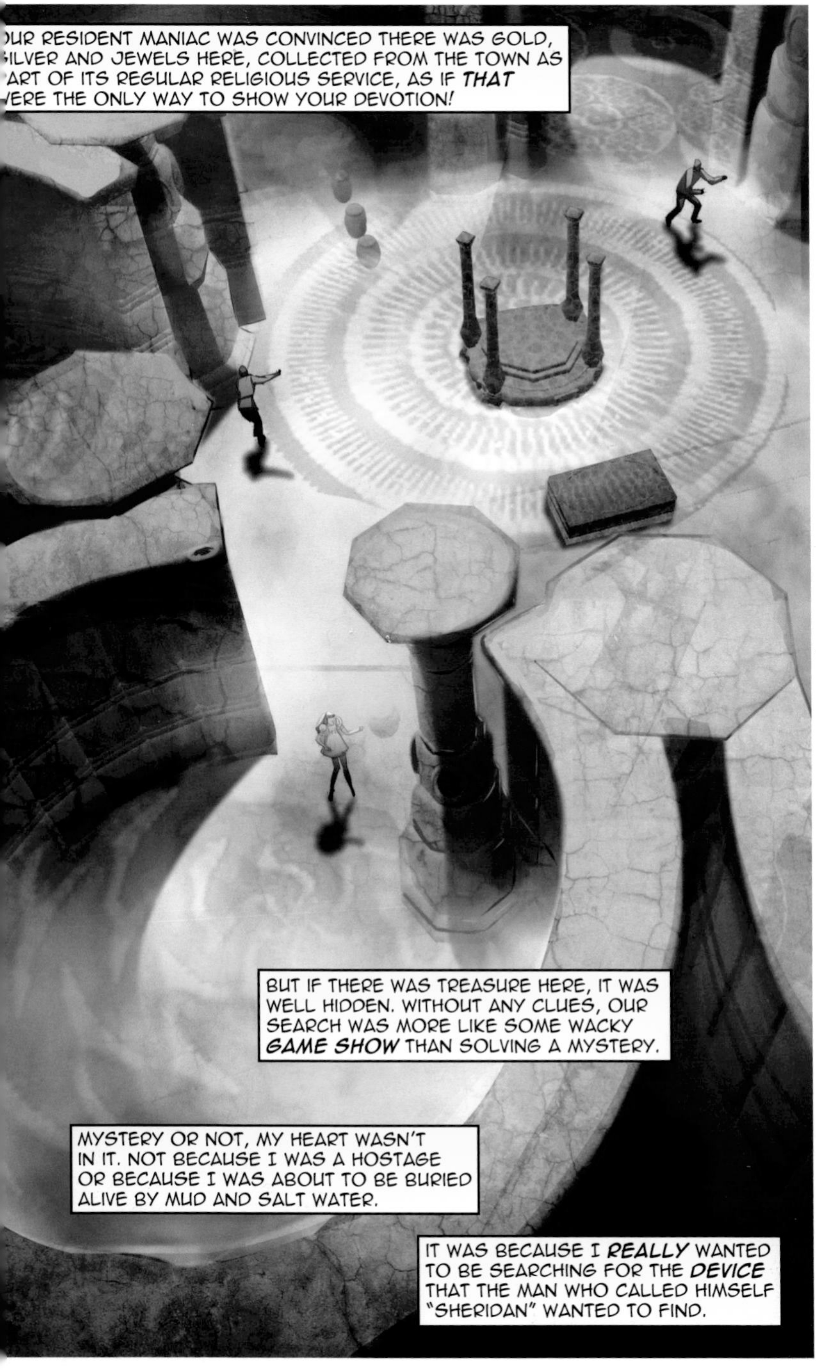
UR RESIDENT MANIAC WAS CONVINCED THERE WAS GOLD, ILVER AND JEWELS HERE, COLLECTED FROM THE TOWN AS ART OF ITS REGULAR RELIGIOUS SERVICE, AS IF *THAT* ERE THE ONLY WAY TO SHOW YOUR DEVOTION!
BUT IF THERE WAS TREASURE HERE, IT WAS WELL HIDDEN. WITHOUT ANY CLUES, OUR SEARCH WAS MORE LIKE SOME WACKY *GAME SHOW* THAN SOLVING A MYSTERY.
MYSTERY OR NOT, MY HEART WASN'T IN IT. NOT BECAUSE I WAS A HOSTAGE OR BECAUSE I WAS ABOUT TO BE BURIED ALIVE BY MUD AND SALT WATER.
IT WAS BECAUSE I *REALLY* WANTED TO BE SEARCHING FOR THE *DEVICE* THAT THE MAN WHO CALLED HIMSELF "SHERIDAN" WANTED TO FIND.

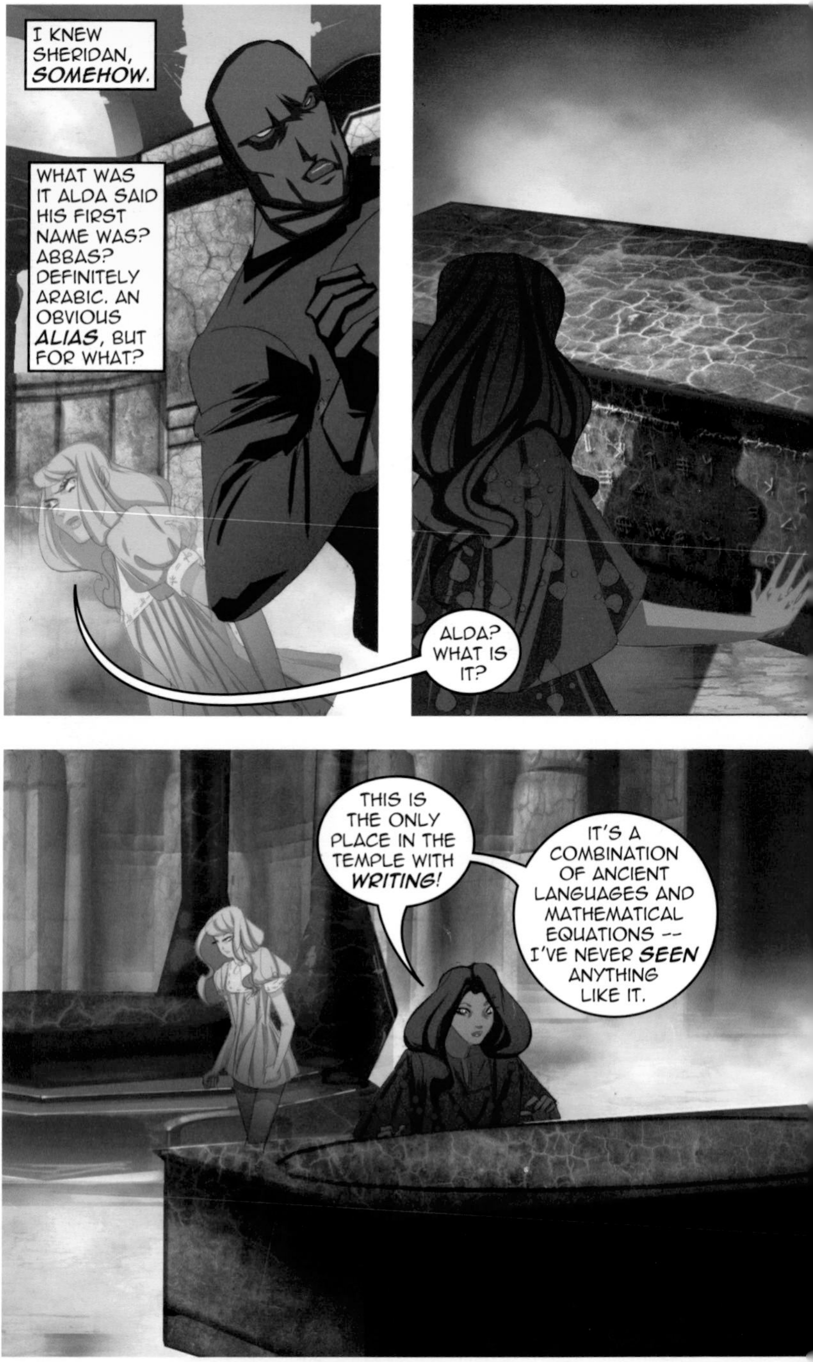
I KNEW SHERIDAN, SOMEHOW.
WHAT WAS IT ALDA SAID HIS FIRST NAME WAS? ABBAS? DEFINITELY ARABIC. AN OBVIOUS ALIAS, BUT FOR WHAT?
ALDA? WHAT IS IT?
THIS IS THE ONLY PLACE IN THE TEMPLE WITH WRITING!
IT'S A COMBINATION OF ANCIENT LANGUAGES AND MATHEMATICAL EQUATIONS -- I'VE NEVER SEEN ANYTHING LIKE IT.

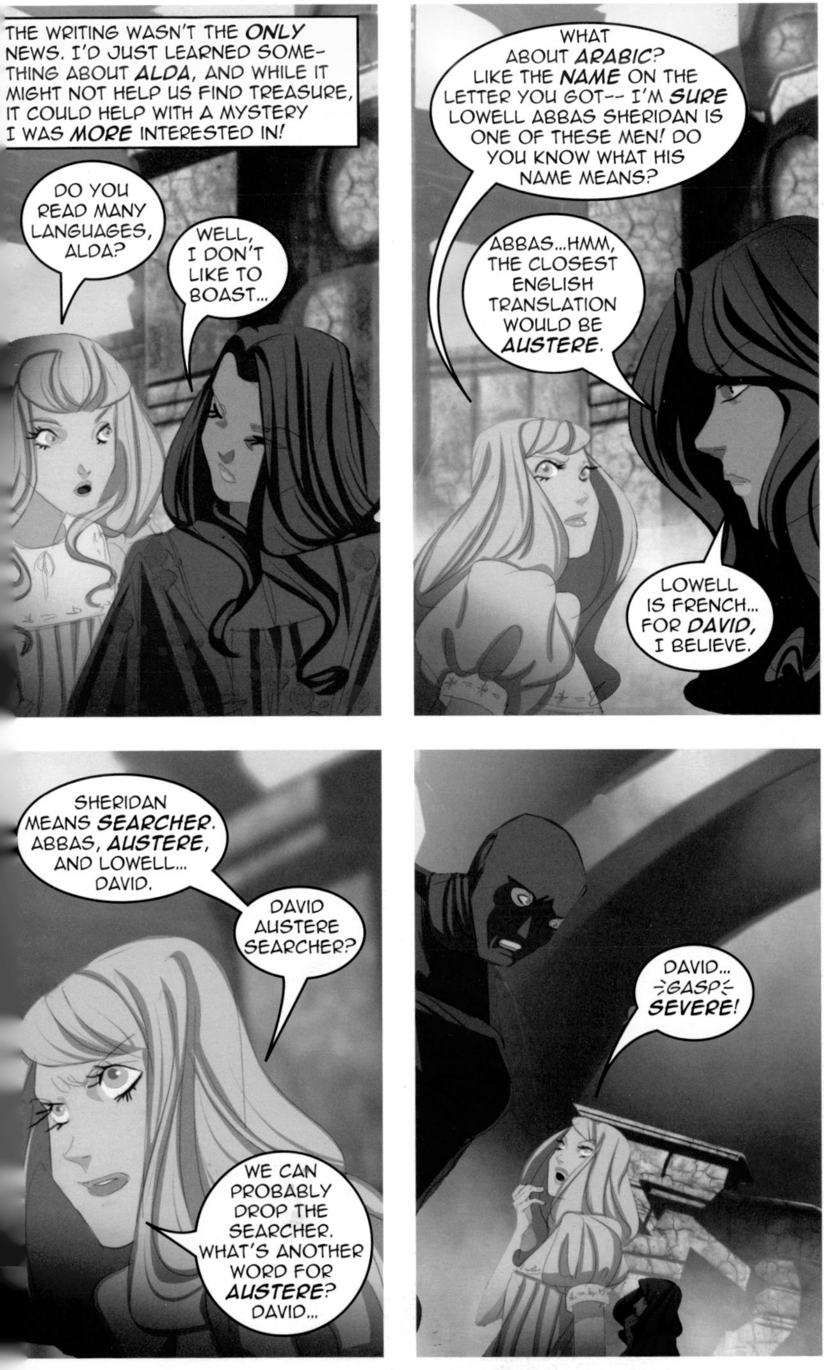
THE WRITING WASN'T THE ONLY NEWS. I'D JUST LEARNED SOMETHING ABOUT ALDA, AND WHILE IT MIGHT NOT HELP US FIND TREASURE, IT COULD HELP WITH A MYSTERY I WAS MORE INTERESTED IN!
DO YOU READ MANY LANGUAGES, ALDA?
WELL, I DON'T LIKE TO BOAST...
WHAT ABOUT ARABIC? LIKE THE NAME ON THE LETTER YOU GOT-- I'M SURE LOWELL ABBAS SHERIDAN IS ONE OF THESE MEN! DO YOU KNOW WHAT HIS NAME MEANS?
ABBAS...HMM, THE CLOSEST ENGLISH TRANSLATION WOULD BE AUSTERE.
LOWELL IS FRENCH... FOR DAVID, I BELIEVE.
SHERIDAN MEANS SEARCHER. ABBAS, AUSTERE, AND LOWELL... DAVID.
DAVID AUSTERE SEARCHER?
WE CAN PROBABLY DROP THE SEARCHER. WHAT'S ANOTHER WORD FOR AUSTERE? DAVID...
DAVID... GASP SEVERE!

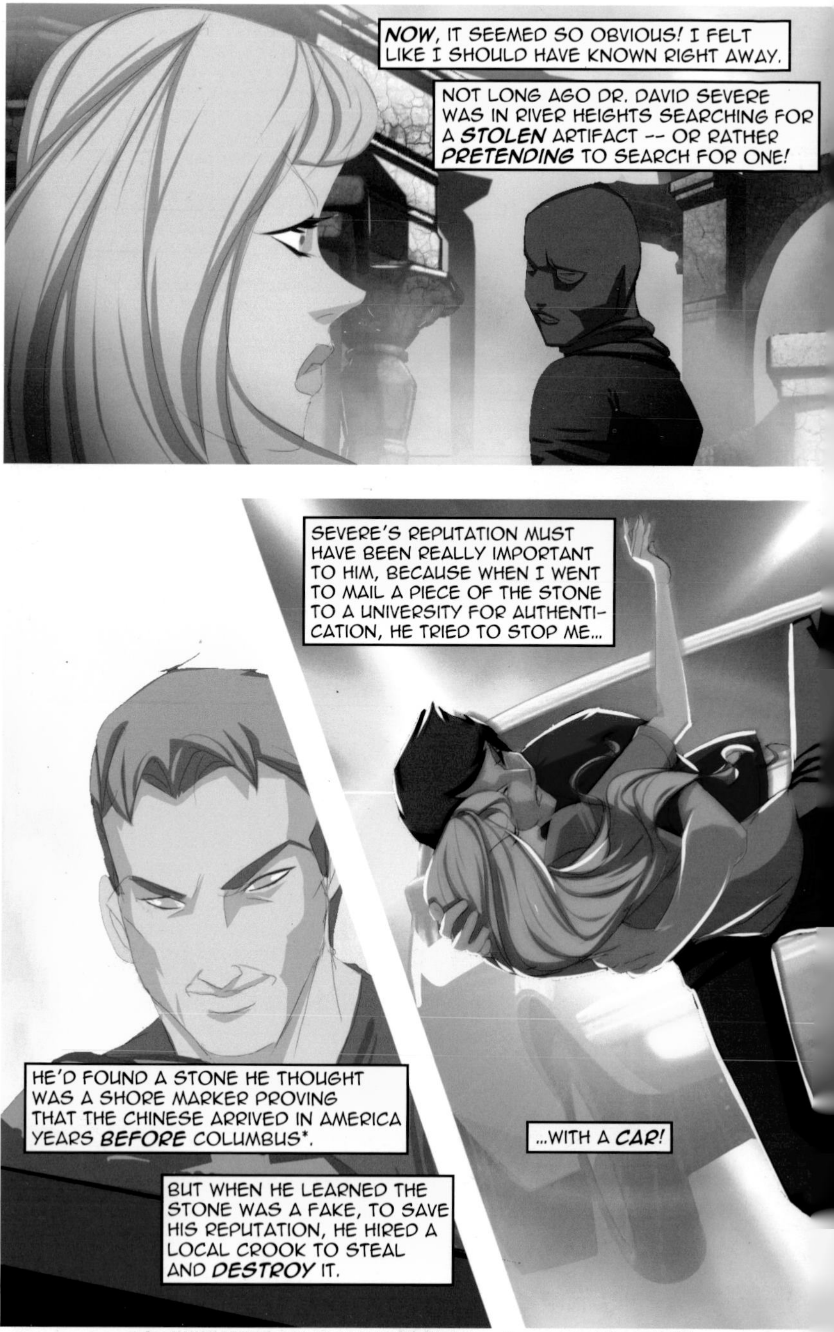
NOW, IT SEEMED SO OBVIOUS! I FELT LIKE I SHOULD HAVE KNOWN RIGHT AWAY.
NOT LONG AGO DR. DAVID SEVERE WAS IN RIVER HEIGHTS SEARCHING FOR A STOLEN ARTIFACT -- OR RATHER PRETENDING TO SEARCH FOR ONE!
HE'D FOUND A STONE HE THOUGHT WAS A SHORE MARKER PROVING THAT THE CHINESE ARRIVED IN AMERICA YEARS BEFORE COLUMBUS*.
BUT WHEN HE LEARNED THE STONE WAS A FAKE, TO SAVE HIS REPUTATION, HE HIRED A LOCAL CROOK TO STEAL AND DESTROY IT.
SEVERE'S REPUTATION MUST HAVE BEEN REALLY IMPORTANT TO HIM, BECAUSE WHEN I WENT TO MAIL A PIECE OF THE STONE TO A UNIVERSITY FOR AUTHENTI-CATION, HE TRIED TO STOP ME...
...WITH A CAR!

****** *See NANCY DREW Graphic Novel #2 "Writ in Stone" or go to www.papercutz.com/nd/fn1***

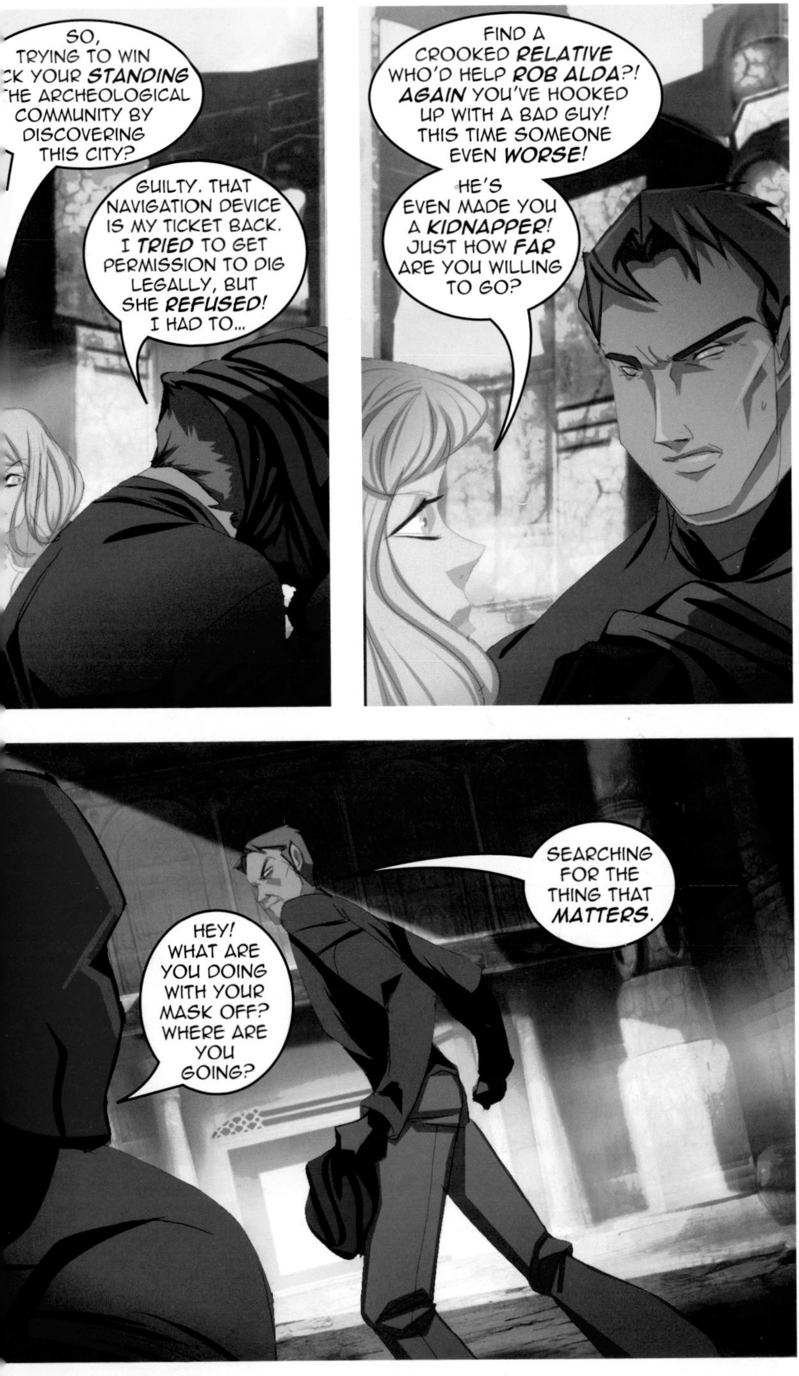
SO, TRYING TO WIN ...CK YOUR STANDING ...THE ARCHEOLOGICAL COMMUNITY BY DISCOVERING THIS CITY?
GUILTY. THAT NAVIGATION DEVICE IS MY TICKET BACK. I TRIED TO GET PERMISSION TO DIG LEGALLY, BUT SHE REFUSED! I HAD TO...
FIND A CROOKED RELATIVE WHO'D HELP ROB ALDA?! AGAIN YOU'VE HOOKED UP WITH A BAD GUY! THIS TIME SOMEONE EVEN WORSE!
HE'S EVEN MADE YOU A KIDNAPPER! JUST HOW FAR ARE YOU WILLING TO GO?
HEY! WHAT ARE YOU DOING WITH YOUR MASK OFF? WHERE ARE YOU GOING?
SEARCHING FOR THE THING THAT MATTERS.

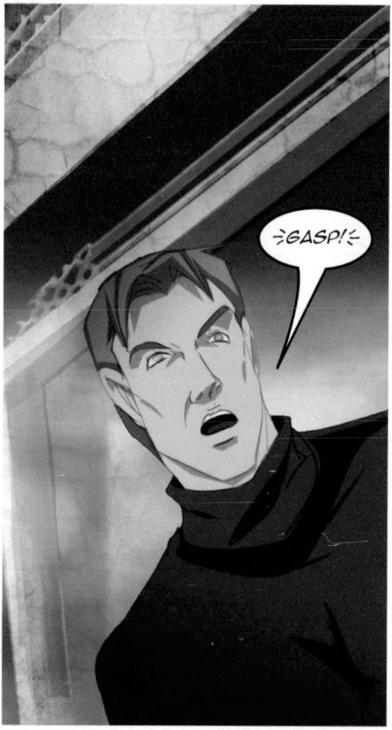
GASP!

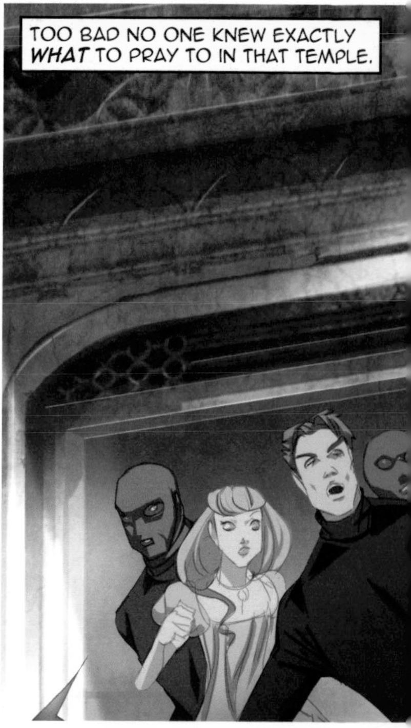
TOO BAD NO ONE KNEW EXACTLY *WHAT* TO PRAY TO IN THAT TEMPLE.

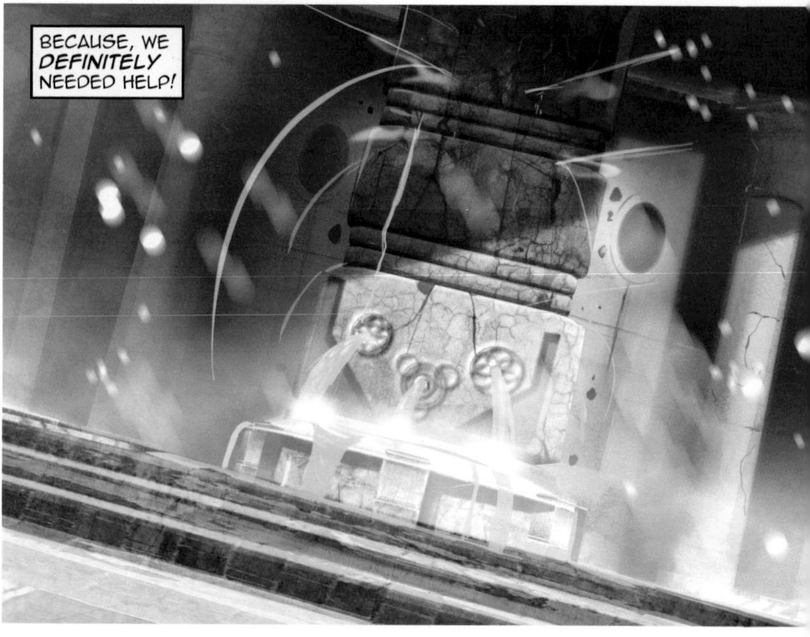
BECAUSE, WE *DEFINITELY* NEEDED HELP!

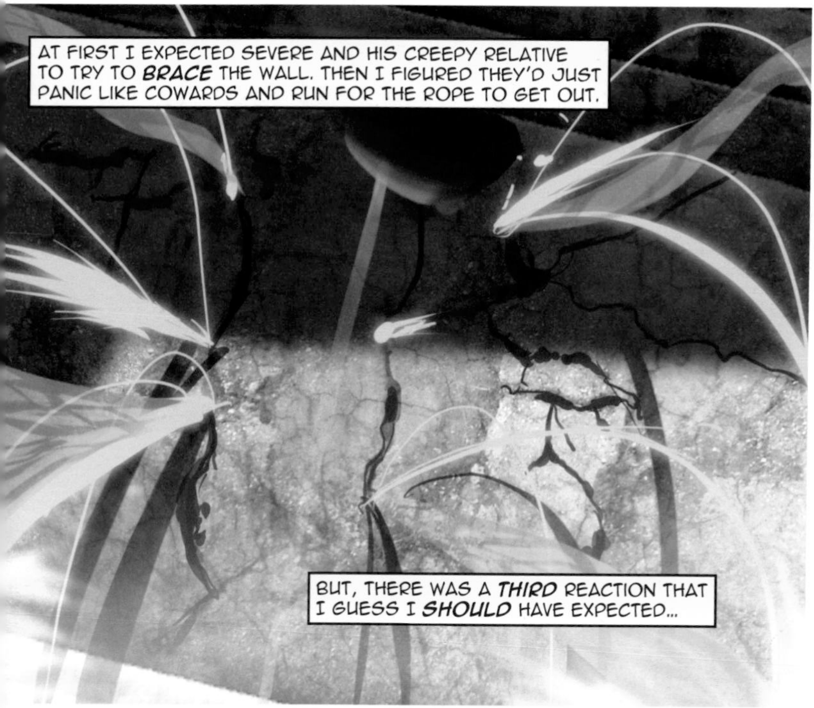
AT FIRST I EXPECTED SEVERE AND HIS CREEPY RELATIVE TO TRY TO *BRACE* THE WALL. THEN I FIGURED THEY'D JUST PANIC LIKE COWARDS AND RUN FOR THE ROPE TO GET OUT.
BUT, THERE WAS A *THIRD* REACTION THAT I GUESS I *SHOULD* HAVE EXPECTED...

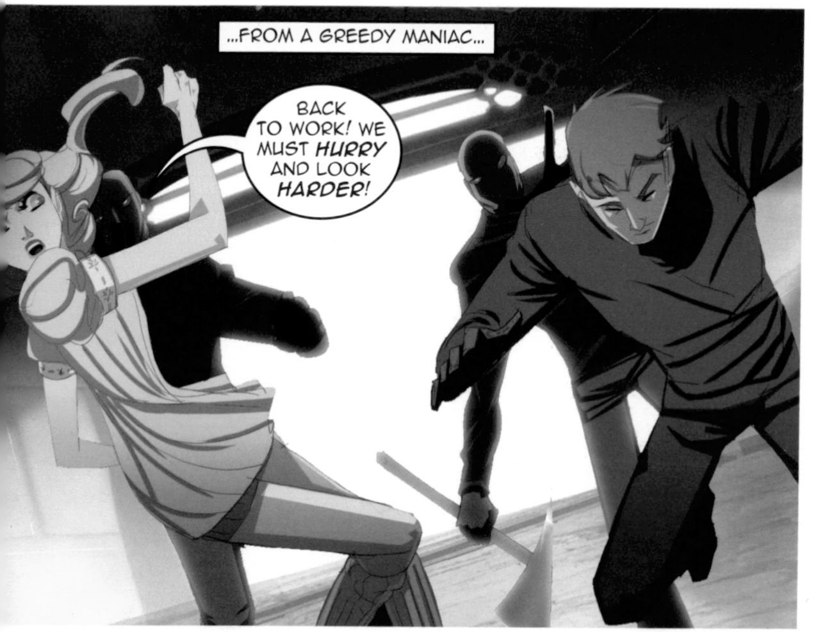
...FROM A GREEDY MANIAC...
BACK TO WORK! WE MUST *HURRY* AND LOOK *HARDER*!

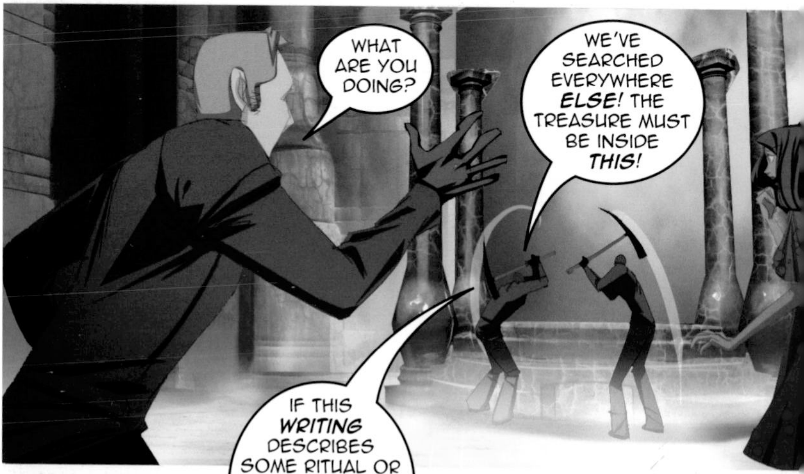
WHAT ARE YOU DOING?
WE'VE SEARCHED EVERYWHERE ELSE! THE TREASURE MUST BE INSIDE THIS!
IF THIS WRITING DESCRIBES SOME RITUAL OR MECHANISM TO OPEN IT, I CAN'T READ IT! NOW, I'M TAKING IT APART!

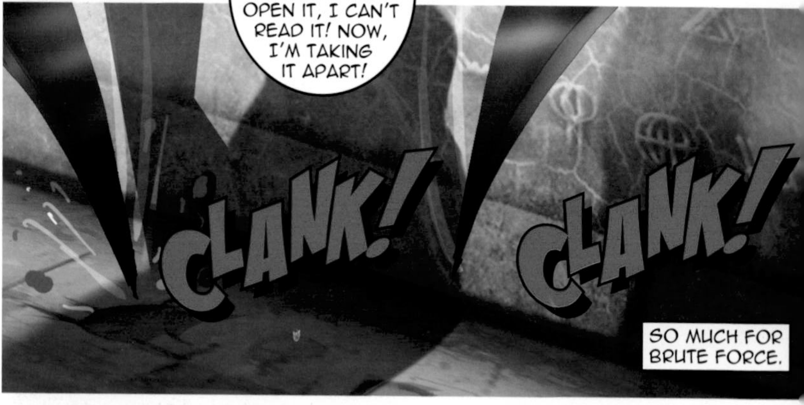
CLANK!
CLANK!
SO MUCH FOR BRUTE FORCE.

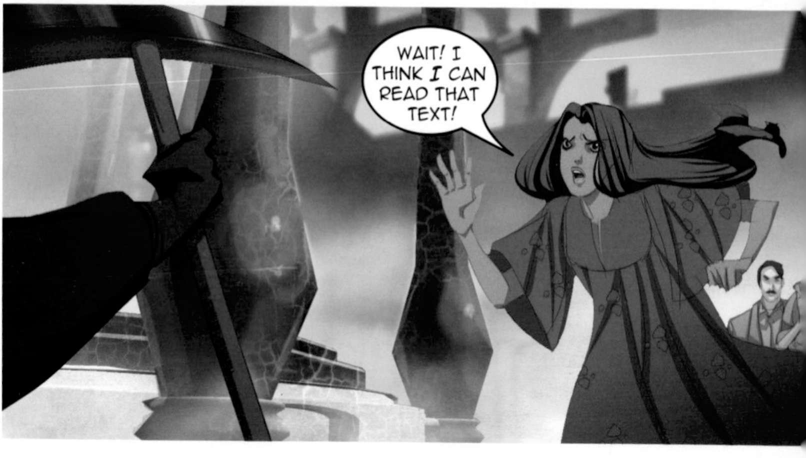
WAIT! I THINK I CAN READ THAT TEXT!

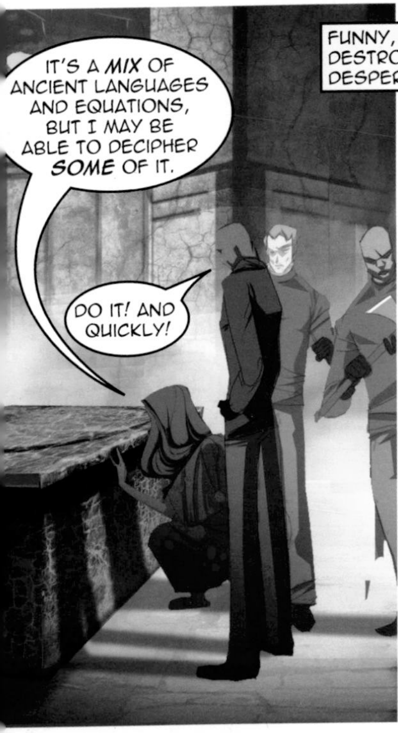
IT'S A MIX OF ANCIENT LANGUAGES AND EQUATIONS, BUT I MAY BE ABLE TO DECIPHER SOME OF IT.
DO IT! AND QUICKLY!

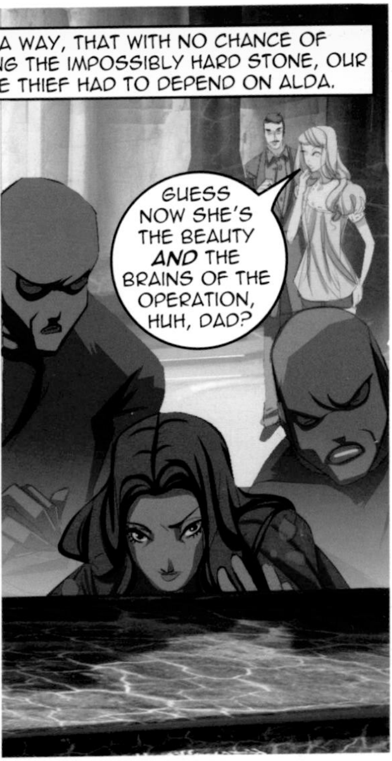
FUNNY, IN A WAY, THAT WITH NO CHANCE OF DESTROYING THE IMPOSSIBLY HARD STONE, OUR DESPERATE THIEF HAD TO DEPEND ON ALDA.
GUESS NOW SHE'S THE BEAUTY AND THE BRAINS OF THE OPERATION, HUH, DAD?

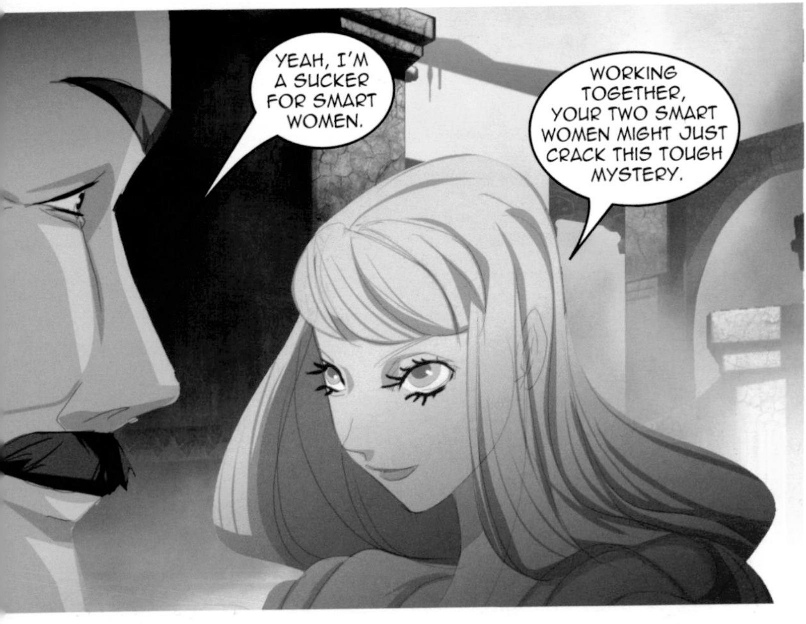
YEAH, I'M A SUCKER FOR SMART WOMEN.
WORKING TOGETHER, YOUR TWO SMART WOMEN MIGHT JUST CRACK THIS TOUGH MYSTERY.

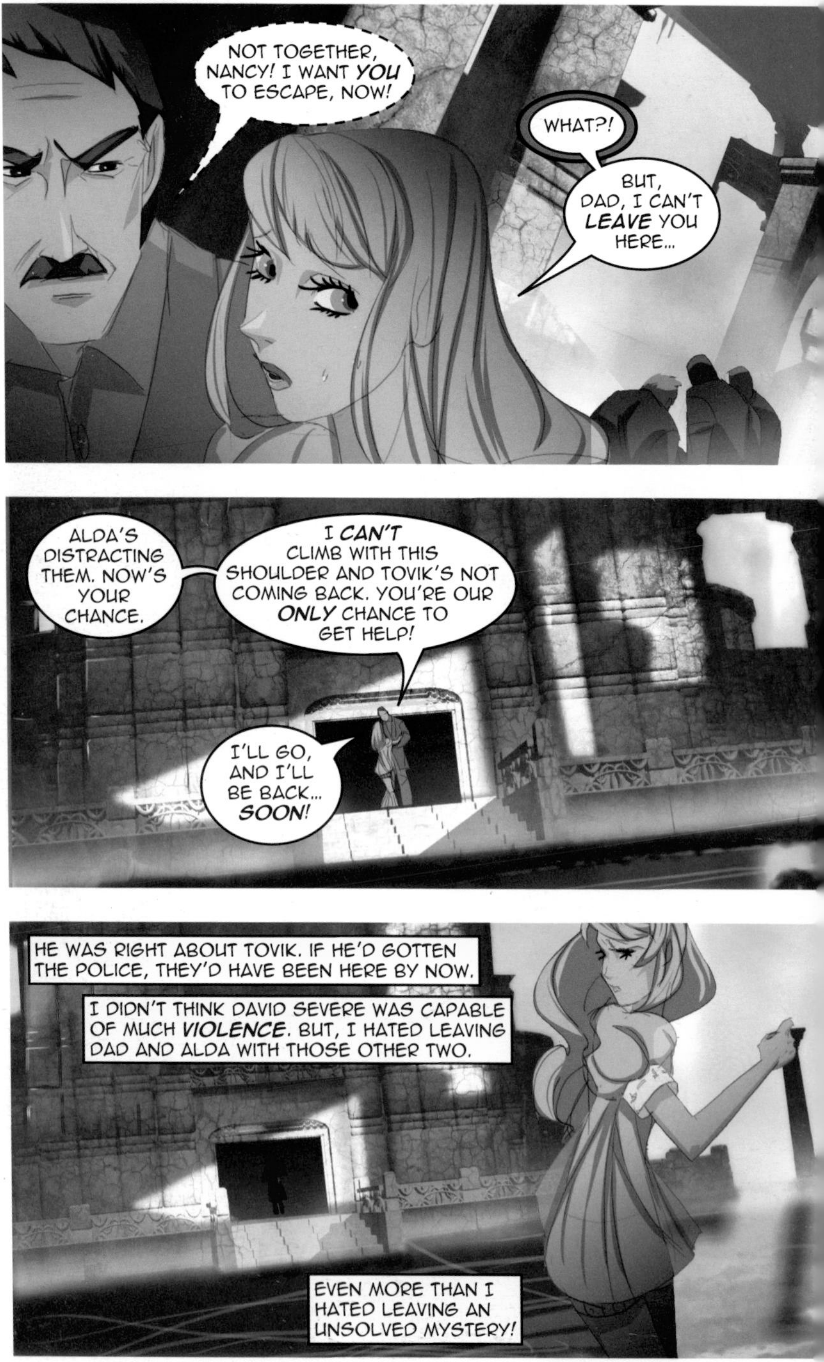
NOT TOGETHER, NANCY! I WANT YOU TO ESCAPE, NOW!
WHAT?!
BUT, DAD, I CAN'T LEAVE YOU HERE...
ALDA'S DISTRACTING THEM. NOW'S YOUR CHANCE.
I CAN'T CLIMB WITH THIS SHOULDER AND TOVIK'S NOT COMING BACK. YOU'RE OUR ONLY CHANCE TO GET HELP!
I'LL GO, AND I'LL BE BACK... SOON!
HE WAS RIGHT ABOUT TOVIK. IF HE'D GOTTEN THE POLICE, THEY'D HAVE BEEN HERE BY NOW.
I DIDN'T THINK DAVID SEVERE WAS CAPABLE OF MUCH VIOLENCE. BUT, I HATED LEAVING DAD AND ALDA WITH THOSE OTHER TWO.
EVEN MORE THAN I HATED LEAVING AN UNSOLVED MYSTERY!

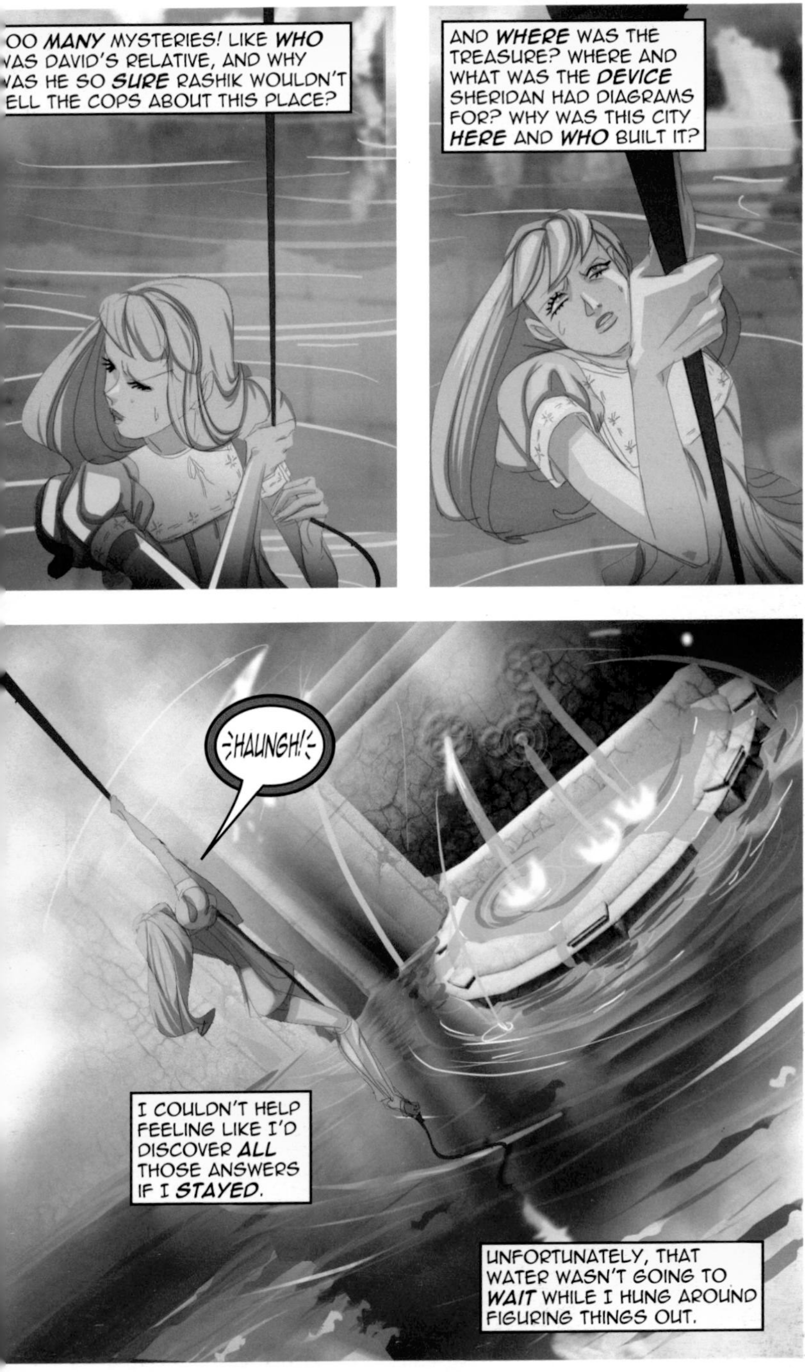

OO MANY MYSTERIES! LIKE WHO VAS DAVID'S RELATIVE, AND WHY VAS HE SO SURE RASHIK WOULDN'T ELL THE COPS ABOUT THIS PLACE?
AND WHERE WAS THE TREASURE? WHERE AND WHAT WAS THE DEVICE SHERIDAN HAD DIAGRAMS FOR? WHY WAS THIS CITY HERE AND WHO BUILT IT?
HAUNGH!
I COULDN'T HELP FEELING LIKE I'D DISCOVER ALL THOSE ANSWERS IF I STAYED.
UNFORTUNATELY, THAT WATER WASN'T GOING TO WAIT WHILE I HUNG AROUND FIGURING THINGS OUT.

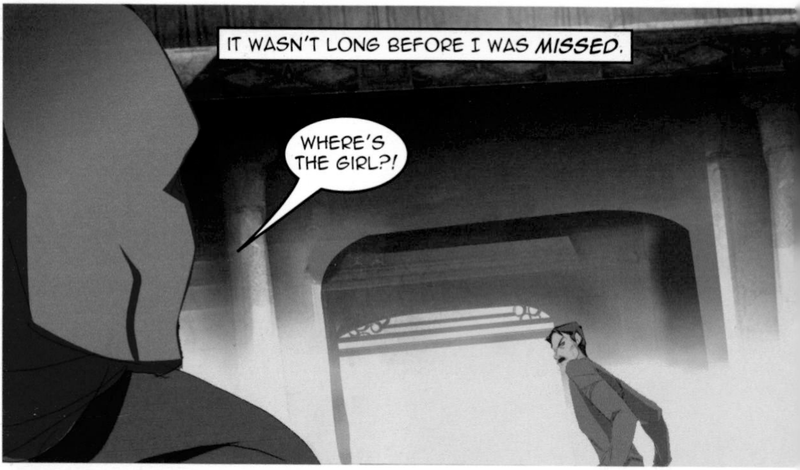
IT WASN'T LONG BEFORE I WAS MISSED.
WHERE'S THE GIRL?!

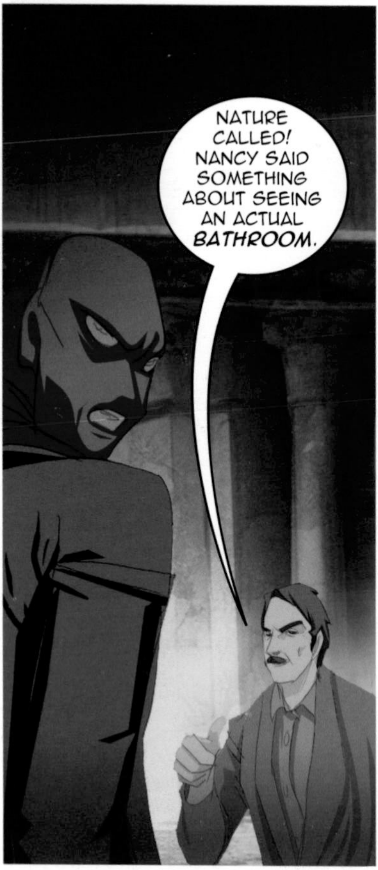
NATURE CALLED! NANCY SAID SOMETHING ABOUT SEEING AN ACTUAL BATHROOM.

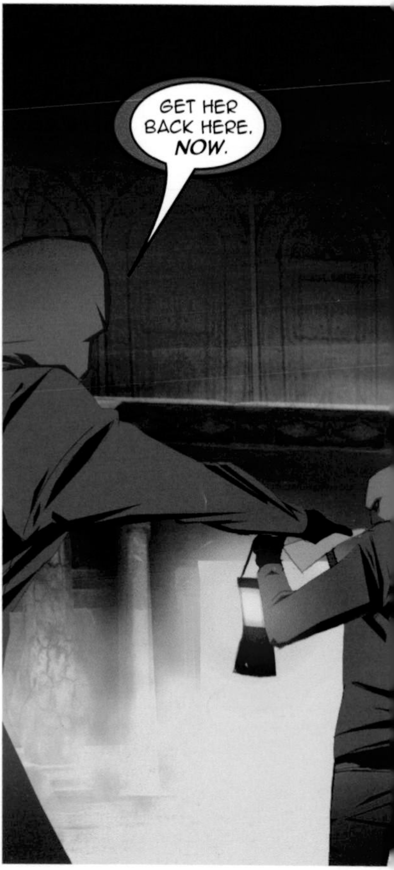
GET HER BACK HERE. NOW.

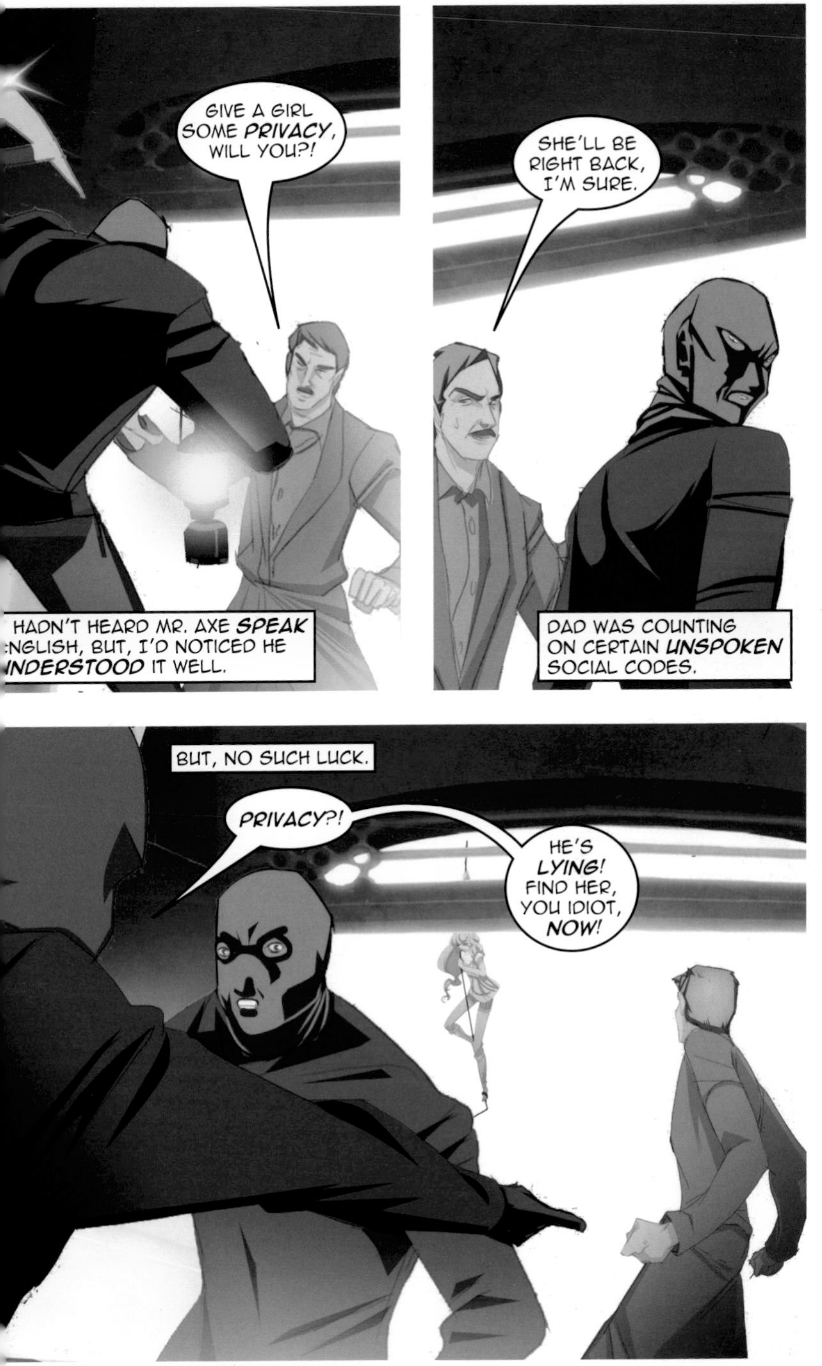

GIVE A GIRL SOME ***PRIVACY***, WILL YOU?!
HADN'T HEARD MR. AXE ***SPEAK***
NGLISH, BUT, I'D NOTICED HE
NDERSTOOD IT WELL.
SHE'LL BE RIGHT BACK, I'M SURE.
DAD WAS COUNTING ON CERTAIN ***UNSPOKEN*** SOCIAL CODES.
BUT, NO SUCH LUCK.
PRIVACY?!
HE'S ***LYING***! FIND HER, YOU IDIOT, ***NOW***!

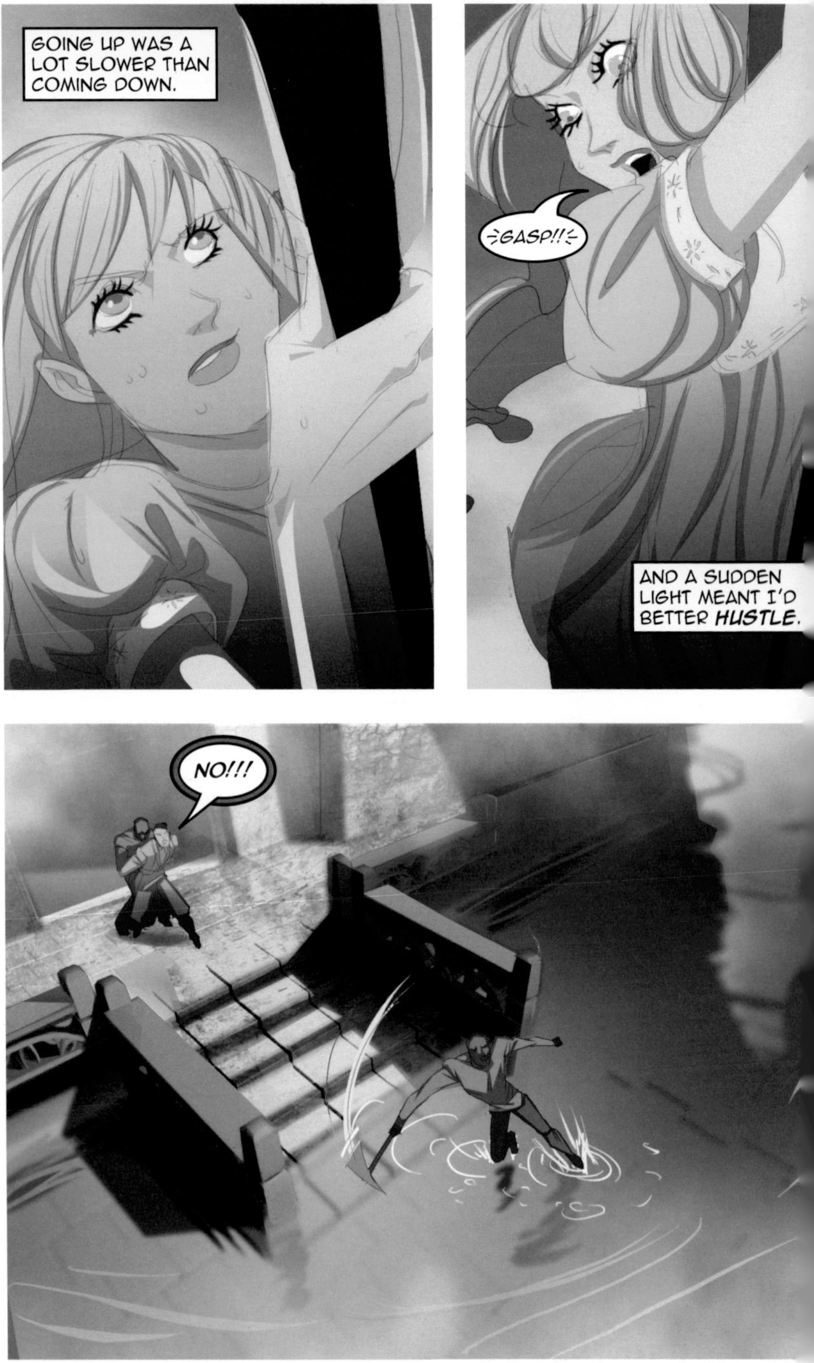
GOING UP WAS A LOT SLOWER THAN COMING DOWN.
GASP!!
AND A SUDDEN LIGHT MEANT I'D BETTER HUSTLE.
NO!!!

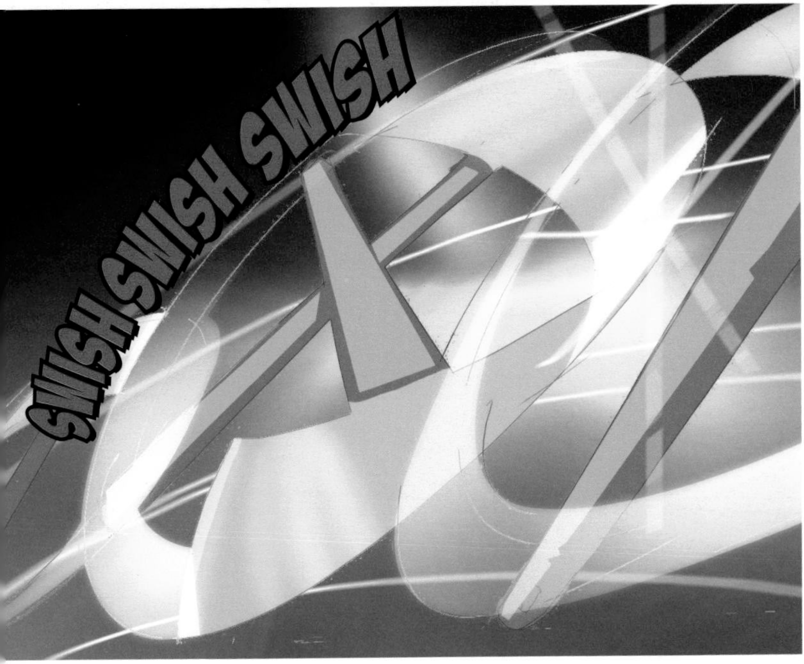
SWISH SWISH SWISH

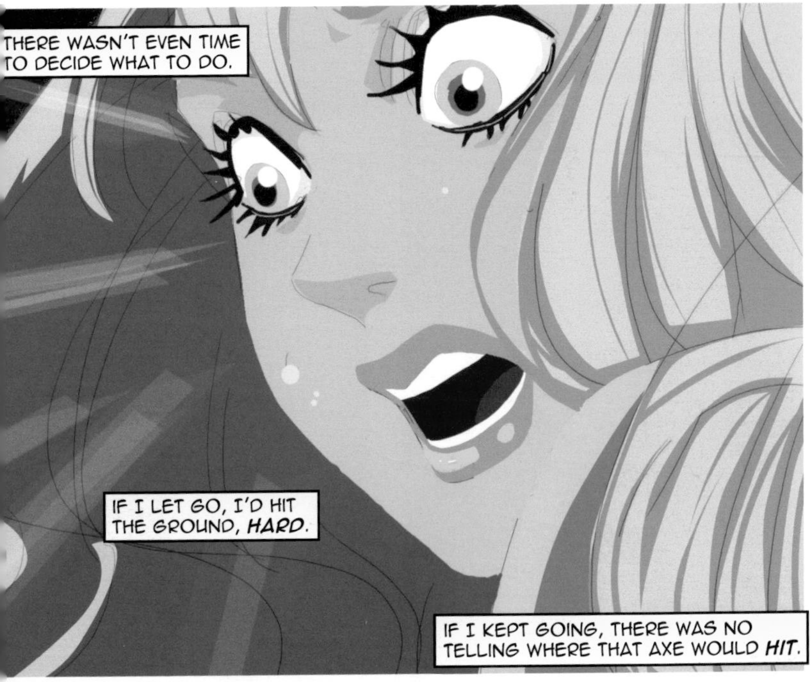
THERE WASN'T EVEN TIME TO DECIDE WHAT TO DO.
IF I LET GO, I'D HIT THE GROUND, HARD.
IF I KEPT GOING, THERE WAS NO TELLING WHERE THAT AXE WOULD HIT.

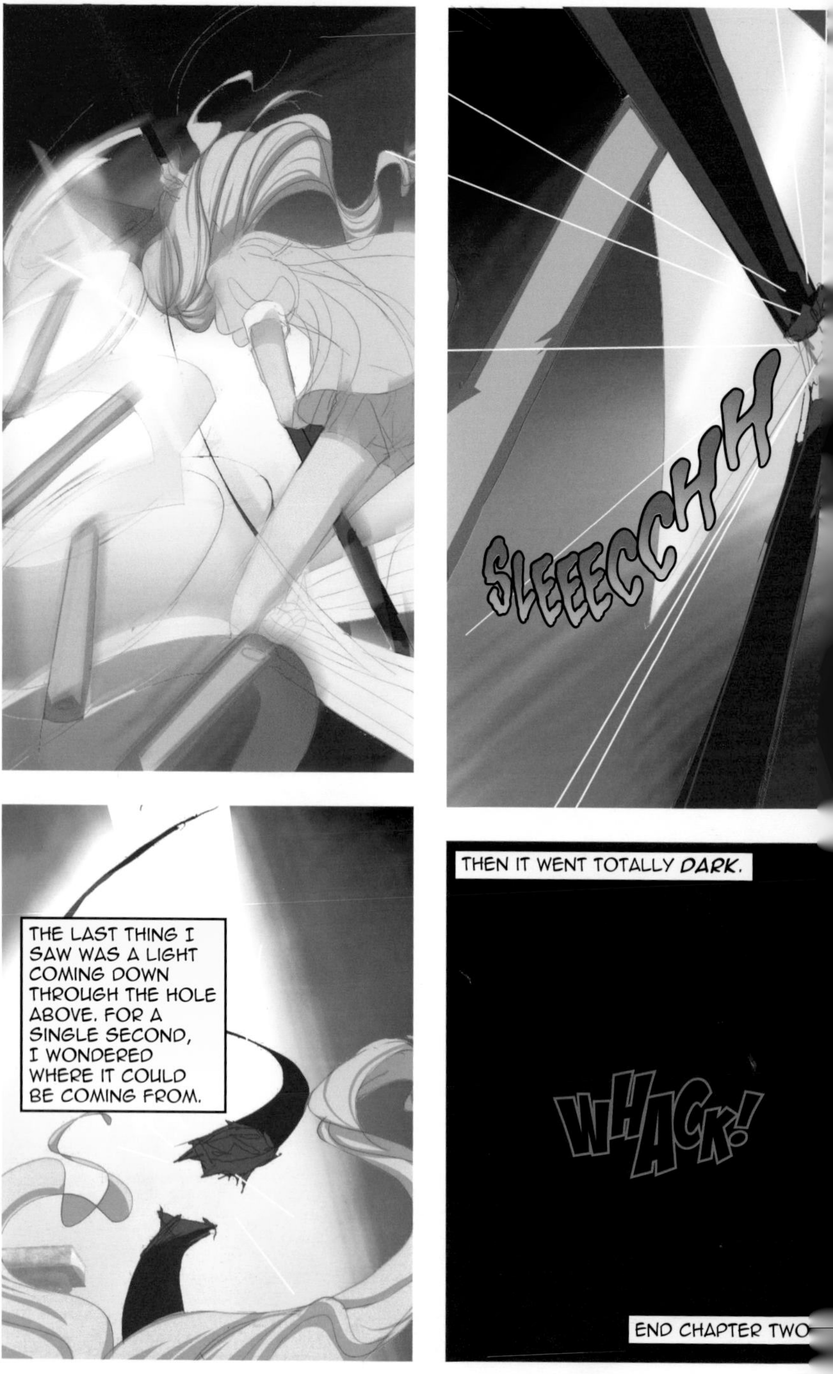
SLEEECCHH
THE LAST THING I SAW WAS A LIGHT COMING DOWN THROUGH THE HOLE ABOVE. FOR A SINGLE SECOND, I WONDERED WHERE IT COULD BE COMING FROM.
THEN IT WENT TOTALLY DARK.
WHACK!
END CHAPTER TWO

NOT SURE HOW LONG IT WAS BEFORE I OPENED MY EYES. BUT, I **WAS** SURE I'D BEEN MOVED. THERE WAS LIGHT. NOT THE LITTLE MYSTERIOUS LIGHT SHINING FROM THE HOLE IN THE CEILING.

THIS LIGHT WAS... ALL AROUND. I REALIZED I WAS IN THE TEMPLE. AT ITS CENTER. HOW WAS IT I HADN'T NOTICED THE GLASS CEILING BEFORE?!

WARM, BEAUTIFUL LIGHT WAS SHINING IN FROM **OUTSIDE** THE TEMPLE -- LIKE THE SUN...OR, MORE LIKE **SEVERAL** SUNS. BUT THAT WAS **IMPOSSIBLE**. WASN'T IT?

I WAS ON THE ROCK. THE TEMPLE'S SACRIFICIAL ROCK. AND I WASN'T **ALONE**.

EVEN WITHOUT FACES, THEIR INTENT WAS CLEAR.

I WAS BEING **SACRIFICED**!

CHAPTER THREE: DEUS EX MACHINA

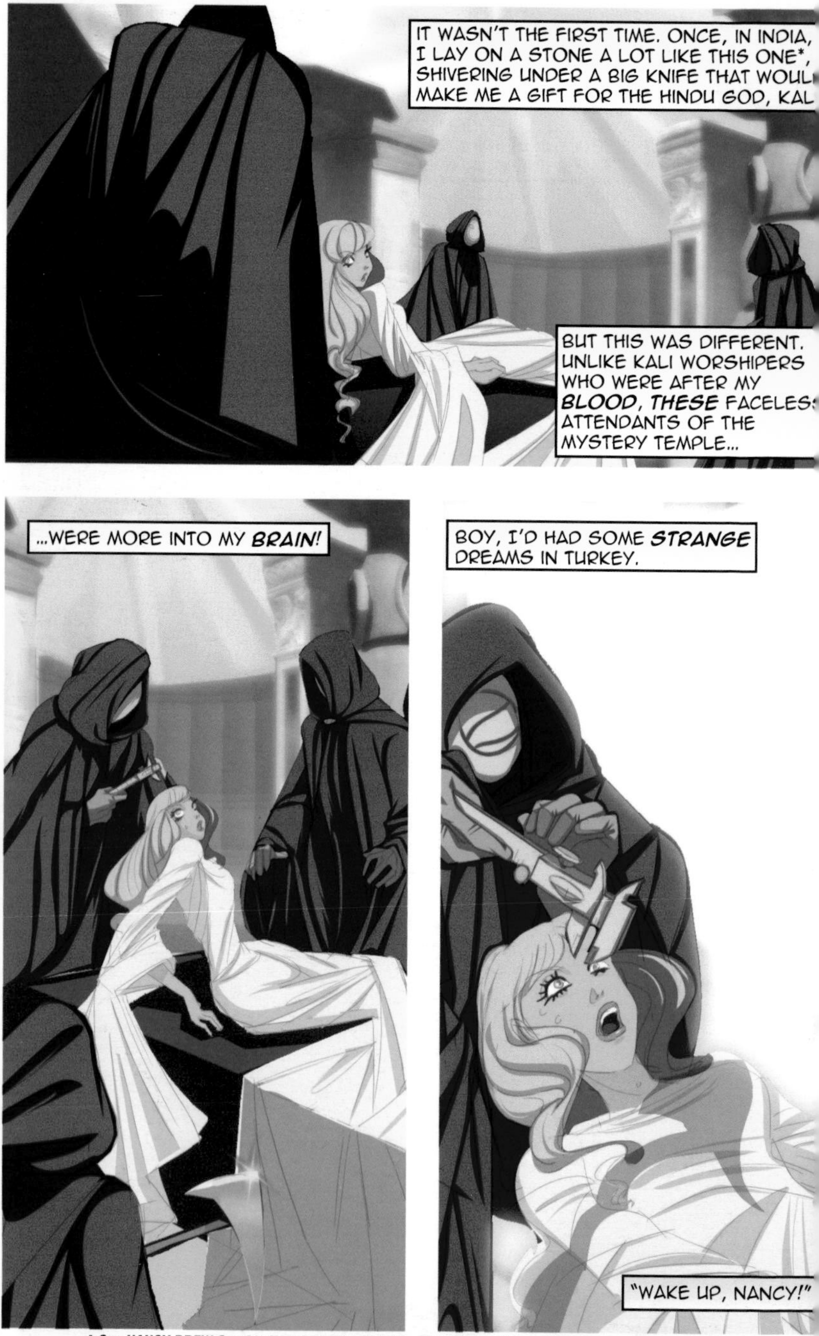
IT WASN'T THE FIRST TIME. ONCE, IN INDIA, I LAY ON A STONE A LOT LIKE THIS ONE*, SHIVERING UNDER A BIG KNIFE THAT WOUL MAKE ME A GIFT FOR THE HINDU GOD, KAL
BUT THIS WAS DIFFERENT. UNLIKE KALI WORSHIPERS WHO WERE AFTER MY BLOOD, THESE FACELES ATTENDANTS OF THE MYSTERY TEMPLE...
...WERE MORE INTO MY BRAIN!
BOY, I'D HAD SOME STRANGE DREAMS IN TURKEY.
"WAKE UP, NANCY!"

*See NANCY DREW Graphic Novel #4 "The Girl Who Wasn't There" or go to www.papercutz.com/nd/fn2

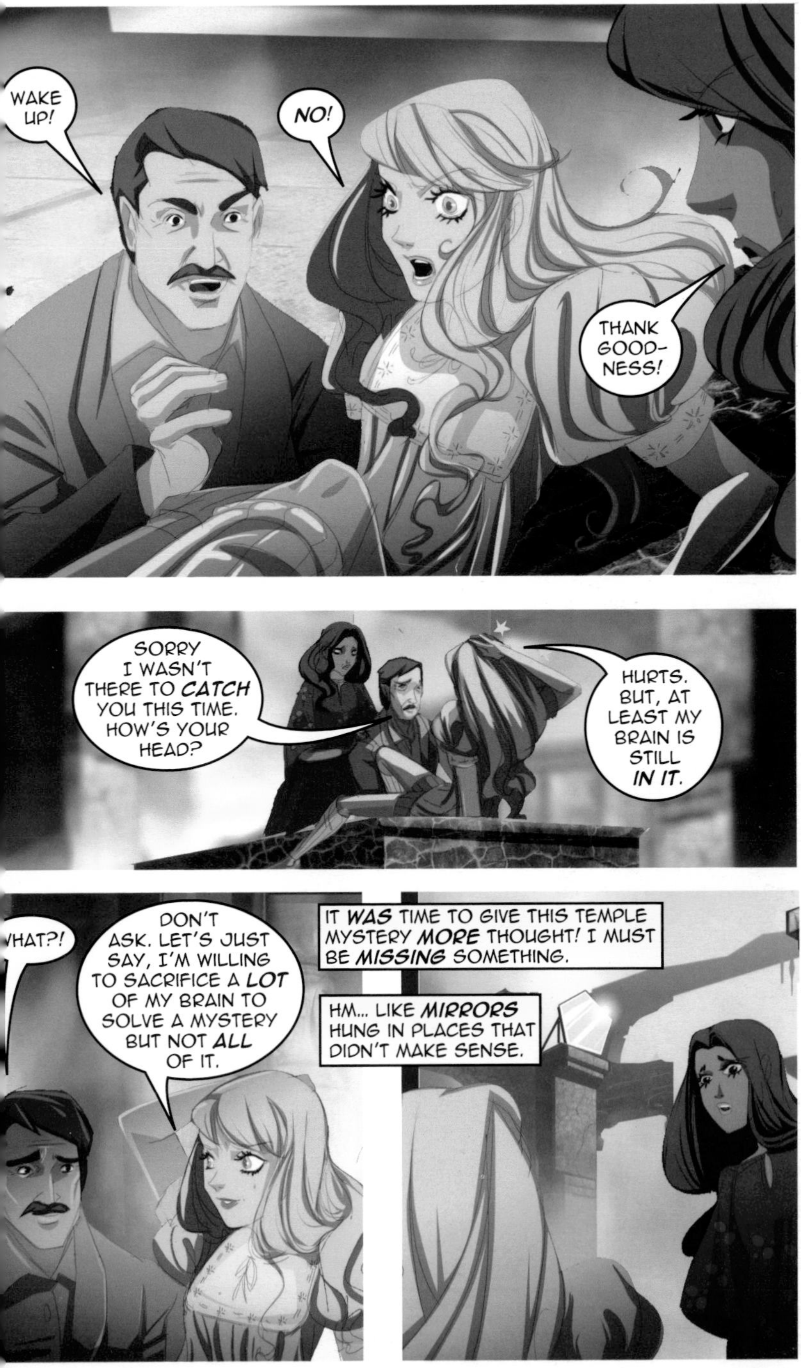

WAKE UP!
NO!
THANK GOODNESS!
SORRY I WASN'T THERE TO *CATCH* YOU THIS TIME. HOW'S YOUR HEAD?
HURTS. BUT, AT LEAST MY BRAIN IS STILL *IN IT*.
HAT?!
DON'T ASK. LET'S JUST SAY, I'M WILLING TO SACRIFICE A *LOT* OF MY BRAIN TO SOLVE A MYSTERY BUT NOT *ALL* OF IT.
IT *WAS* TIME TO GIVE THIS TEMPLE MYSTERY *MORE* THOUGHT! I MUST BE *MISSING* SOMETHING.
HM... LIKE *MIRRORS* HUNG IN PLACES THAT DIDN'T MAKE SENSE.

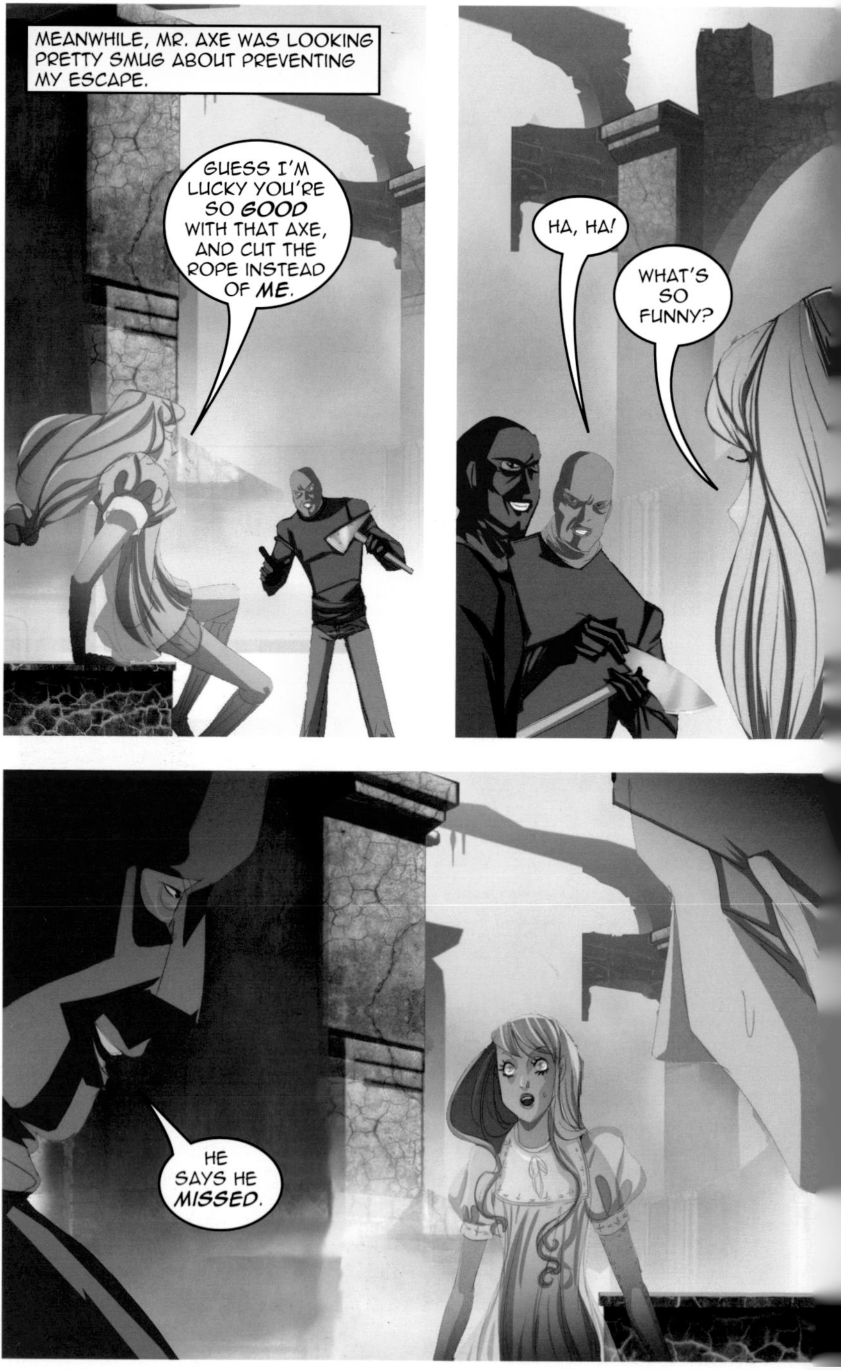
MEANWHILE, MR. AXE WAS LOOKING PRETTY SMUG ABOUT PREVENTING MY ESCAPE.
GUESS I'M LUCKY YOU'RE SO GOOD WITH THAT AXE, AND CUT THE ROPE INSTEAD OF ME.
HA, HA!
WHAT'S SO FUNNY?
HE SAYS HE MISSED.

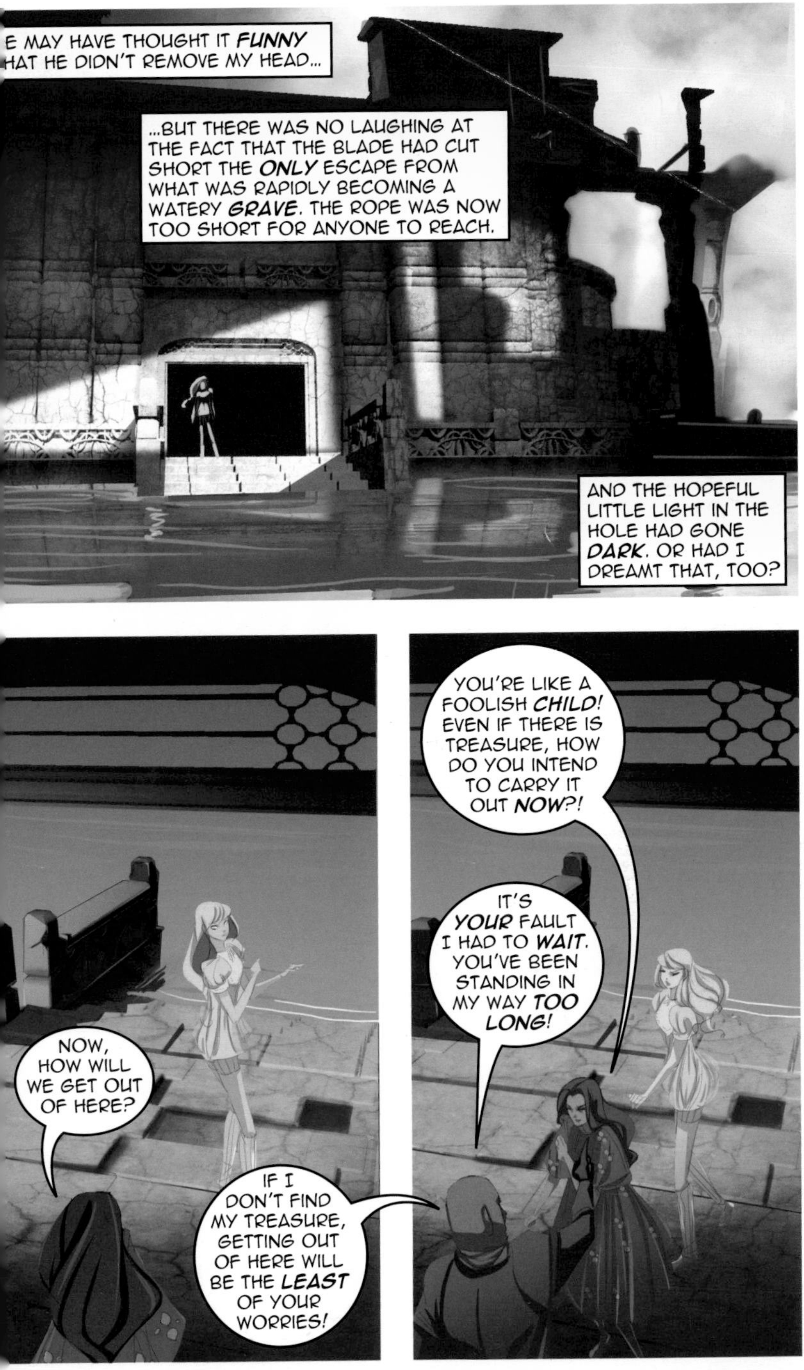
E MAY HAVE THOUGHT IT FUNNY HAT HE DIDN'T REMOVE MY HEAD...
...BUT THERE WAS NO LAUGHING AT THE FACT THAT THE BLADE HAD CUT SHORT THE ONLY ESCAPE FROM WHAT WAS RAPIDLY BECOMING A WATERY GRAVE. THE ROPE WAS NOW TOO SHORT FOR ANYONE TO REACH.
AND THE HOPEFUL LITTLE LIGHT IN THE HOLE HAD GONE DARK. OR HAD I DREAMT THAT, TOO?
NOW, HOW WILL WE GET OUT OF HERE?
IF I DON'T FIND MY TREASURE, GETTING OUT OF HERE WILL BE THE LEAST OF YOUR WORRIES!
YOU'RE LIKE A FOOLISH CHILD! EVEN IF THERE IS TREASURE, HOW DO YOU INTEND TO CARRY IT OUT NOW?!
IT'S YOUR FAULT I HAD TO WAIT. YOU'VE BEEN STANDING IN MY WAY TOO LONG!

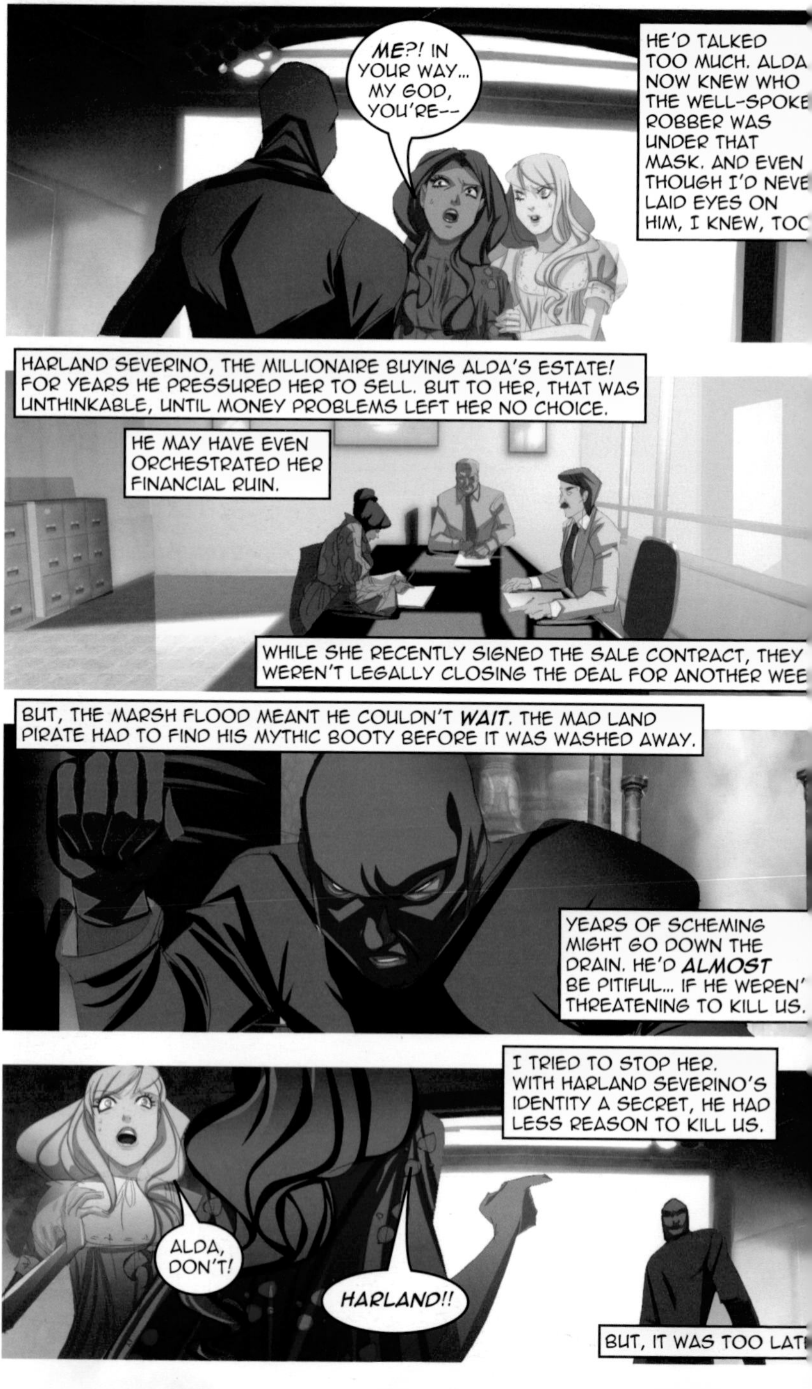

ME?! IN YOUR WAY... MY GOD, YOU'RE--
HE'D TALKED TOO MUCH. ALDA NOW KNEW WHO THE WELL-SPOKE ROBBER WAS UNDER THAT MASK. AND EVEN THOUGH I'D NEVE LAID EYES ON HIM, I KNEW, TOC
HARLAND SEVERINO, THE MILLIONAIRE BUYING ALDA'S ESTATE! FOR YEARS HE PRESSURED HER TO SELL. BUT TO HER, THAT WAS UNTHINKABLE, UNTIL MONEY PROBLEMS LEFT HER NO CHOICE.
HE MAY HAVE EVEN ORCHESTRATED HER FINANCIAL RUIN.
WHILE SHE RECENTLY SIGNED THE SALE CONTRACT, THEY WEREN'T LEGALLY CLOSING THE DEAL FOR ANOTHER WEE
BUT, THE MARSH FLOOD MEANT HE COULDN'T ***WAIT***. THE MAD LAND PIRATE HAD TO FIND HIS MYTHIC BOOTY BEFORE IT WAS WASHED AWAY.
YEARS OF SCHEMING MIGHT GO DOWN THE DRAIN. HE'D ***ALMOST*** BE PITIFUL... IF HE WEREN' THREATENING TO KILL US.
I TRIED TO STOP HER. WITH HARLAND SEVERINO'S IDENTITY A SECRET, HE HAD LESS REASON TO KILL US.
ALDA, DON'T!
HARLAND!!
BUT, IT WAS TOO LAT

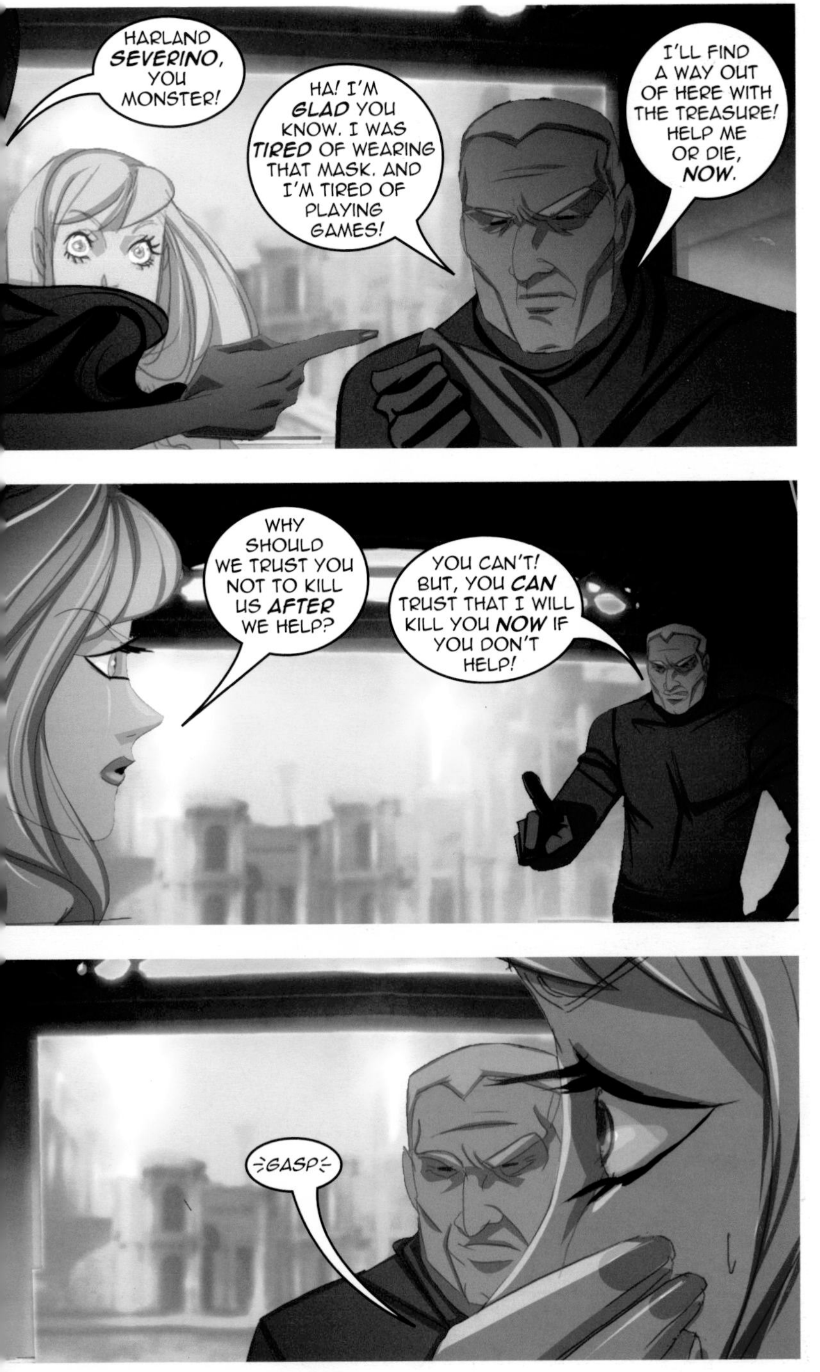
HARLAND SEVERINO, YOU MONSTER!
HA! I'M GLAD YOU KNOW. I WAS TIRED OF WEARING THAT MASK. AND I'M TIRED OF PLAYING GAMES!
I'LL FIND A WAY OUT OF HERE WITH THE TREASURE! HELP ME OR DIE, NOW.
WHY SHOULD WE TRUST YOU NOT TO KILL US AFTER WE HELP?
YOU CAN'T! BUT, YOU CAN TRUST THAT I WILL KILL YOU NOW IF YOU DON'T HELP!
GASP

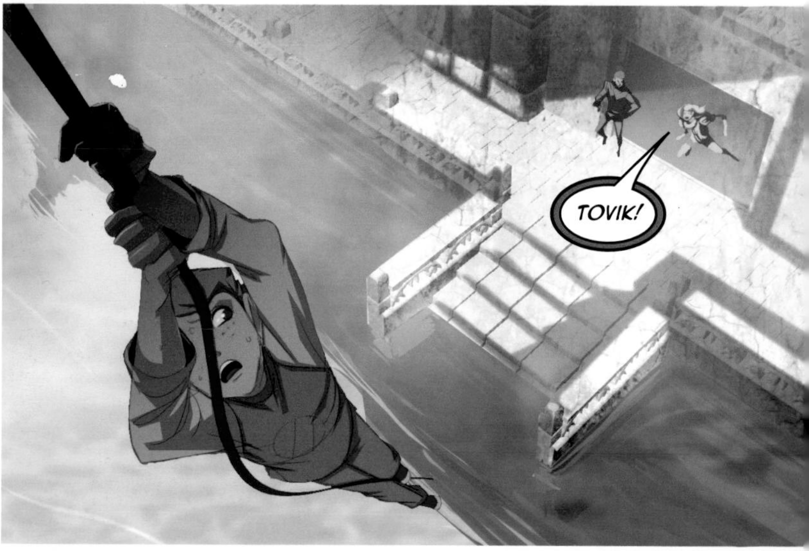
TOVIK!

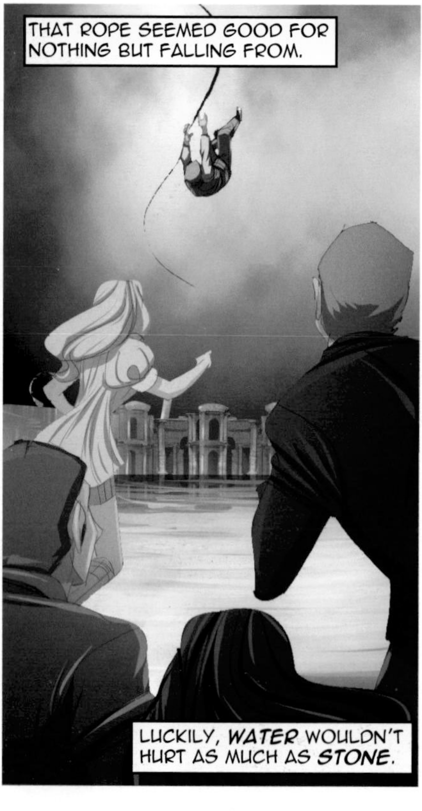
THAT ROPE SEEMED GOOD FOR NOTHING BUT FALLING FROM.
LUCKILY, WATER WOULDN'T HURT AS MUCH AS STONE.

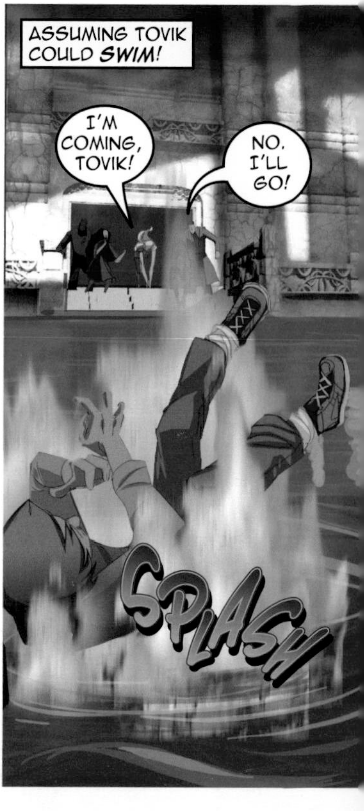
ASSUMING TOVIK COULD SWIM!
I'M COMING, TOVIK!
NO. I'LL GO!
SPLASH

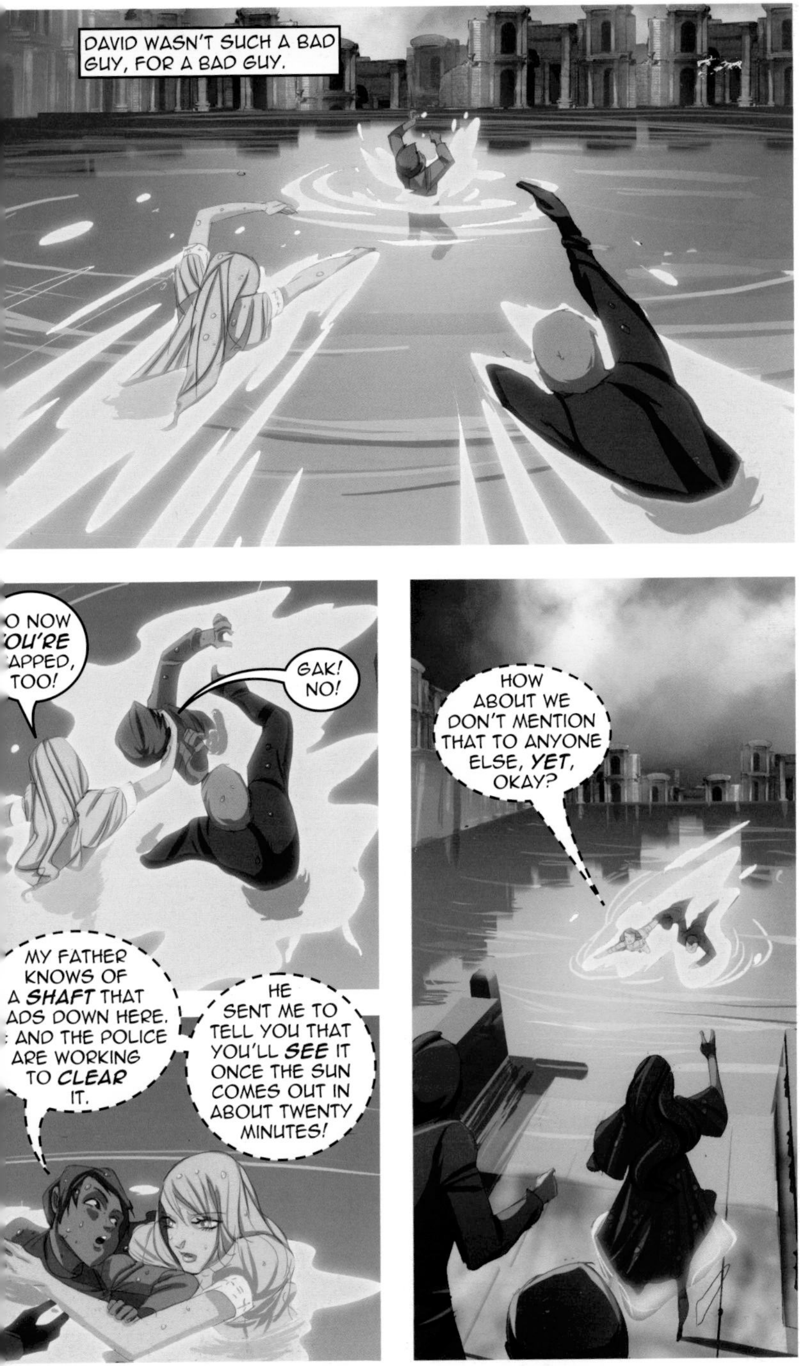

DAVID WASN'T SUCH A BAD GUY, FOR A BAD GUY.
O NOW OU'RE APPED, TOO!
GAK! NO!
MY FATHER KNOWS OF A SHAFT THAT ADS DOWN HERE. AND THE POLICE ARE WORKING TO CLEAR IT.
HE SENT ME TO TELL YOU THAT YOU'LL SEE IT ONCE THE SUN COMES OUT IN ABOUT TWENTY MINUTES!
HOW ABOUT WE DON'T MENTION THAT TO ANYONE ELSE, YET, OKAY?

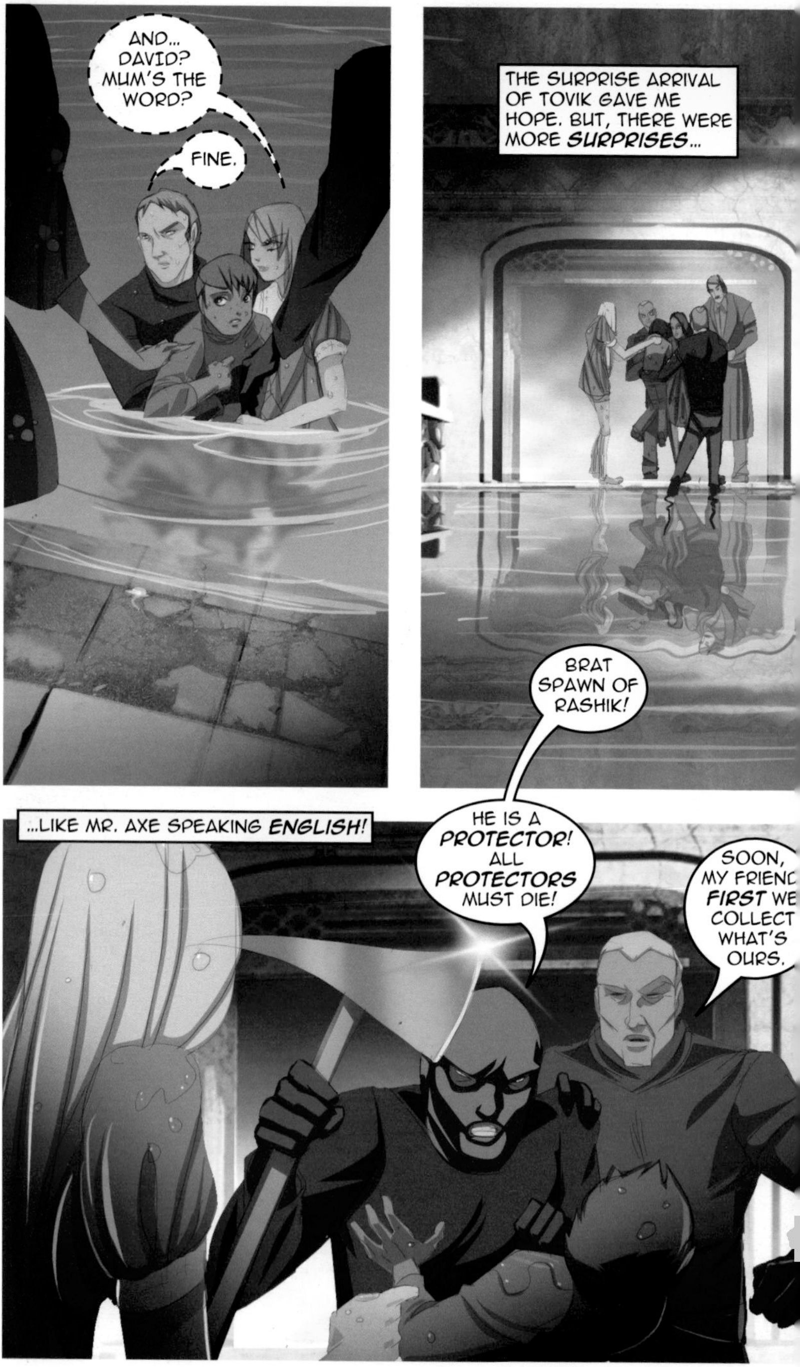
AND... DAVID? MUM'S THE WORD?
FINE.
THE SURPRISE ARRIVAL OF TOVIK GAVE ME HOPE. BUT, THERE WERE MORE SURPRISES...
BRAT SPAWN OF RASHIK!
...LIKE MR. AXE SPEAKING ENGLISH!
HE IS A PROTECTOR! ALL PROTECTORS MUST DIE!
SOON, MY FRIEND FIRST WE COLLECT WHAT'S OURS.

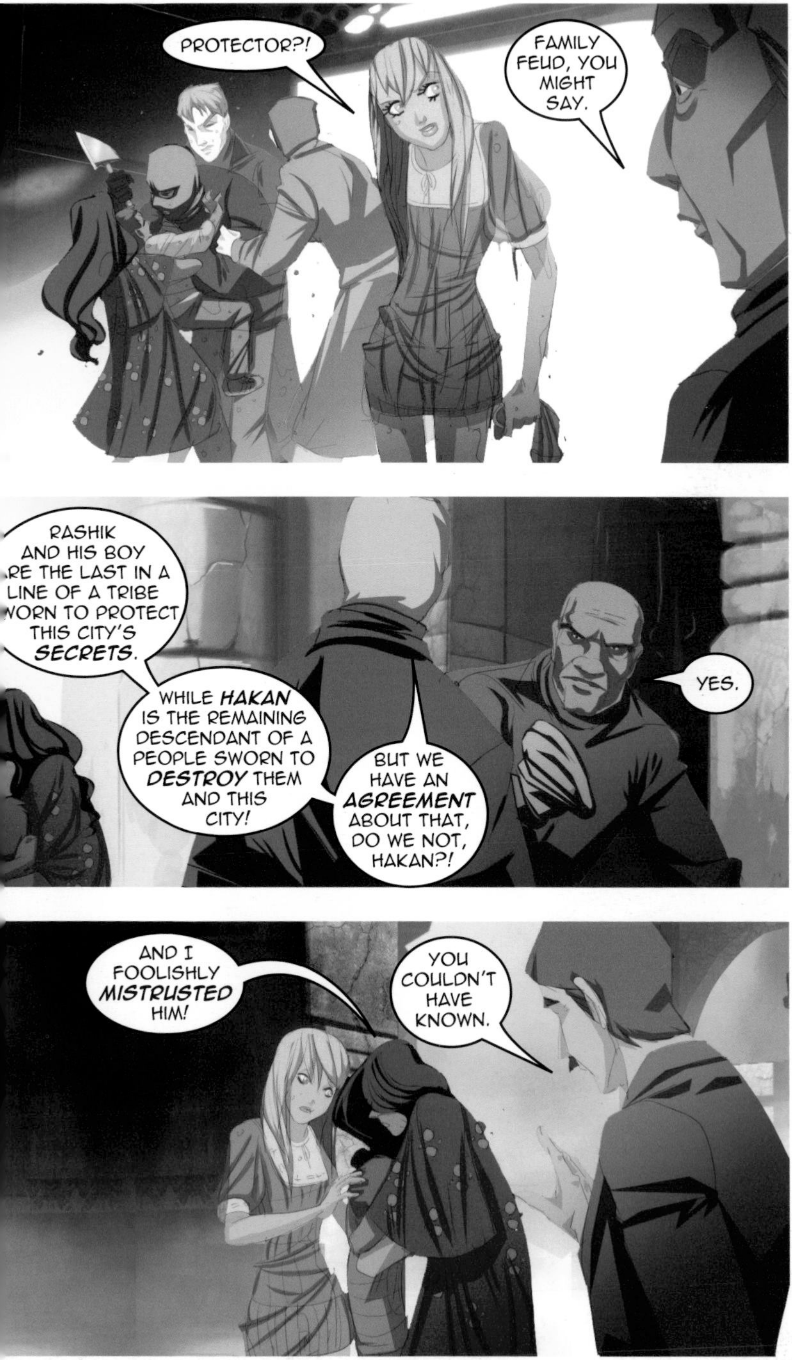
PROTECTOR?!
FAMILY FEUD, YOU MIGHT SAY.
RASHIK AND HIS BOY RE THE LAST IN A LINE OF A TRIBE ORN TO PROTECT THIS CITY'S SECRETS.
WHILE HAKAN IS THE REMAINING DESCENDANT OF A PEOPLE SWORN TO DESTROY THEM AND THIS CITY!
BUT WE HAVE AN AGREEMENT ABOUT THAT, DO WE NOT, HAKAN?!
YES.
AND I FOOLISHLY MISTRUSTED HIM!
YOU COULDN'T HAVE KNOWN.

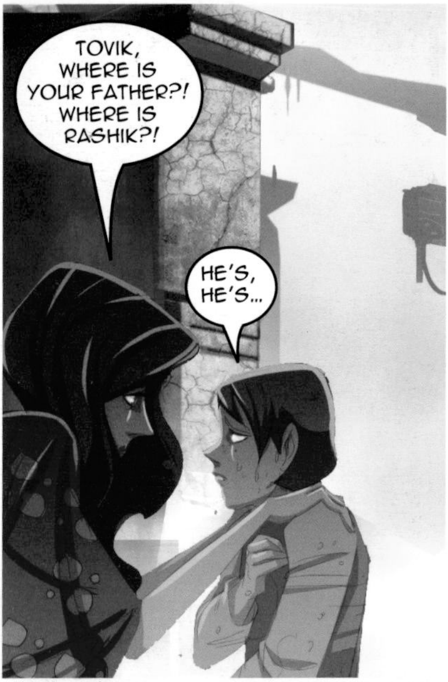
TOVIK, WHERE IS YOUR FATHER?! WHERE IS RASHIK?!
HE'S, HE'S...

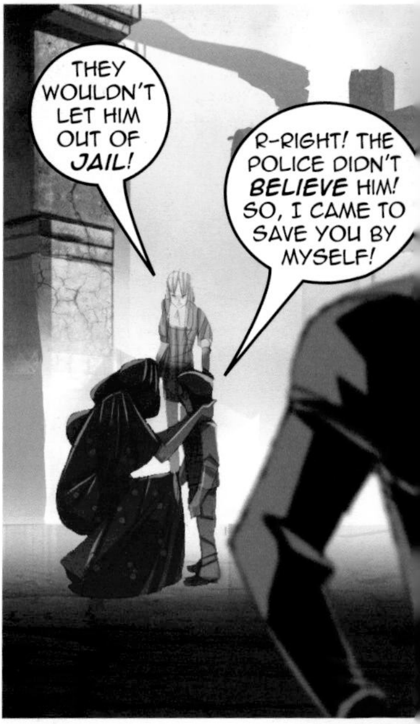
THEY WOULDN'T LET HIM OUT OF JAIL!
R-RIGHT! THE POLICE DIDN'T BELIEVE HIM! SO, I CAME TO SAVE YOU BY MYSELF!

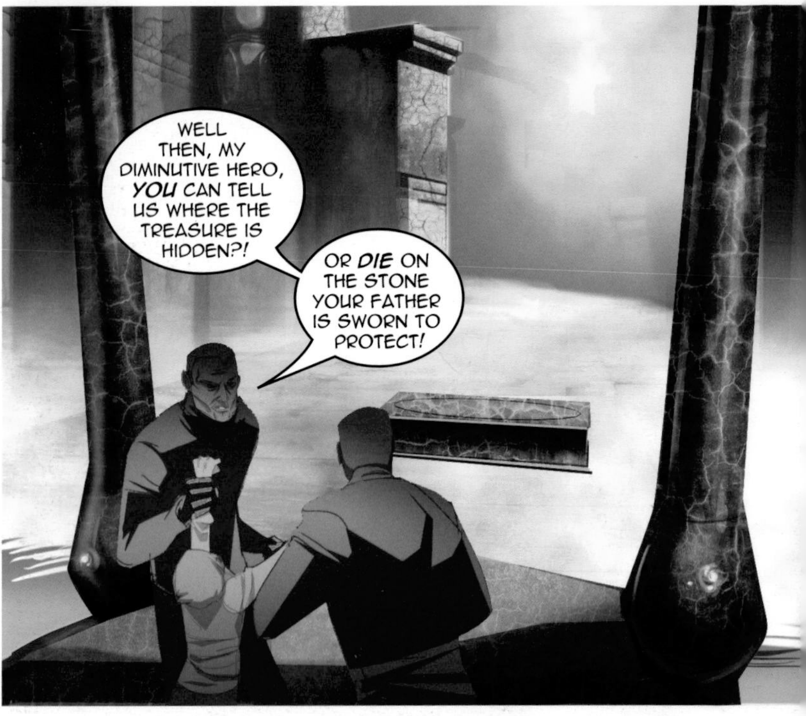
WELL THEN, MY DIMINUTIVE HERO, YOU CAN TELL US WHERE THE TREASURE IS HIDDEN?!
OR DIE ON THE STONE YOUR FATHER IS SWORN TO PROTECT!

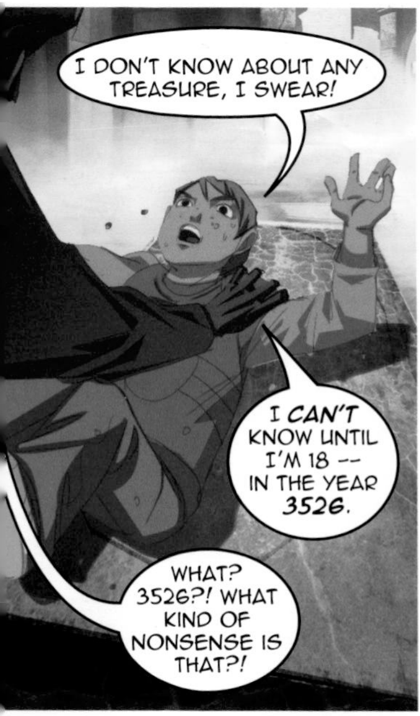
I DON'T KNOW ABOUT ANY TREASURE, I SWEAR!
I *CAN'T* KNOW UNTIL I'M 18 -- IN THE YEAR **3526**.
WHAT? 3526?! WHAT KIND OF NONSENSE IS THAT?!

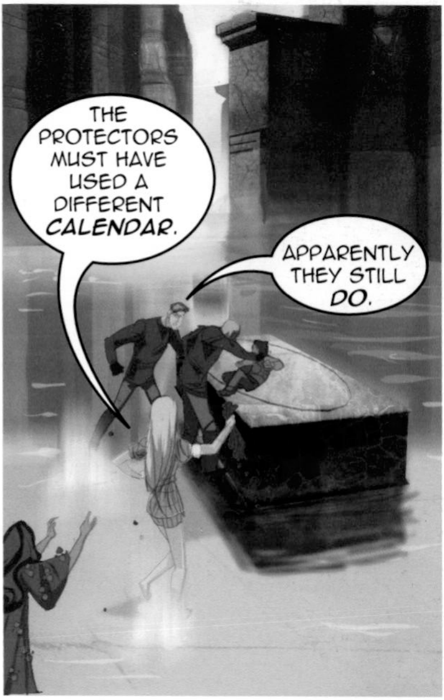
THE PROTECTORS MUST HAVE USED A DIFFERENT **CALENDAR**.
APPARENTLY THEY STILL *DO*.

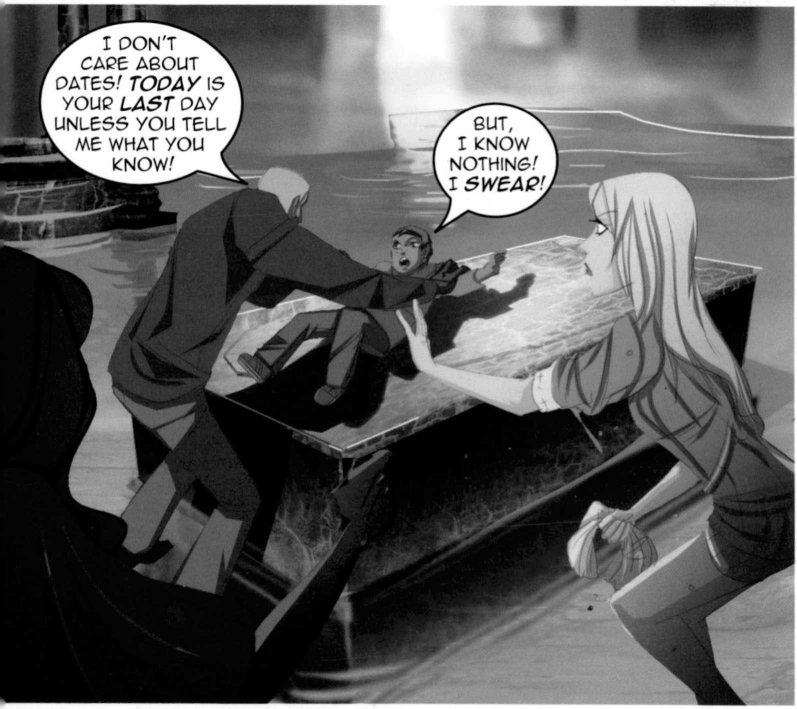
I DON'T CARE ABOUT DATES! *TODAY* IS YOUR *LAST* DAY UNLESS YOU TELL ME WHAT YOU KNOW!
BUT, I KNOW NOTHING! I *SWEAR!*

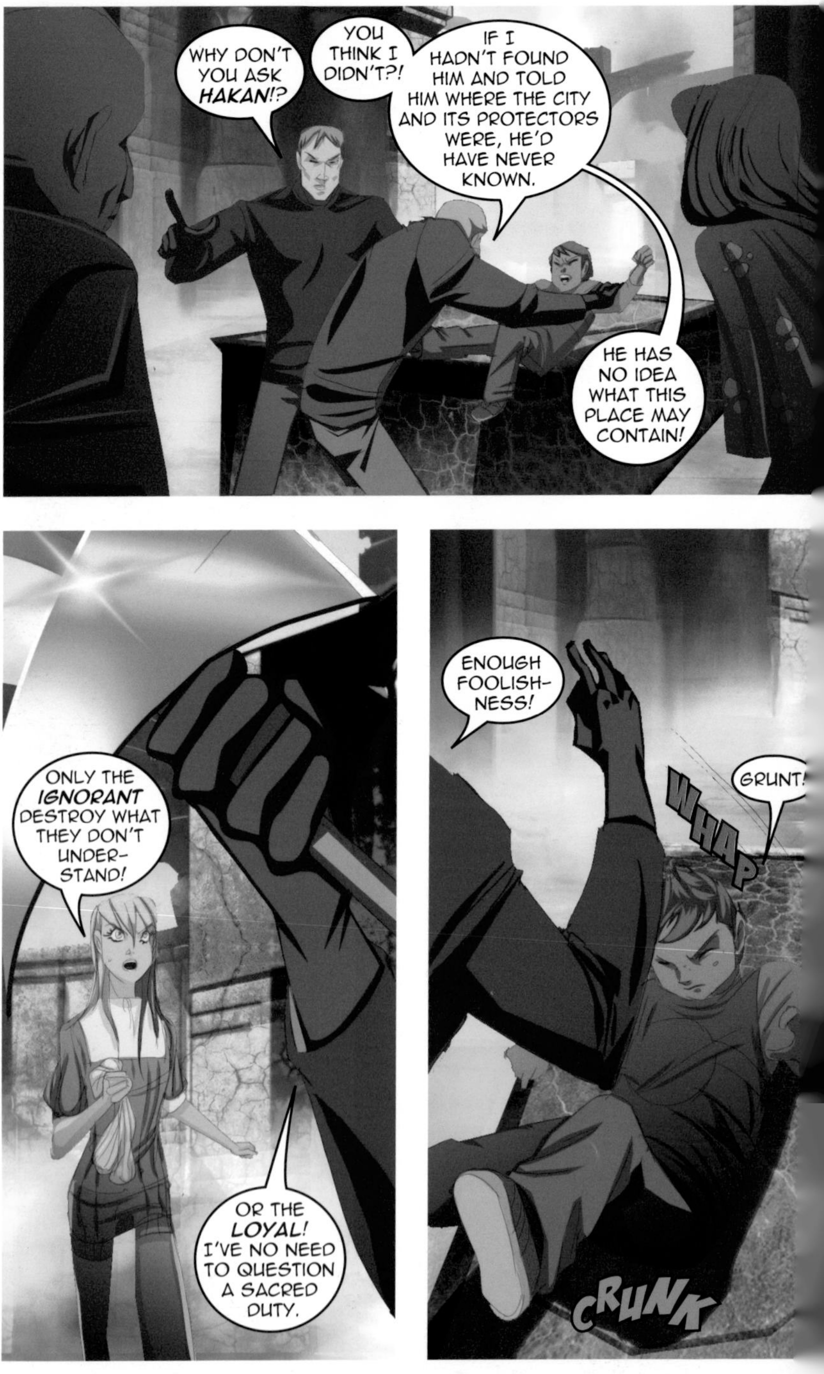
WHY DON'T YOU ASK HAKAN!?
YOU THINK I DIDN'T?!
IF I HADN'T FOUND HIM AND TOLD HIM WHERE THE CITY AND ITS PROTECTORS WERE, HE'D HAVE NEVER KNOWN.
HE HAS NO IDEA WHAT THIS PLACE MAY CONTAIN!
ONLY THE IGNORANT DESTROY WHAT THEY DON'T UNDER-STAND!
OR THE LOYAL! I'VE NO NEED TO QUESTION A SACRED DUTY.
ENOUGH FOOLISH-NESS!
WHAP
GRUNT!
CRUNK

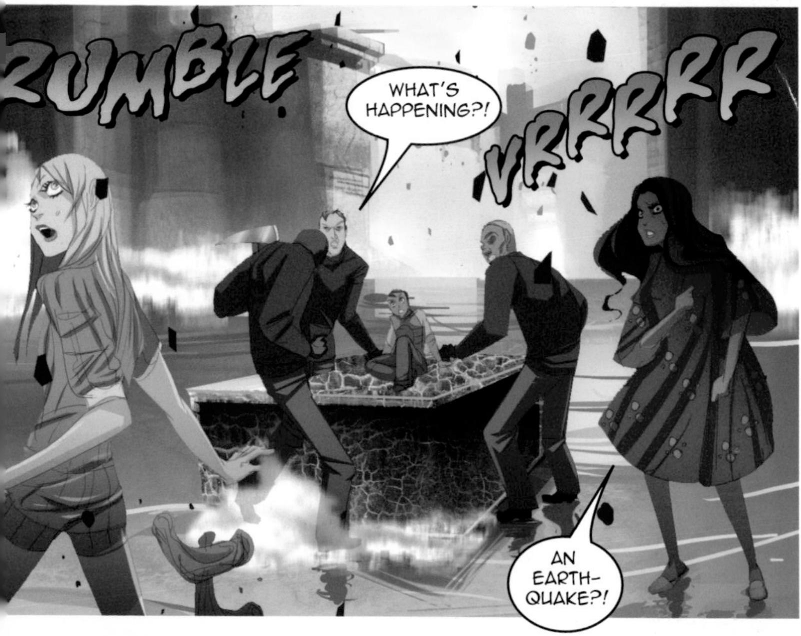
RUMBLE
WHAT'S HAPPENING?!
VRRRRR
AN EARTH-QUAKE?!

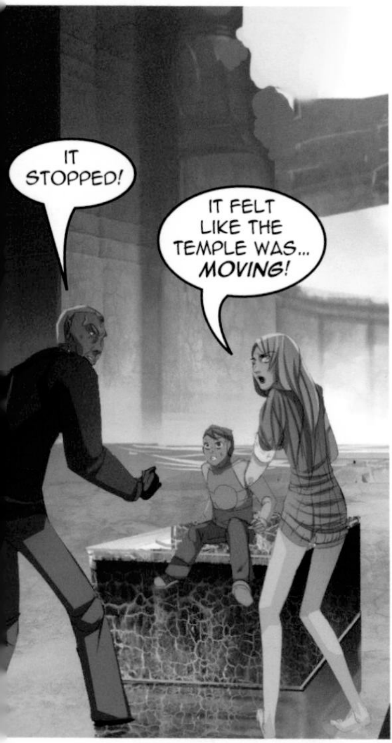
IT STOPPED!
IT FELT LIKE THE TEMPLE WAS... *MOVING*!

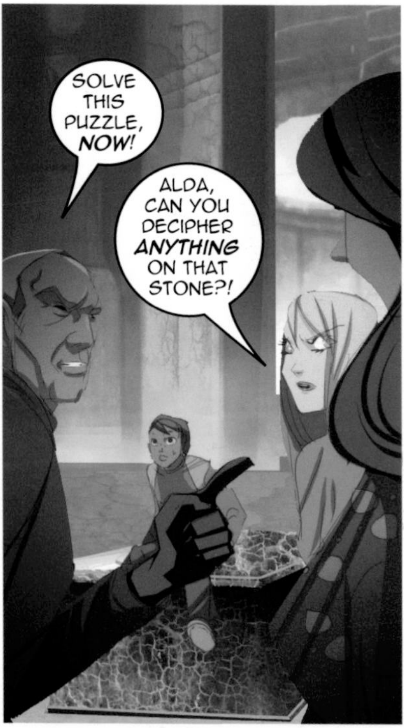
SOLVE THIS PUZZLE, *NOW*!
ALDA, CAN YOU DECIPHER *ANYTHING* ON THAT STONE?!

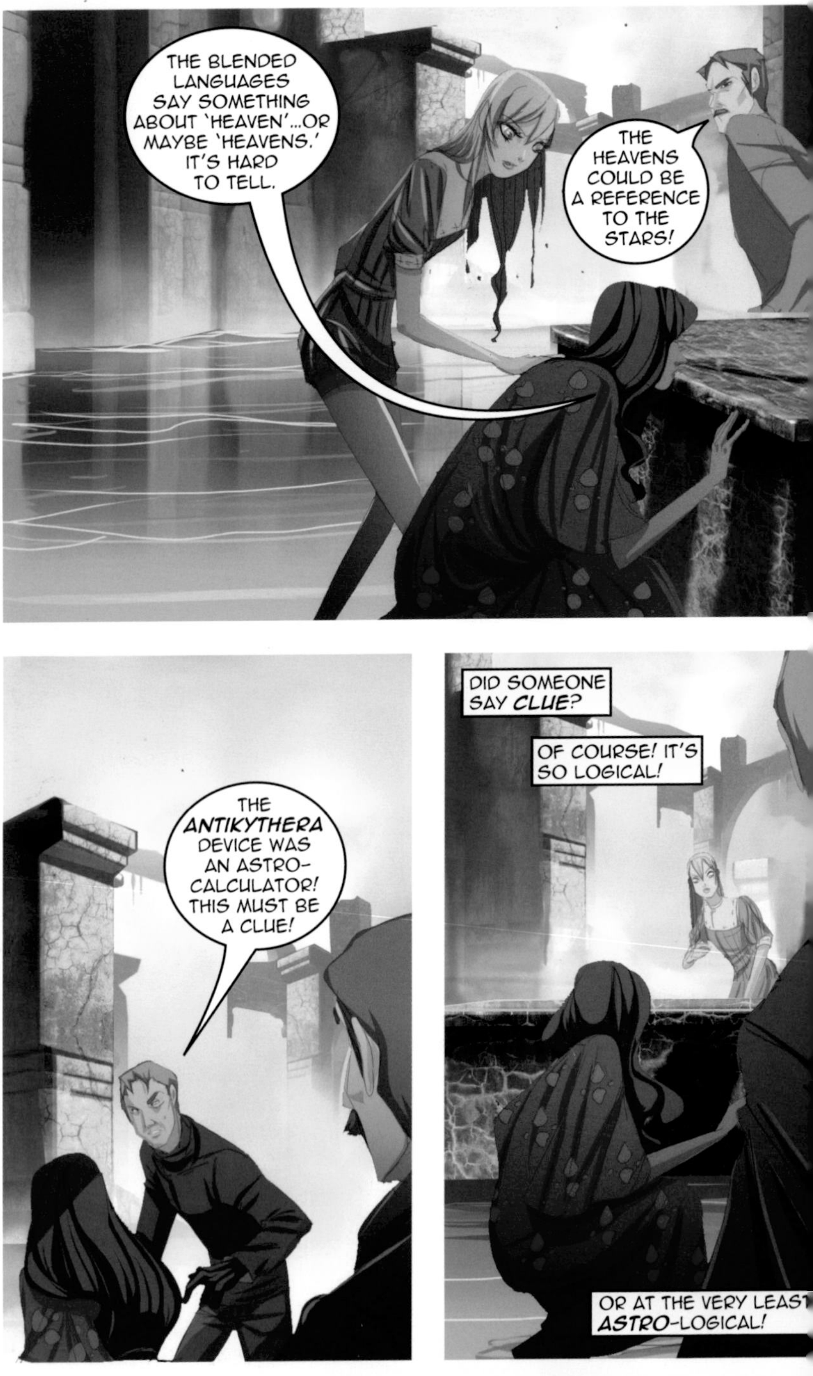
THE BLENDED LANGUAGES SAY SOMETHING ABOUT 'HEAVEN'...OR MAYBE 'HEAVENS.' IT'S HARD TO TELL.
THE HEAVENS COULD BE A REFERENCE TO THE STARS!
THE *ANTIKYTHERA* DEVICE WAS AN ASTRO-CALCULATOR! THIS MUST BE A CLUE!
DID SOMEONE SAY *CLUE*?
OF COURSE! IT'S SO LOGICAL!
OR AT THE VERY LEAST *ASTRO*-LOGICAL!

TOVIK TRIGGERED A MECHANISM WHEN HE BOUNCED ON THE STONE. NOW THE SHAKING WATER WASHED AWAY THE MURKY MYSTERY OF THIS PLACE.

LOOK!

MY DREAM *WAS* TELLING ME SOMETHING! THE SECRET WAS IN MY *BRAIN*. IT WAS JUST *COVERED* WITH DUST.

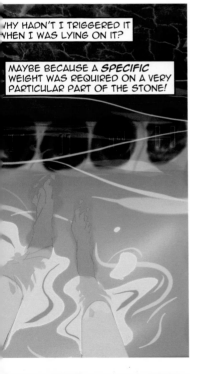

WHY HADN'T I TRIGGERED IT WHEN I WAS LYING ON IT?

MAYBE BECAUSE A *SPECIFIC* WEIGHT WAS REQUIRED ON A VERY PARTICULAR PART OF THE STONE!

A BIT OF A HUNCH. BUT, I'D SOLVED CASES ON *WEAKER* HUNCHES THAN THIS.

QUICKLY, TOVIK! HELP ME CLEAN THE STONE!

NO PROBLEM!

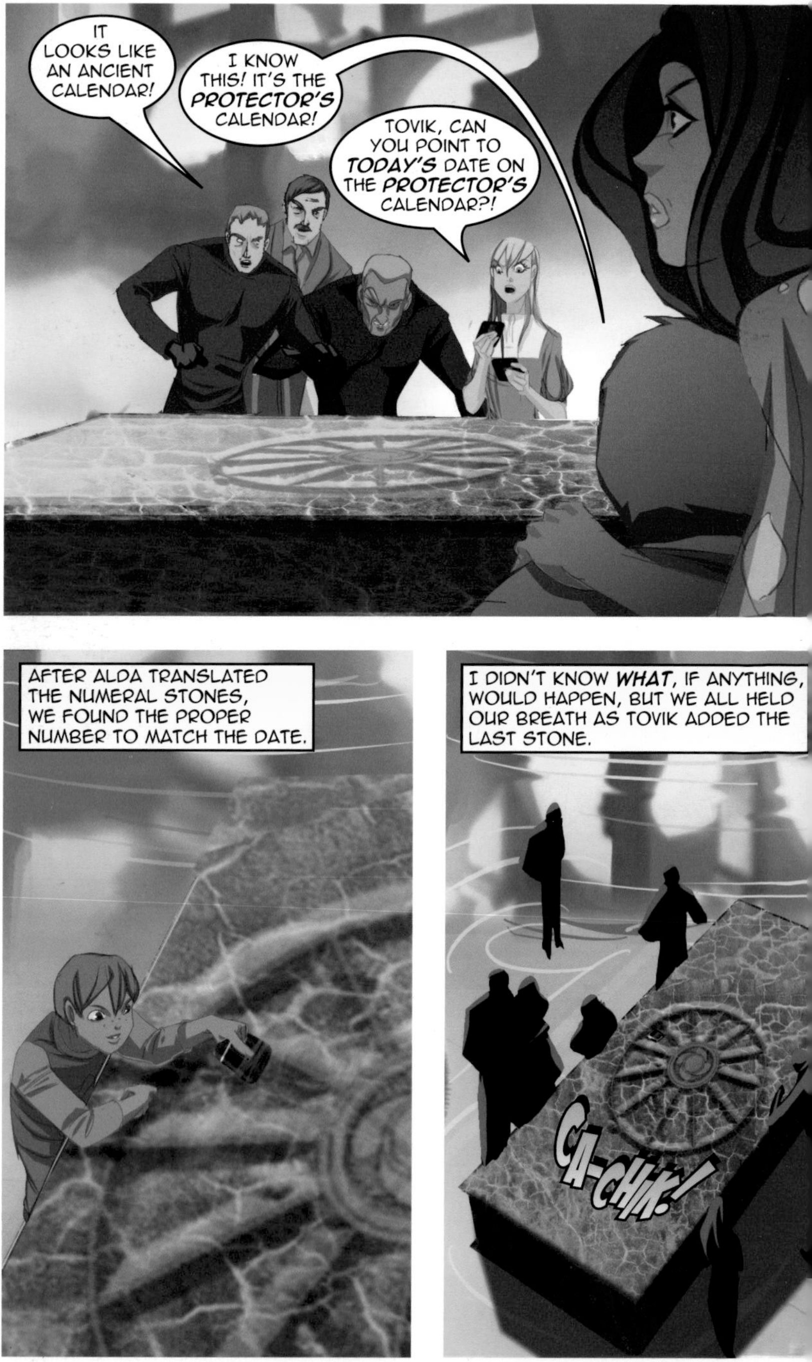
IT LOOKS LIKE AN ANCIENT CALENDAR!
I KNOW THIS! IT'S THE *PROTECTOR'S* CALENDAR!
TOVIK, CAN YOU POINT TO *TODAY'S* DATE ON THE *PROTECTOR'S* CALENDAR?!
AFTER ALDA TRANSLATED THE NUMERAL STONES, WE FOUND THE PROPER NUMBER TO MATCH THE DATE.
I DIDN'T KNOW *WHAT*, IF ANYTHING, WOULD HAPPEN, BUT WE ALL HELD OUR BREATH AS TOVIK ADDED THE LAST STONE.
CA-CHIK!

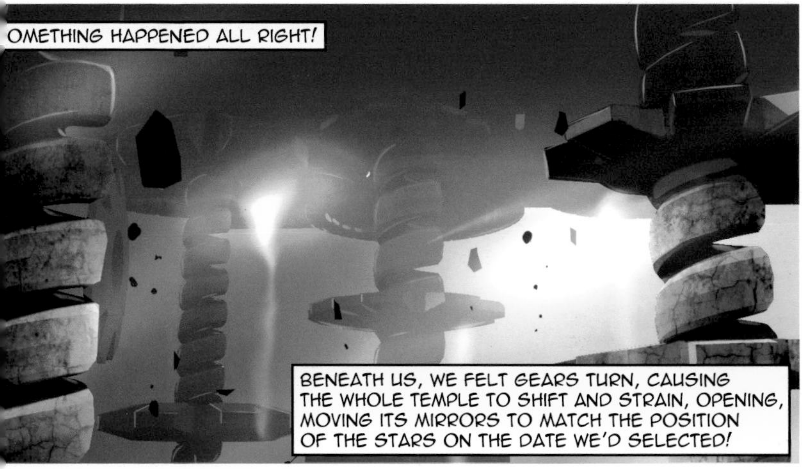
OMETHING HAPPENED ALL RIGHT!
BENEATH US, WE FELT GEARS TURN, CAUSING THE WHOLE TEMPLE TO SHIFT AND STRAIN, OPENING, MOVING ITS MIRRORS TO MATCH THE POSITION OF THE STARS ON THE DATE WE'D SELECTED!

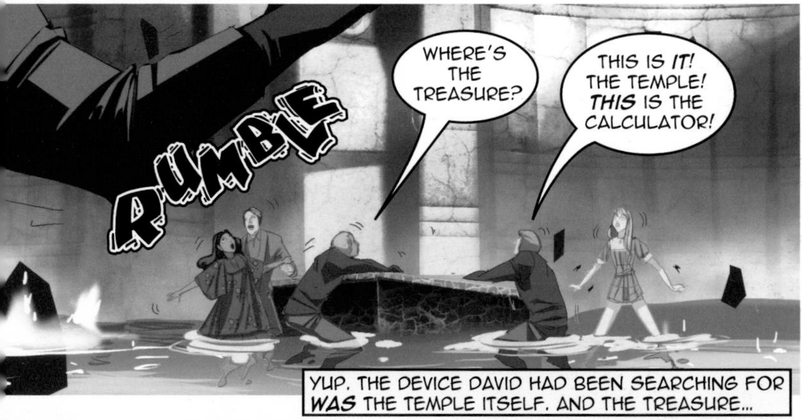
RUMBLE
WHERE'S THE TREASURE?
THIS IS *IT!* THE TEMPLE! ***THIS*** IS THE CALCULATOR!
YUP. THE DEVICE DAVID HAD BEEN SEARCHING FOR ***WAS*** THE TEMPLE ITSELF. AND THE TREASURE...

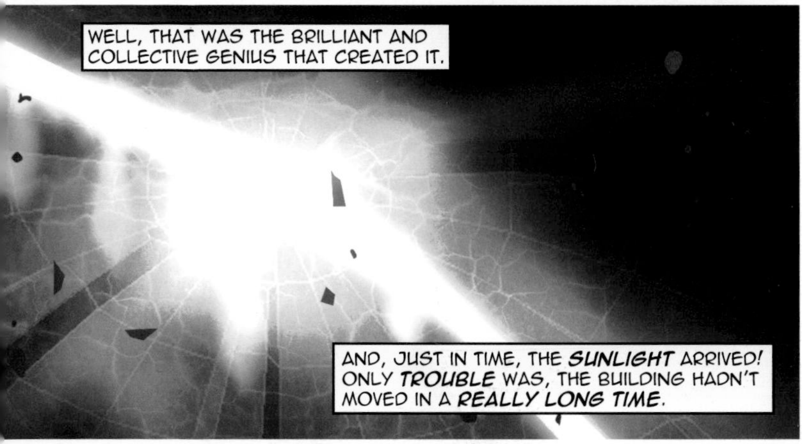
WELL, THAT WAS THE BRILLIANT AND COLLECTIVE GENIUS THAT CREATED IT.
AND, JUST IN TIME, THE ***SUNLIGHT*** ARRIVED! ONLY ***TROUBLE*** WAS, THE BUILDING HADN'T MOVED IN A ***REALLY LONG TIME***.

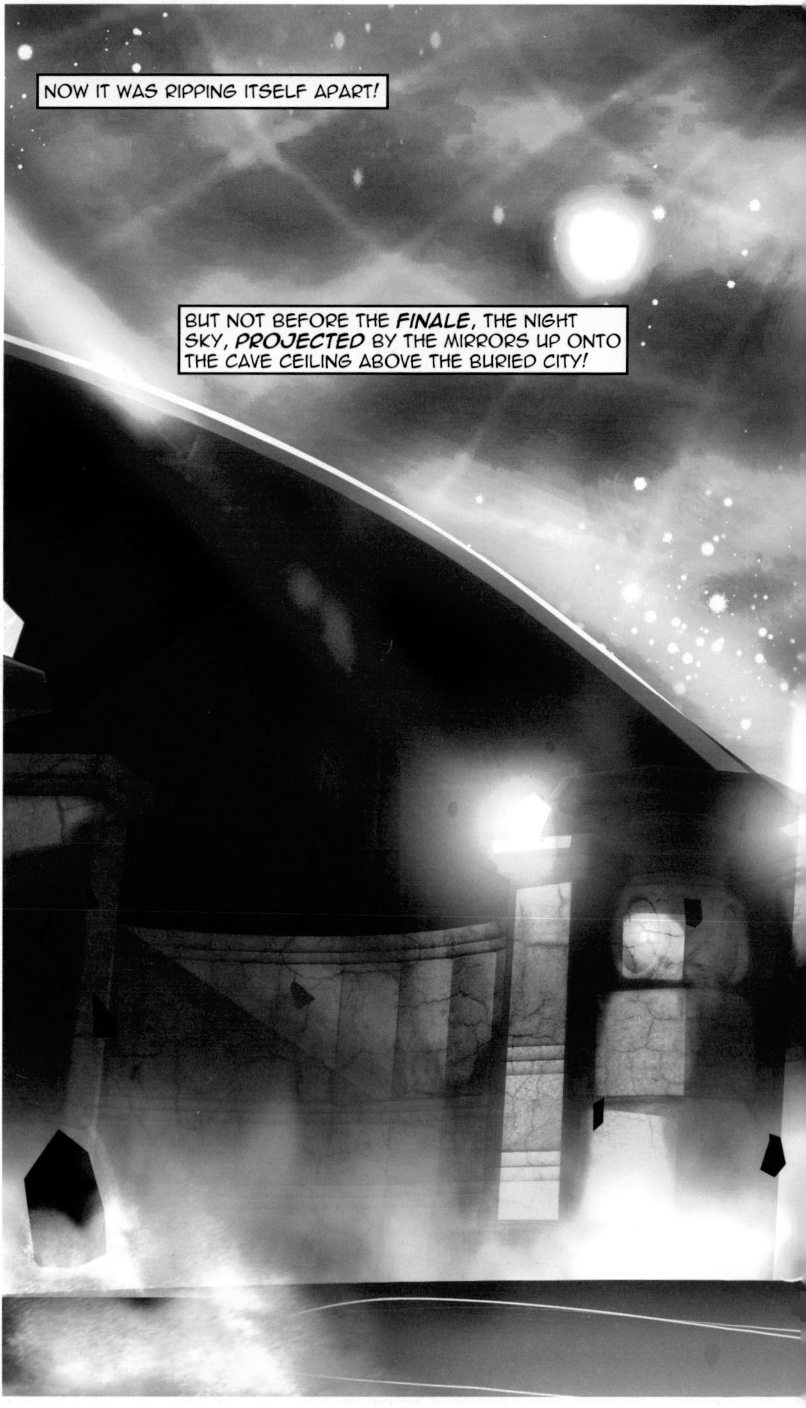
NOW IT WAS RIPPING ITSELF APART!
BUT NOT BEFORE THE *FINALE*, THE NIGHT SKY, *PROJECTED* BY THE MIRRORS UP ONTO THE CAVE CEILING ABOVE THE BURIED CITY!

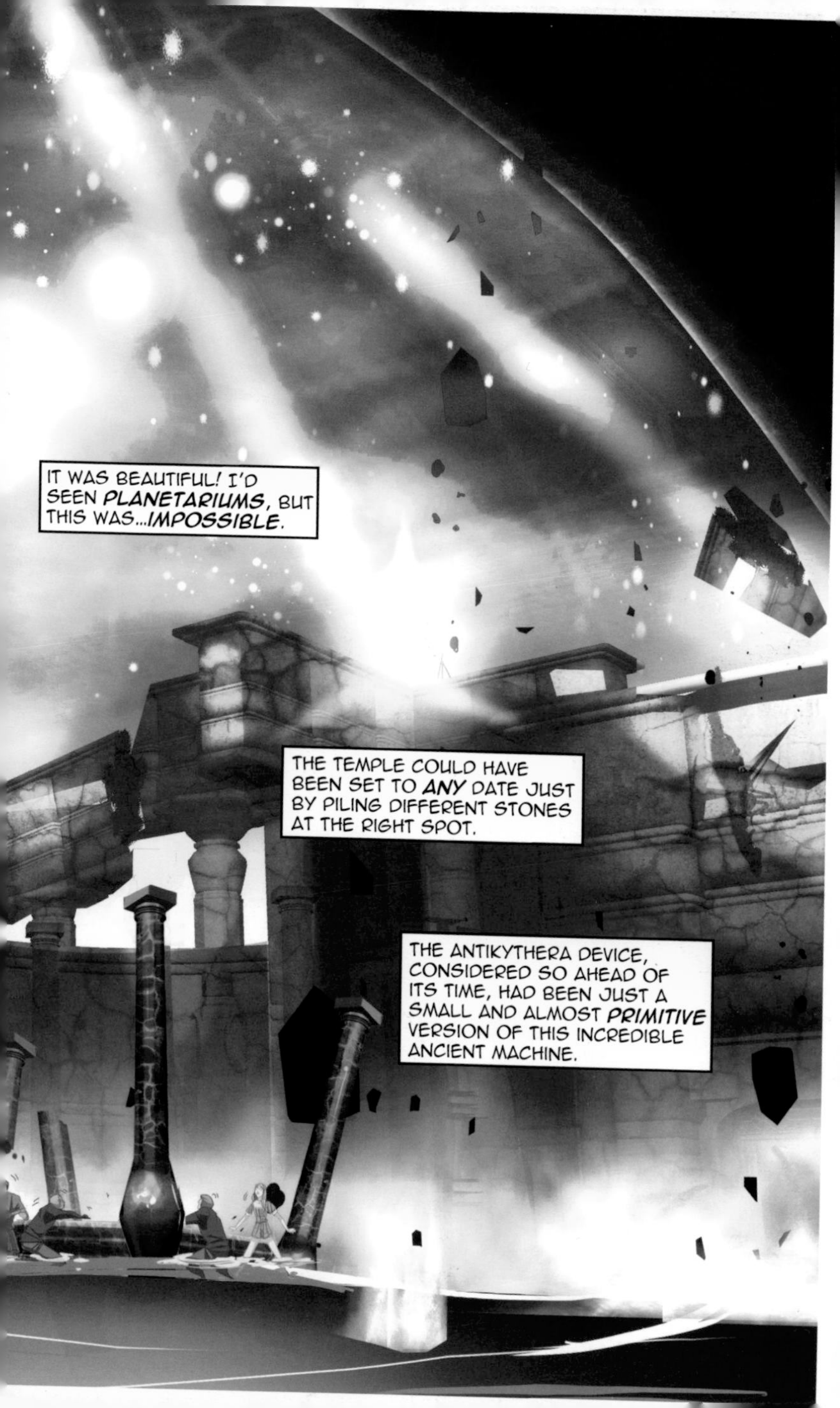
IT WAS BEAUTIFUL! I'D SEEN PLANETARIUMS, BUT THIS WAS...IMPOSSIBLE.
THE TEMPLE COULD HAVE BEEN SET TO ANY DATE JUST BY PILING DIFFERENT STONES AT THE RIGHT SPOT.
THE ANTIKYTHERA DEVICE, CONSIDERED SO AHEAD OF ITS TIME, HAD BEEN JUST A SMALL AND ALMOST PRIMITIVE VERSION OF THIS INCREDIBLE ANCIENT MACHINE.

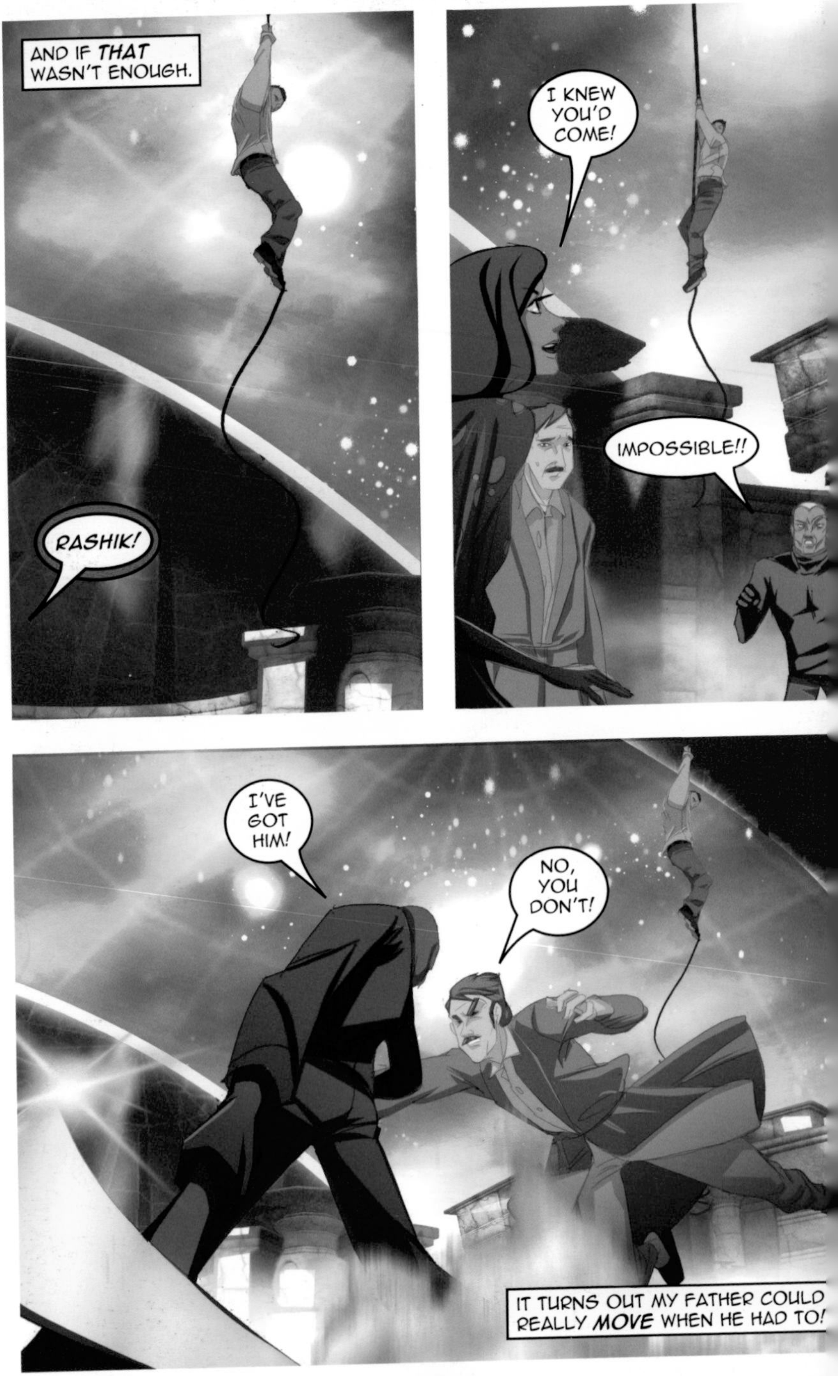
AND IF THAT WASN'T ENOUGH.
RASHIK!
I KNEW YOU'D COME!
IMPOSSIBLE!!
I'VE GOT HIM!
NO, YOU DON'T!
IT TURNS OUT MY FATHER COULD REALLY MOVE WHEN HE HAD TO!

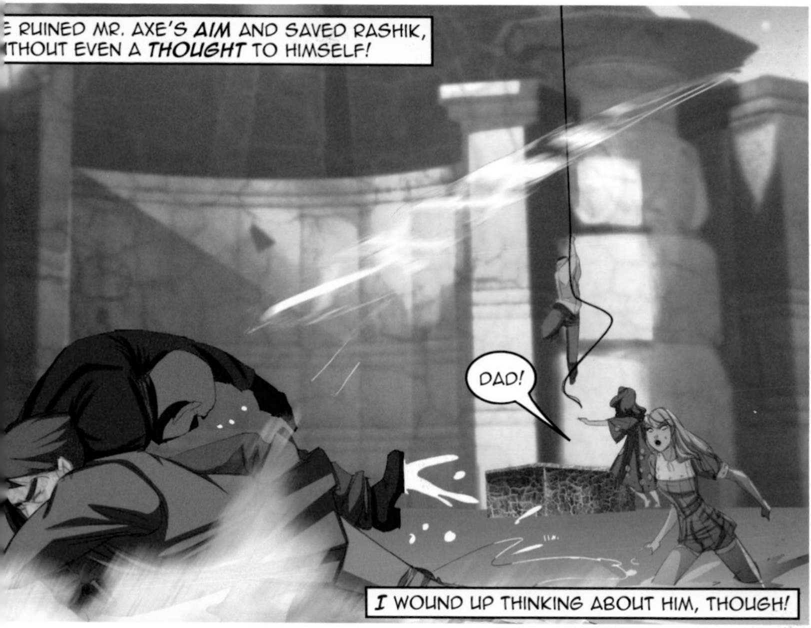
E RUINED MR. AXE'S AIM AND SAVED RASHIK,
ITHOUT EVEN A THOUGHT TO HIMSELF!
DAD!
I WOUND UP THINKING ABOUT HIM, THOUGH!

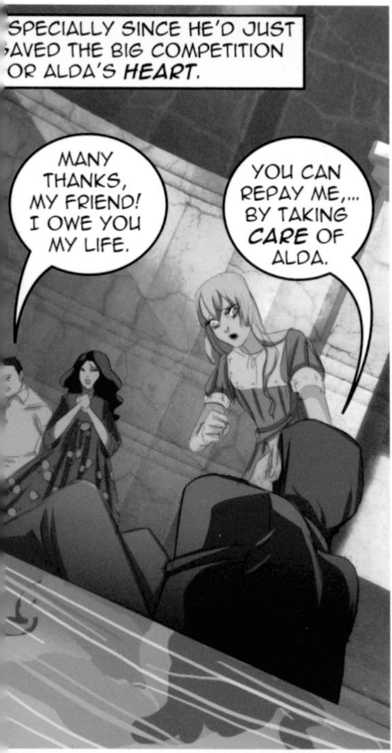
SPECIALLY SINCE HE'D JUST
AVED THE BIG COMPETITION
OR ALDA'S HEART.
MANY THANKS, MY FRIEND! I OWE YOU MY LIFE.
YOU CAN REPAY ME,... BY TAKING CARE OF ALDA.

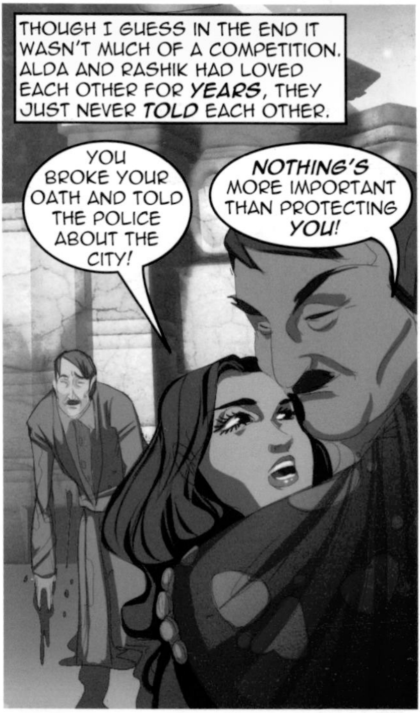
THOUGH I GUESS IN THE END IT WASN'T MUCH OF A COMPETITION. ALDA AND RASHIK HAD LOVED EACH OTHER FOR YEARS, THEY JUST NEVER TOLD EACH OTHER.
YOU BROKE YOUR OATH AND TOLD THE POLICE ABOUT THE CITY!
NOTHING'S MORE IMPORTANT THAN PROTECTING YOU!

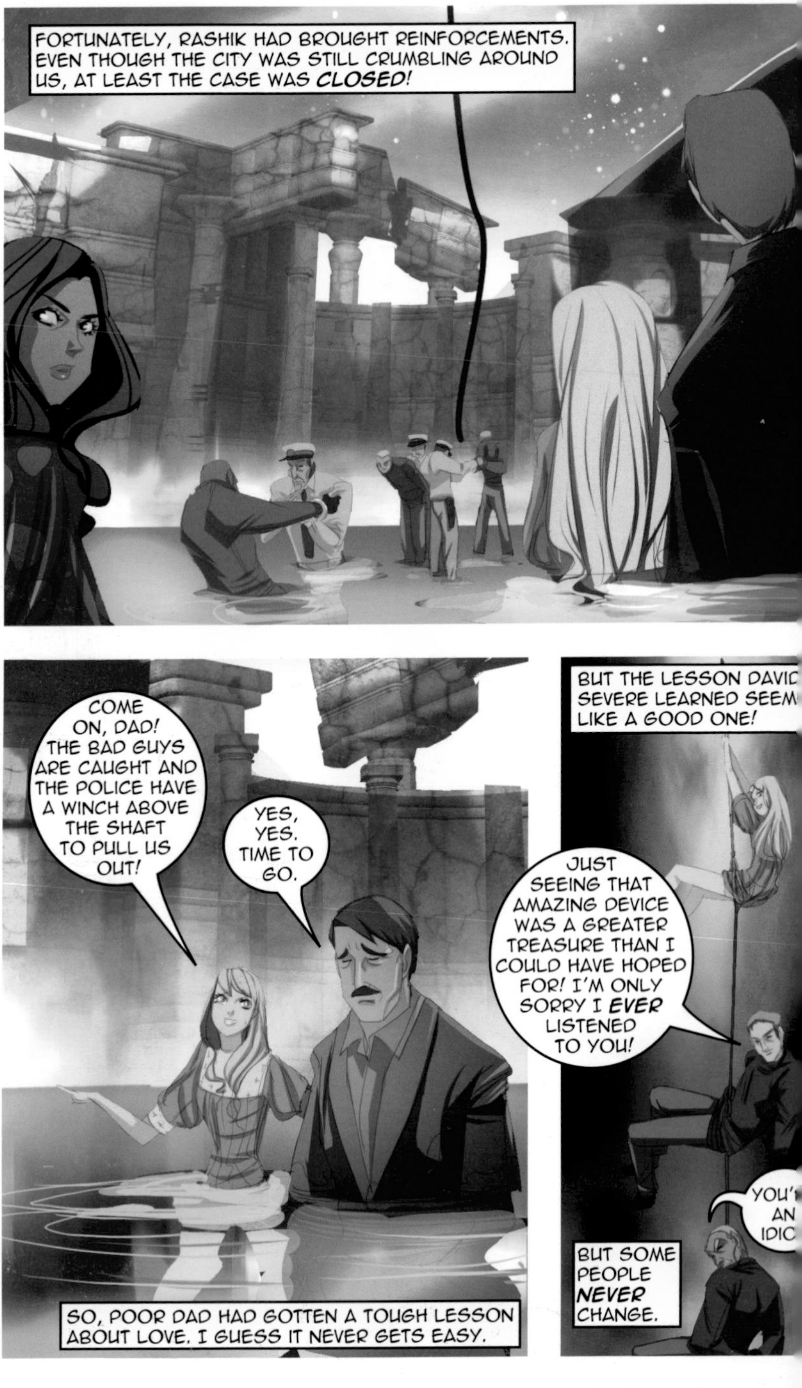

FORTUNATELY, RASHIK HAD BROUGHT REINFORCEMENTS. EVEN THOUGH THE CITY WAS STILL CRUMBLING AROUND US, AT LEAST THE CASE WAS ***CLOSED***!
COME ON, DAD! THE BAD GUYS ARE CAUGHT AND THE POLICE HAVE A WINCH ABOVE THE SHAFT TO PULL US OUT!
YES, YES. TIME TO GO.
SO, POOR DAD HAD GOTTEN A TOUGH LESSON ABOUT LOVE. I GUESS IT NEVER GETS EASY.
BUT THE LESSON DAVI SEVERE LEARNED SEEM LIKE A GOOD ONE!
JUST SEEING THAT AMAZING DEVICE WAS A GREATER TREASURE THAN I COULD HAVE HOPED FOR! I'M ONLY SORRY I ***EVER*** LISTENED TO YOU!
YOU' AN IDI
BUT SOME PEOPLE ***NEVER*** CHANGE.

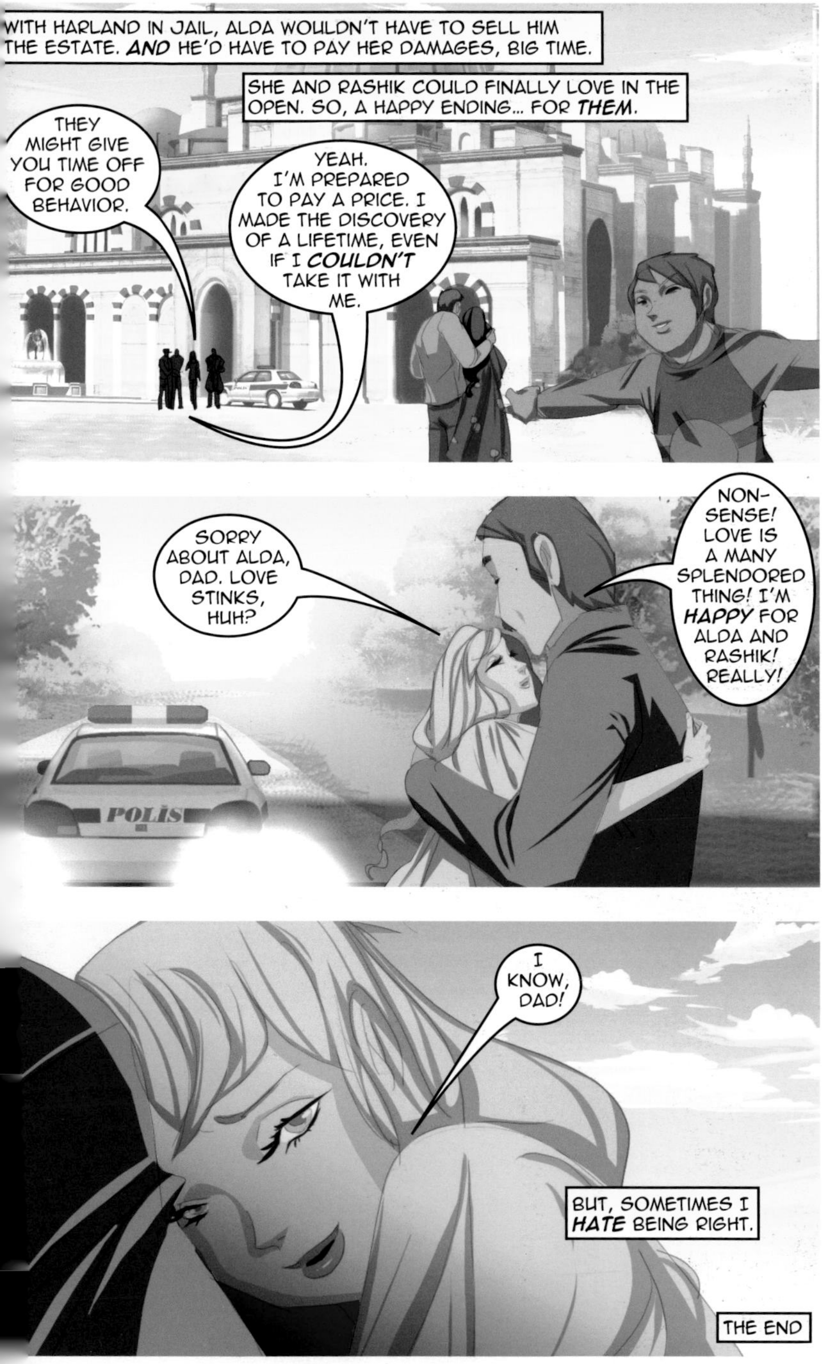
WITH HARLAND IN JAIL, ALDA WOULDN'T HAVE TO SELL HIM THE ESTATE. AND HE'D HAVE TO PAY HER DAMAGES, BIG TIME.
SHE AND RASHIK COULD FINALLY LOVE IN THE OPEN. SO, A HAPPY ENDING... FOR THEM.
THEY MIGHT GIVE YOU TIME OFF FOR GOOD BEHAVIOR.
YEAH. I'M PREPARED TO PAY A PRICE. I MADE THE DISCOVERY OF A LIFETIME, EVEN IF I COULDN'T TAKE IT WITH ME.
SORRY ABOUT ALDA, DAD. LOVE STINKS, HUH?
NON-SENSE! LOVE IS A MANY SPLENDORED THING! I'M HAPPY FOR ALDA AND RASHIK! REALLY!
POLIS
I KNOW, DAD!
BUT, SOMETIMES I HATE BEING RIGHT.
THE END

SPECIAL PREVIEW OF NANCY DREW GRAPHIC NOVEL #19 – "CLIFFHANGER"

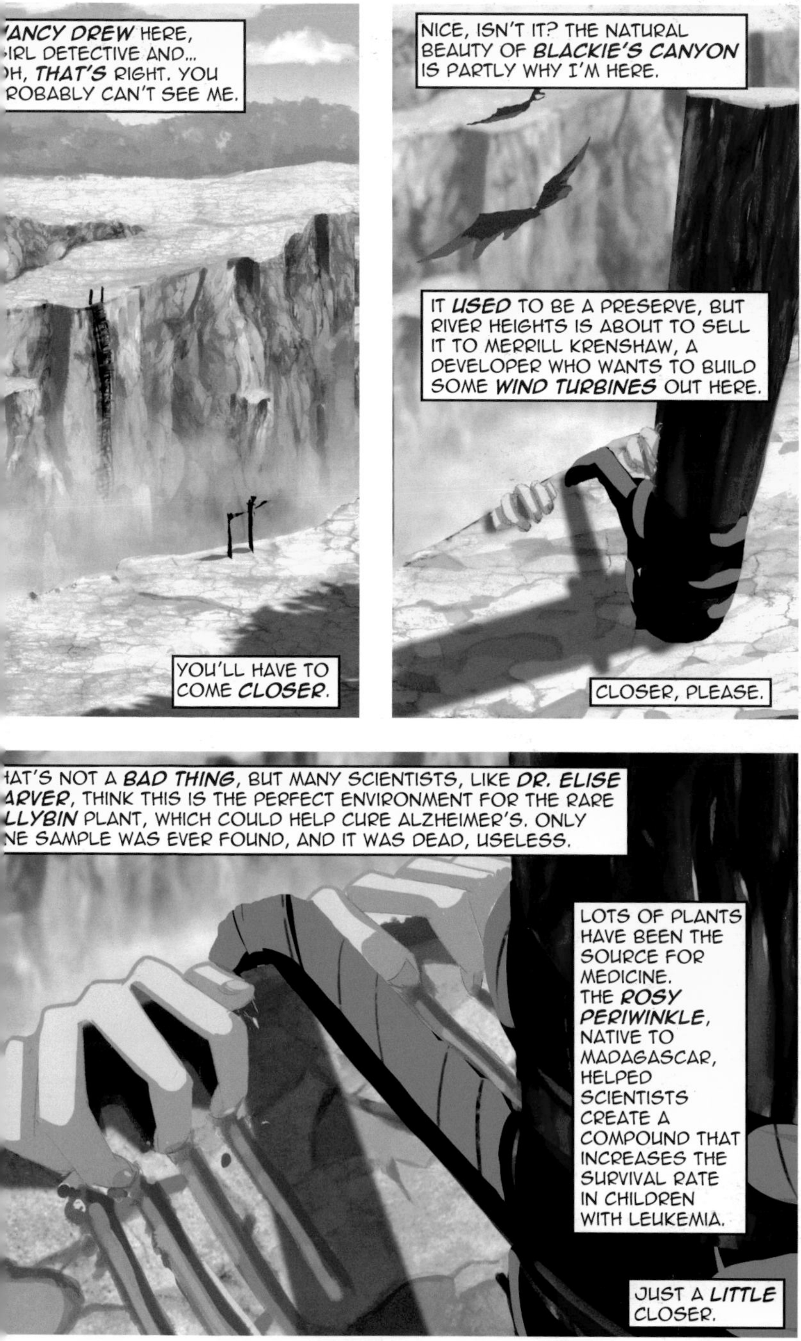
ANCY DREW HERE,
IRL DETECTIVE AND...
H, THAT'S RIGHT. YOU
ROBABLY CAN'T SEE ME.
YOU'LL HAVE TO COME CLOSER.
NICE, ISN'T IT? THE NATURAL BEAUTY OF BLACKIE'S CANYON IS PARTLY WHY I'M HERE.
IT USED TO BE A PRESERVE, BUT RIVER HEIGHTS IS ABOUT TO SELL IT TO MERRILL KRENSHAW, A DEVELOPER WHO WANTS TO BUILD SOME WIND TURBINES OUT HERE.
CLOSER, PLEASE.
HAT'S NOT A BAD THING, BUT MANY SCIENTISTS, LIKE DR. ELISE
ARVER, THINK THIS IS THE PERFECT ENVIRONMENT FOR THE RARE
LLYBIN PLANT, WHICH COULD HELP CURE ALZHEIMER'S. ONLY
NE SAMPLE WAS EVER FOUND, AND IT WAS DEAD, USELESS.
LOTS OF PLANTS HAVE BEEN THE SOURCE FOR MEDICINE. THE ROSY PERIWINKLE, NATIVE TO MADAGASCAR, HELPED SCIENTISTS CREATE A COMPOUND THAT INCREASES THE SURVIVAL RATE IN CHILDREN WITH LEUKEMIA.
JUST A LITTLE CLOSER.

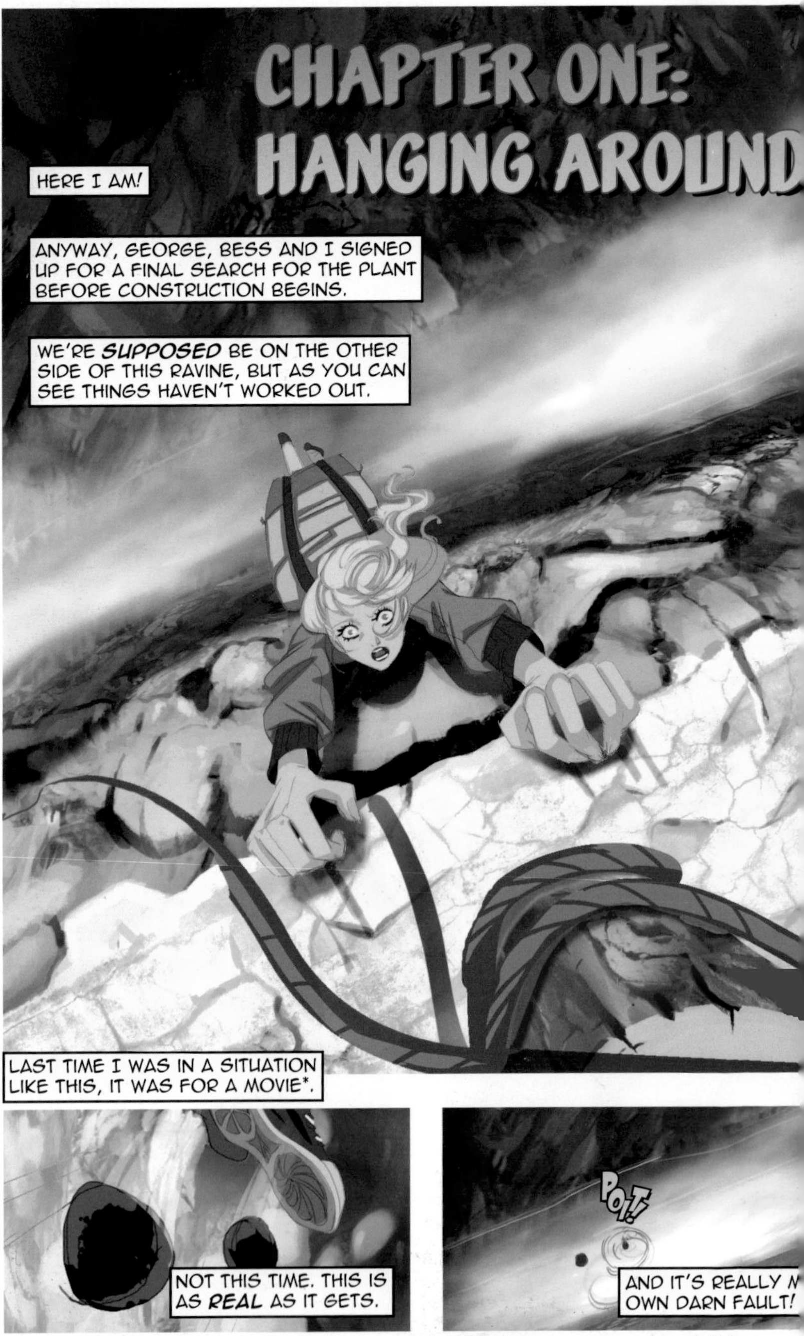
CHAPTER ONE: HANGING AROUND
HERE I AM!
ANYWAY, GEORGE, BESS AND I SIGNED UP FOR A FINAL SEARCH FOR THE PLANT BEFORE CONSTRUCTION BEGINS.
WE'RE *SUPPOSED* BE ON THE OTHER SIDE OF THIS RAVINE, BUT AS YOU CAN SEE THINGS HAVEN'T WORKED OUT.
LAST TIME I WAS IN A SITUATION LIKE THIS, IT WAS FOR A MOVIE*.
NOT THIS TIME. THIS IS AS *REAL* AS IT GETS.
POT!
AND IT'S REALLY M
OWN DARN FAULT!

** See NANCY DREW Graphic Novel #1 "The Demon of River Heights" or go to www.papercutz.com/nd/fn3*

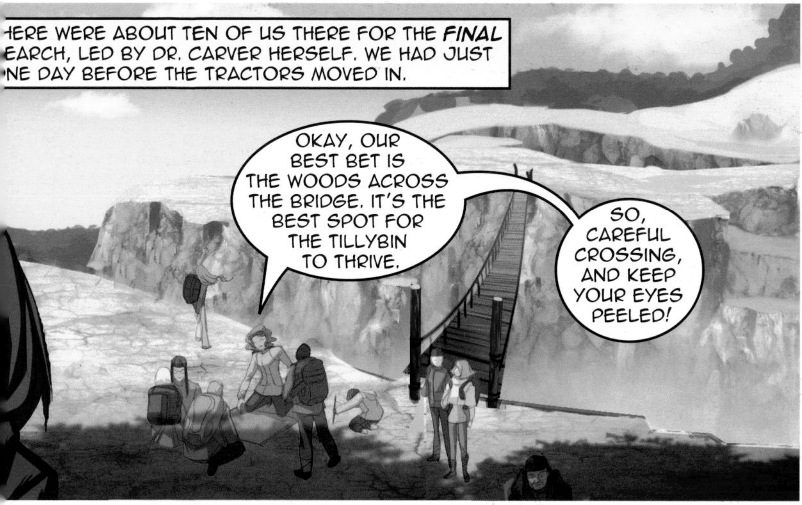
HERE WERE ABOUT TEN OF US THERE FOR THE *FINAL* EARCH, LED BY DR. CARVER HERSELF. WE HAD JUST NE DAY BEFORE THE TRACTORS MOVED IN.
OKAY, OUR BEST BET IS THE WOODS ACROSS THE BRIDGE. IT'S THE BEST SPOT FOR THE TILLYBIN TO THRIVE.
SO, CAREFUL CROSSING, AND KEEP YOUR EYES PEELED!

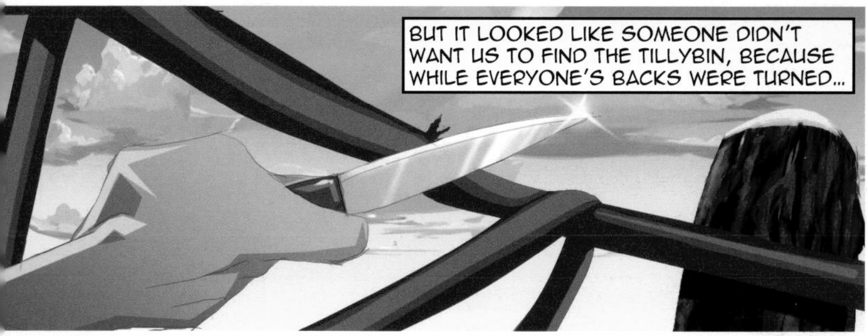
BUT IT LOOKED LIKE SOMEONE DIDN'T WANT US TO FIND THE TILLYBIN, BECAUSE WHILE EVERYONE'S BACKS WERE TURNED...

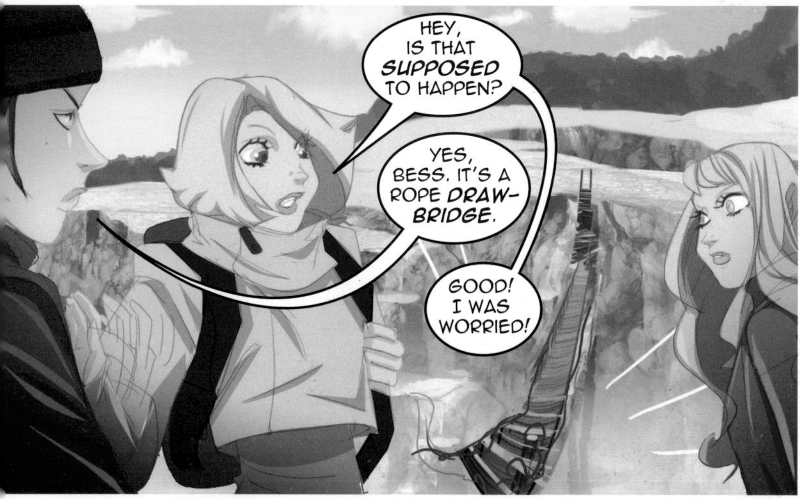
HEY, IS THAT *SUPPOSED* TO HAPPEN?
YES, BESS. IT'S A ROPE *DRAW-BRIDGE*.
GOOD! I WAS WORRIED!

WE CAN'T DEAL WITH THIS NOW, WE'RE ALREADY SHORT ON TIME!

WE'LL HAVE TO WALK DOWN, CROSS THE RIVER, THEN CLIMB BACK UP! COME ON!

YOU ALL GO AHEAD. I'LL CATCH UP IN A SECOND! I *KNOW* WHO DID THIS, AND I THINK I CAN *PROVE* IT!

THAT'S OUR GIRL DETECTIVE! I'LL CALL CHIEF McGINNIS!

I HAD TO DO SOMETHING *QUICK*. IF THEY TRIED TO SLOW US DOWN ONCE, NO REASON THEY WOULDN'T DO IT AGAIN!

HONESTLY, THOUGH, I HAD NO IDEA *WHO* WAS GUILTY, BUT IT HAD TO BE ONE OF US, AND I FIGURED IF THE CREEP *THOUGHT* I KNEW WHO THEY WERE, THEY'D DO SOMETHING TO GIVE THEMSELVES AWAY!

ME AND MY BIG IDEAS.

AND *THAT'S* HO I GOT TO WHER I AM RIGHT NOW

DON'T MISS NANCY DREW GRAPHIC NOVEL #19 – "CLIFFHANGER"

THE HARDY BOYS

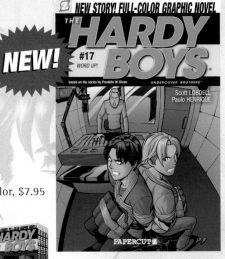

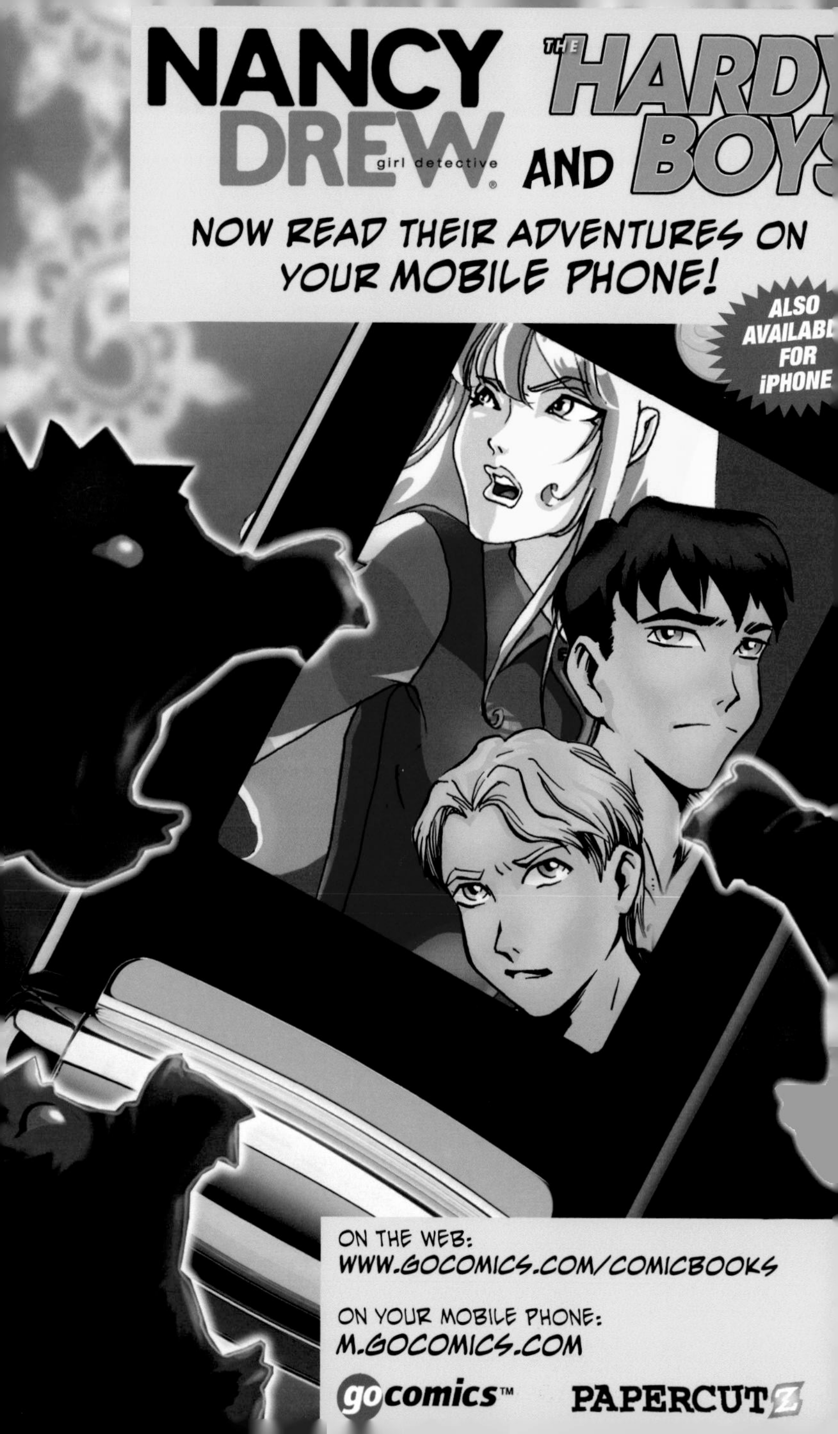
NANCY DREW girl detective®
AND
THE HARDY BOYS
NOW READ THEIR ADVENTURES ON YOUR MOBILE PHONE!
ALSO AVAILABLE FOR iPHONE
ON THE WEB:
WWW.GOCOMICS.COM/COMICBOOKS
ON YOUR MOBILE PHONE:
M.GOCOMICS.COM
gocomics™
PAPERCUTZ

WATCH OUT FOR PAPERCUTZ™

Welcome to the Backpages of NANCY DREW Graphic Novel #17 "City Under the Basement." I'm Jim Salicrup, Boy Editor (-in-Chief) of Papercutz, the publisher of all sorts of cool graphic novels. In these Backpages, we tell you all the exciting things going on at Papercutz, and there's so much to report, we better get right to it before we run out of room!

First, as you noticed, this volume of NANCY DREW is the second and concluding part of "The Secret Within." Back in NANCY DREW Graphic Novels #9 –11 we ran the three-part "The High Miles Mystery." What do you think about continued stories in the Papercutz NANCY DREW graphic novels? Love it? Hate it? Do you want each graphic novel to have one complete story? Do you want more continued stories? Or do you want a mix, like we're doing now? Please let us know!

Second, the best way to let us know what you think is to post a message on our blog at www.papercutz.com! Not only do NANCY DREW writers Stefan Petrucha and Sarah Kinney blog, we hope Sho Murase will be blogging there soon too!

Third, starting with #19 "Cliffhanger" our NANCY DREW Graphic Novels will have a bold, new look! Just as the Simon & Schuster ND novels have switched to a new logo, we'll be switching to the new bigger logo too! The covers may look different, but never fear -- the insides will still have the comics by Stefan Petrucha, Sarah Kinney, and Sho Murase that we all love so much!

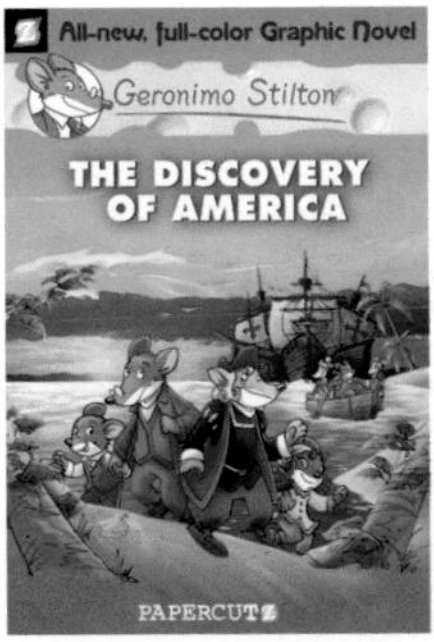

All-new, full-color Graphic Novel
Geronimo Stilton
THE DISCOVERY OF AMERICA
PAPERCUTZ

Fourth, the April 3rd, 2009 issue of ENTERTAINMENT WEEKLY named Nancy Drew as one of their Top 20 Heroes! Nancy Drew came in at #17, beating out Batman, who had to settle for being #18! How cool is that? We already know how cool Nancy is -- it's nice to see EW recognize it too!

Fifth, we wanted to share some BIG NEWS with you! GERONIMO STILTON will be starring in an all-new series of big full-color graphic novels from Papercutz. The first two are coming your way in August – GERONIMO STILTON Graphic Novel #1 "The Discovery of America" and GERONIMO STILTON Graphic Novel #2 "The Secret of the Sphinx" – but we've got a special preview of GERONIMO STILTON Graphic Novel #1 "The Discovery of America" on the following pages!

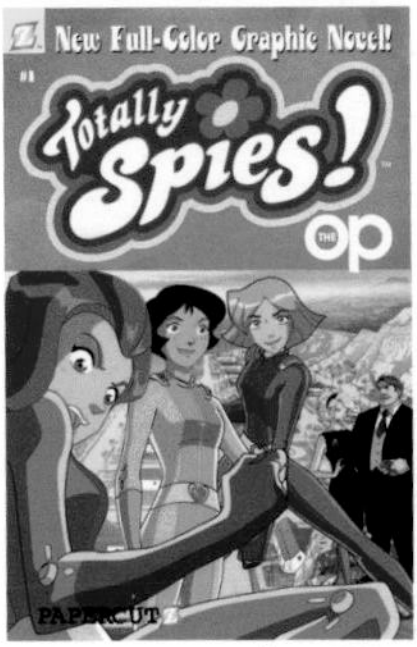

New Full-Color Graphic Novel!
Totally Spies!
OP
PAPERCUTZ

Sixth, we also thought you'd might like a peek at TOTALLY SPIES! Graphic Novel #1 "The OP." If you haven't already picked up the four, fabulous full-color TOTALLY SPIES! Graphic Novels, they're all available right now at booksellers everywhere!

Finally, thanks for picking up this Papercutz graphic novel. We greatly appreciate your support. Talk to you on the Papercutz blog!

Thanks,
Jim

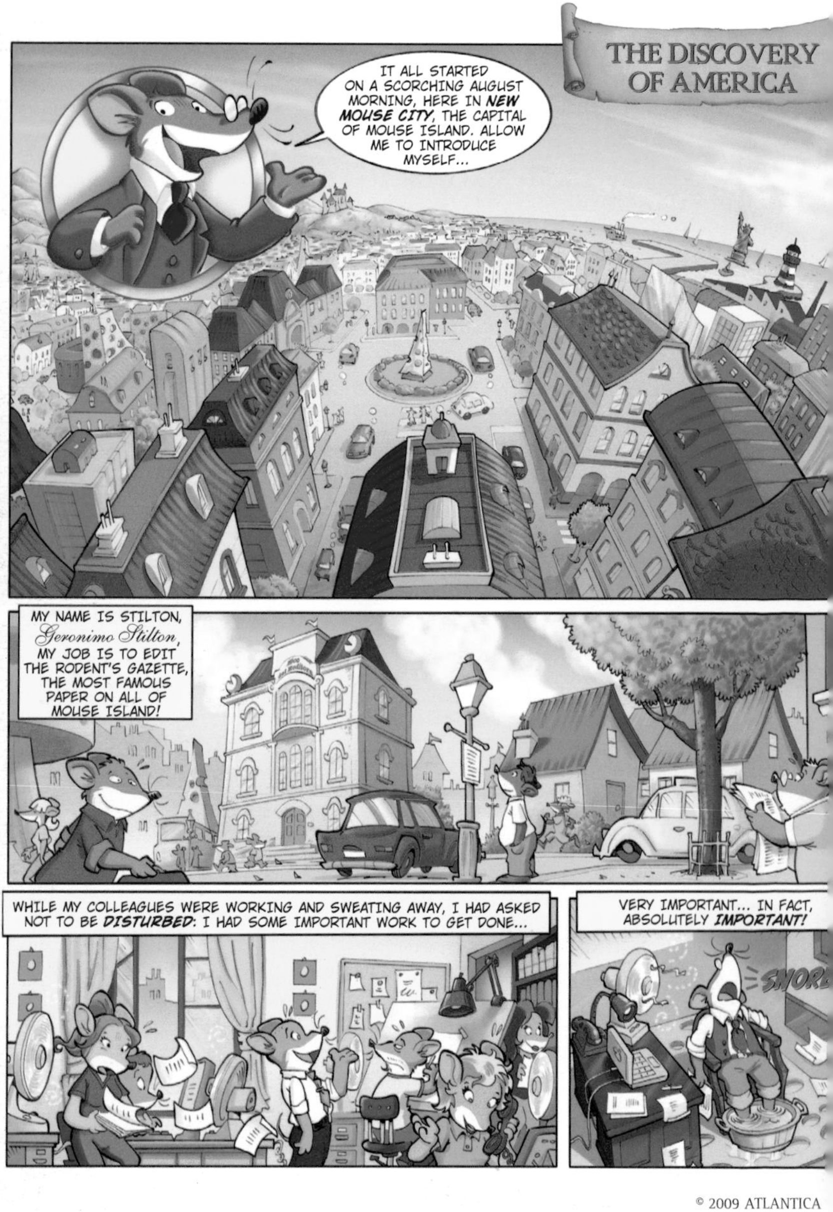
THE DISCOVERY OF AMERICA
IT ALL STARTED ON A SCORCHING AUGUST MORNING, HERE IN NEW MOUSE CITY, THE CAPITAL OF MOUSE ISLAND. ALLOW ME TO INTRODUCE MYSELF...
MY NAME IS STILTON, Geronimo Stilton, MY JOB IS TO EDIT THE RODENT'S GAZETTE, THE MOST FAMOUS PAPER ON ALL OF MOUSE ISLAND!
WHILE MY COLLEAGUES WERE WORKING AND SWEATING AWAY, I HAD ASKED NOT TO BE DISTURBED: I HAD SOME IMPORTANT WORK TO GET DONE...
VERY IMPORTANT... IN FACT, ABSOLUTELY IMPORTANT!

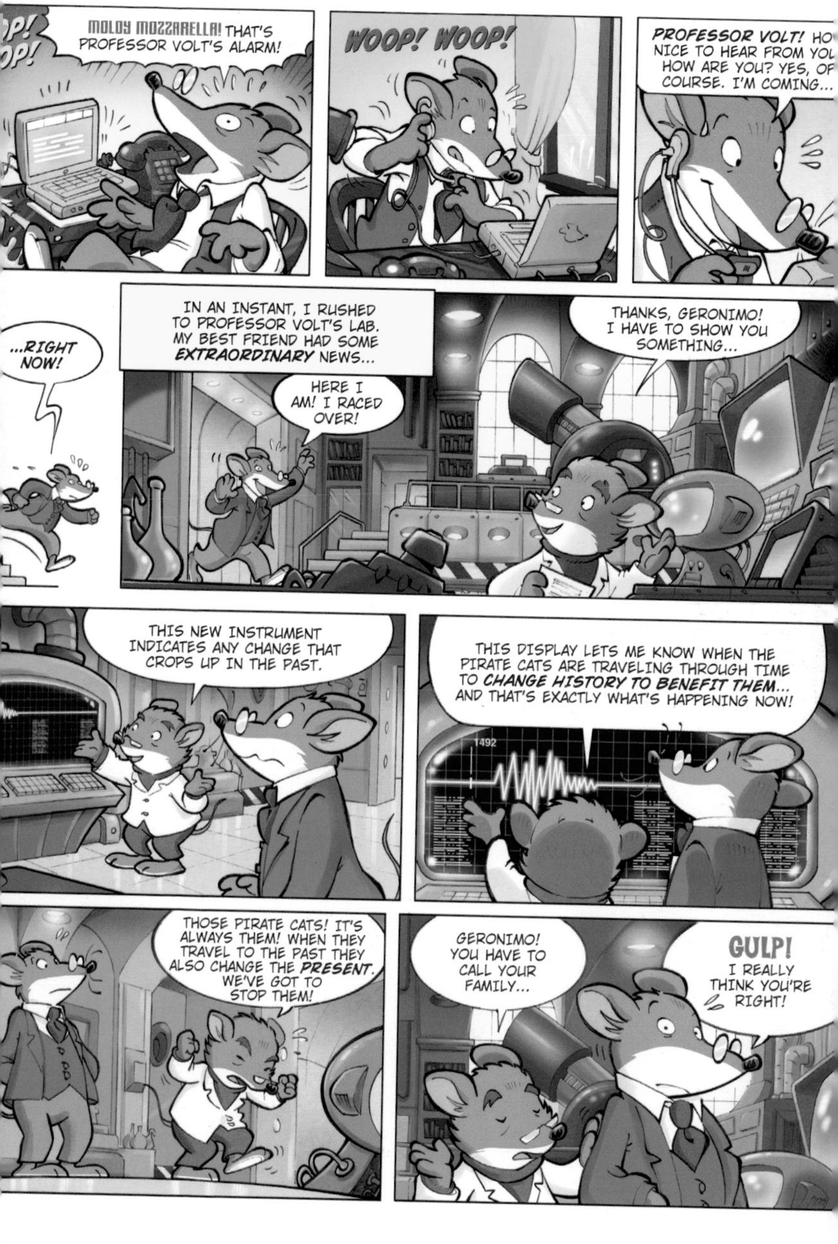

MOLDY MOZZARELLA! THAT'S PROFESSOR VOLT'S ALARM!
WOOP! WOOP!
PROFESSOR VOLT! HO
NICE TO HEAR FROM YO
HOW ARE YOU? YES, OF
COURSE. I'M COMING...
...RIGHT NOW!
IN AN INSTANT, I RUSHED TO PROFESSOR VOLT'S LAB. MY BEST FRIEND HAD SOME EXTRAORDINARY NEWS...
HERE I AM! I RACED OVER!
THANKS, GERONIMO! I HAVE TO SHOW YOU SOMETHING...
THIS NEW INSTRUMENT INDICATES ANY CHANGE THAT CROPS UP IN THE PAST.
THIS DISPLAY LETS ME KNOW WHEN THE PIRATE CATS ARE TRAVELING THROUGH TIME TO CHANGE HISTORY TO BENEFIT THEM... AND THAT'S EXACTLY WHAT'S HAPPENING NOW!
1492
THOSE PIRATE CATS! IT'S ALWAYS THEM! WHEN THEY TRAVEL TO THE PAST THEY ALSO CHANGE THE PRESENT. WE'VE GOT TO STOP THEM!
GERONIMO! YOU HAVE TO CALL YOUR FAMILY...
GULP! I REALLY THINK YOU'RE RIGHT!

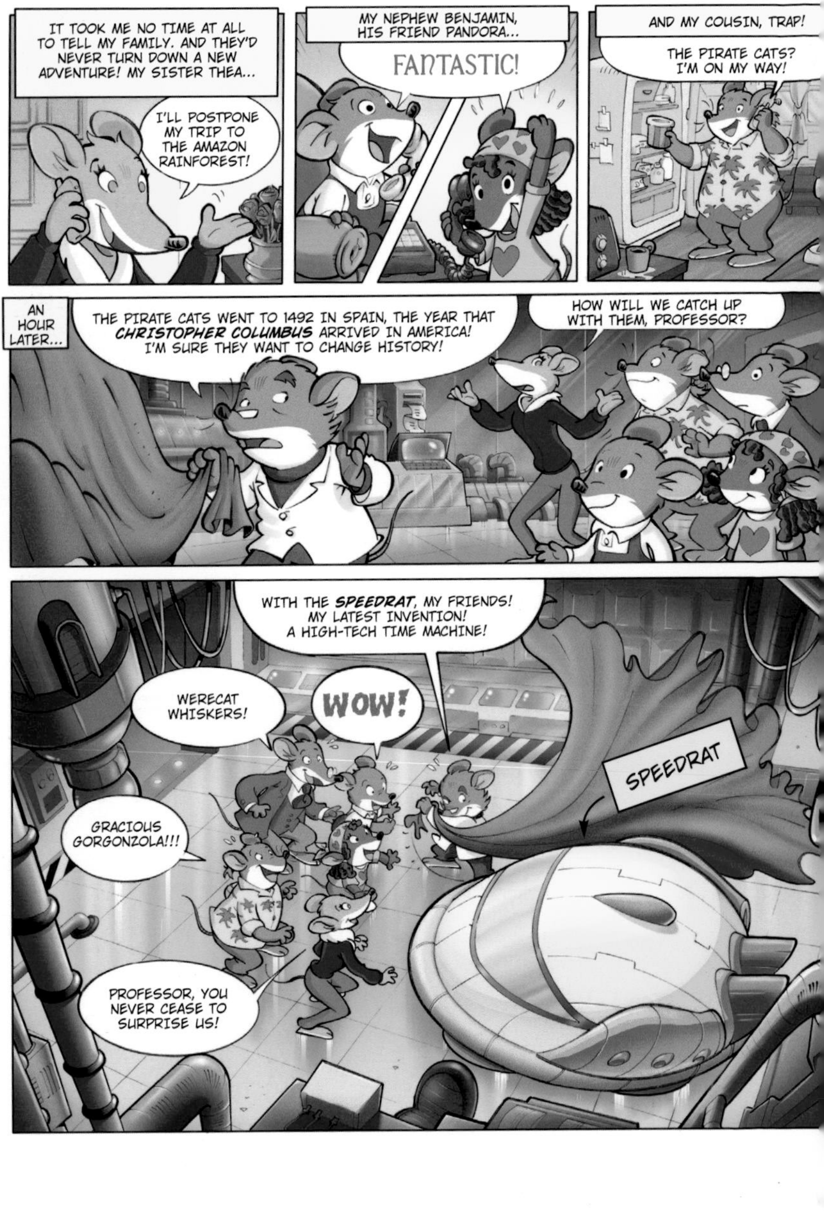
IT TOOK ME NO TIME AT ALL TO TELL MY FAMILY. AND THEY'D NEVER TURN DOWN A NEW ADVENTURE! MY SISTER THEA...
I'LL POSTPONE MY TRIP TO THE AMAZON RAINFOREST!
MY NEPHEW BENJAMIN, HIS FRIEND PANDORA...
FANTASTIC!
AND MY COUSIN, TRAP!
THE PIRATE CATS? I'M ON MY WAY!
AN HOUR LATER...
THE PIRATE CATS WENT TO 1492 IN SPAIN, THE YEAR THAT CHRISTOPHER COLUMBUS ARRIVED IN AMERICA! I'M SURE THEY WANT TO CHANGE HISTORY!
HOW WILL WE CATCH UP WITH THEM, PROFESSOR?
WITH THE SPEEDRAT, MY FRIENDS! MY LATEST INVENTION! A HIGH-TECH TIME MACHINE!
WERECAT WHISKERS!
WOW!
SPEEDRAT
GRACIOUS GORGONZOLA!!!
PROFESSOR, YOU NEVER CEASE TO SURPRISE US!

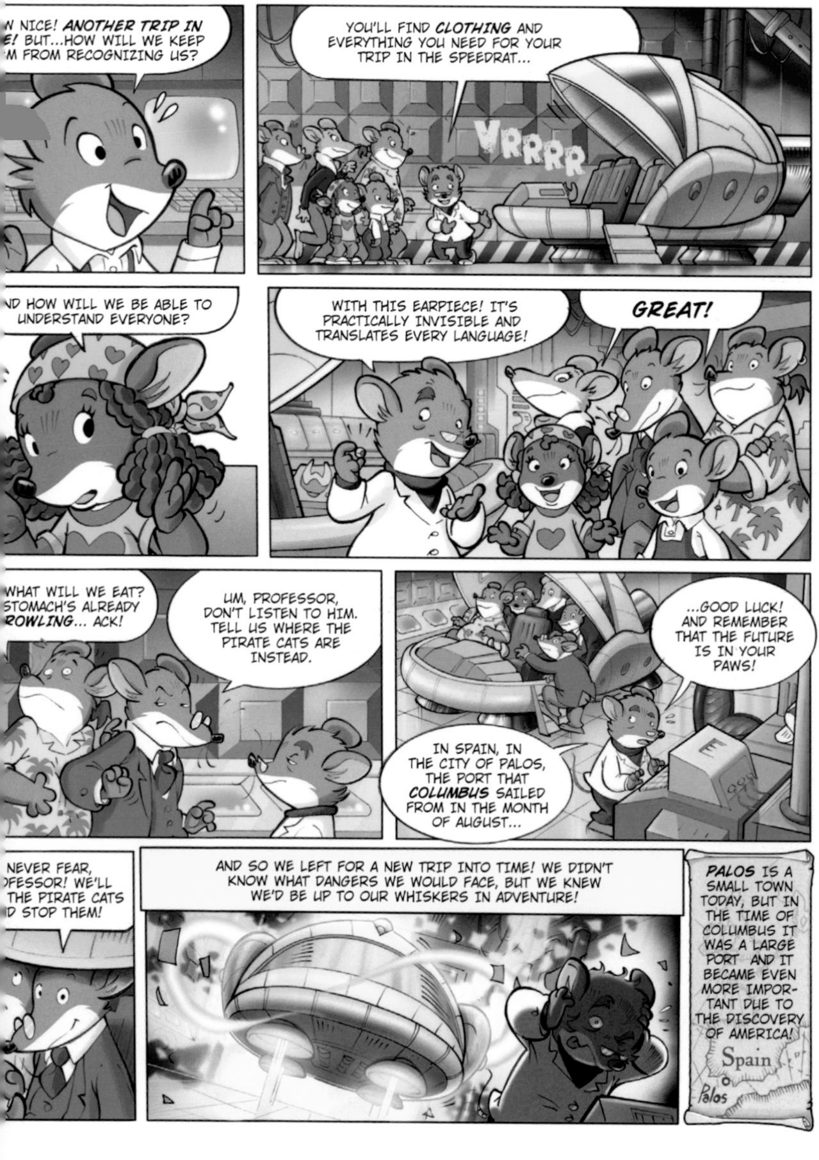
N NICE! ANOTHER TRIP IN E! BUT...HOW WILL WE KEEP M FROM RECOGNIZING US?
YOU'LL FIND CLOTHING AND EVERYTHING YOU NEED FOR YOUR TRIP IN THE SPEEDRAT...
VRRRR
D HOW WILL WE BE ABLE TO UNDERSTAND EVERYONE?
WITH THIS EARPIECE! IT'S PRACTICALLY INVISIBLE AND TRANSLATES EVERY LANGUAGE!
GREAT!
WHAT WILL WE EAT? STOMACH'S ALREADY ROWLING... ACK!
UM, PROFESSOR, DON'T LISTEN TO HIM. TELL US WHERE THE PIRATE CATS ARE INSTEAD.
IN SPAIN, IN THE CITY OF PALOS, THE PORT THAT COLUMBUS SAILED FROM IN THE MONTH OF AUGUST...
...GOOD LUCK! AND REMEMBER THAT THE FUTURE IS IN YOUR PAWS!
NEVER FEAR, FESSOR! WE'LL THE PIRATE CATS D STOP THEM!
AND SO WE LEFT FOR A NEW TRIP INTO TIME! WE DIDN'T KNOW WHAT DANGERS WE WOULD FACE, BUT WE KNEW WE'D BE UP TO OUR WHISKERS IN ADVENTURE!
PALOS IS A SMALL TOWN TODAY, BUT IN THE TIME OF COLUMBUS IT WAS A LARGE PORT AND IT BECAME EVEN MORE IMPORTANT DUE TO THE DISCOVERY OF AMERICA!
Spain
Palos

'T MISS GERONIMO STILTON GRAPHIC NOVEL #1 "THE DISCOVERY OF AMERICA" COMING IN AUGUST '09!

CAROLYN KEENE

NANCY DREW

GIRL DETECTIVE®

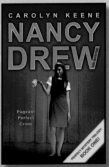

Pageant Perfect Crime

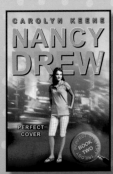

Perfect Cover

Perfect Escape

Secret Identity

Identity Theft

Identity Revealed

INVESTIGATE THESE TWO THRILLING MYSTERY TRILOGIES

SPECIAL PEEK AT TOTALLY SPIES! GRAPHIC NOVEL #1 "THE OP"

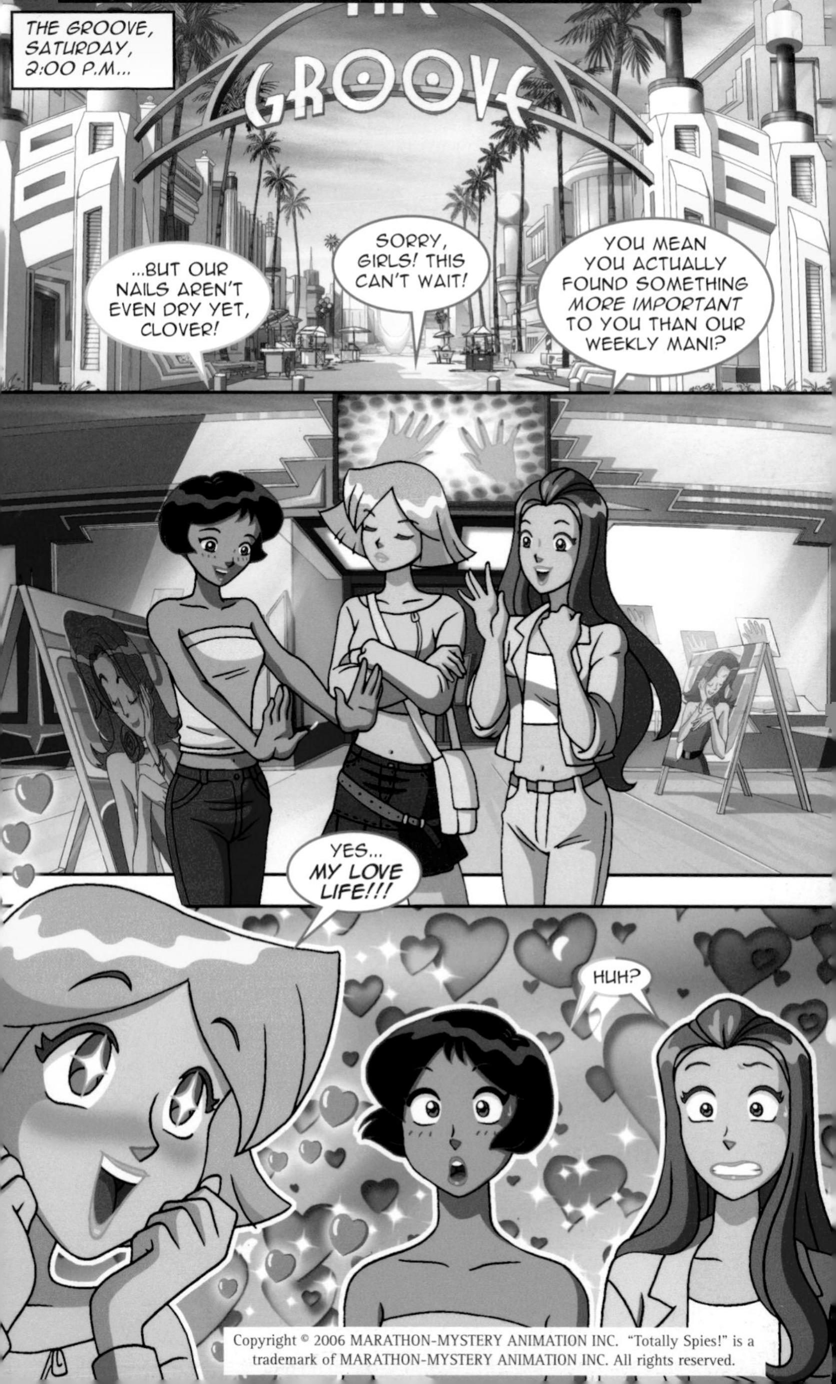
THE GROOVE, SATURDAY, 2:00 P.M...
GROOVE
...BUT OUR NAILS AREN'T EVEN DRY YET, CLOVER!
SORRY, GIRLS! THIS CAN'T WAIT!
YOU MEAN YOU ACTUALLY FOUND SOMETHING *MORE IMPORTANT* TO YOU THAN OUR WEEKLY MANI?
YES... *MY LOVE LIFE!!!*
HUH?

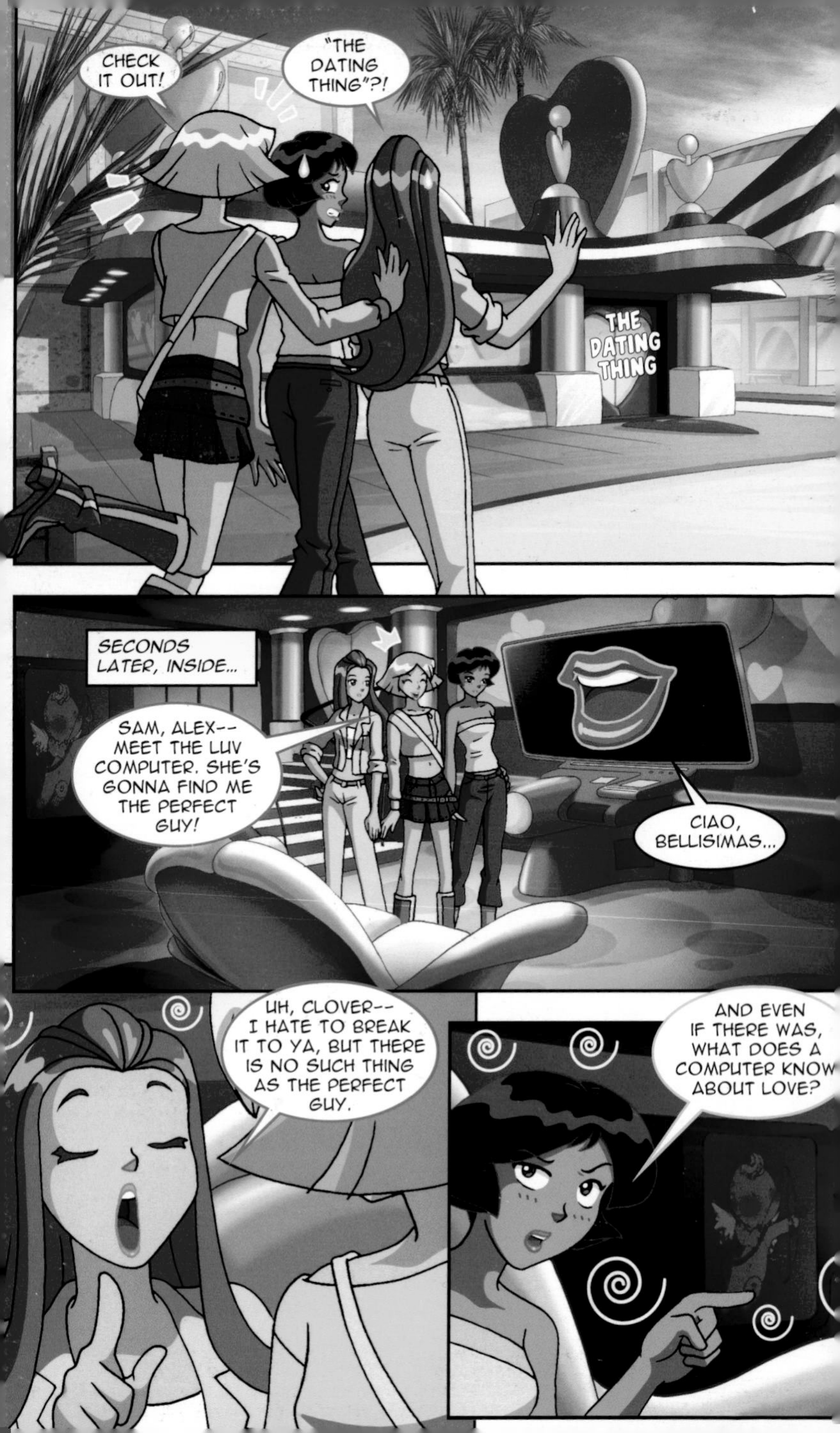
CHECK IT OUT!
"THE DATING THING"?!
THE DATING THING
SECONDS LATER, INSIDE...
SAM, ALEX-- MEET THE LUV COMPUTER. SHE'S GONNA FIND ME THE PERFECT GUY!
CIAO, BELLISIMAS...
UH, CLOVER-- I HATE TO BREAK IT TO YA, BUT THERE IS NO SUCH THING AS THE PERFECT GUY.
AND EVEN IF THERE WAS, WHAT DOES A COMPUTER KNOW ABOUT LOVE?

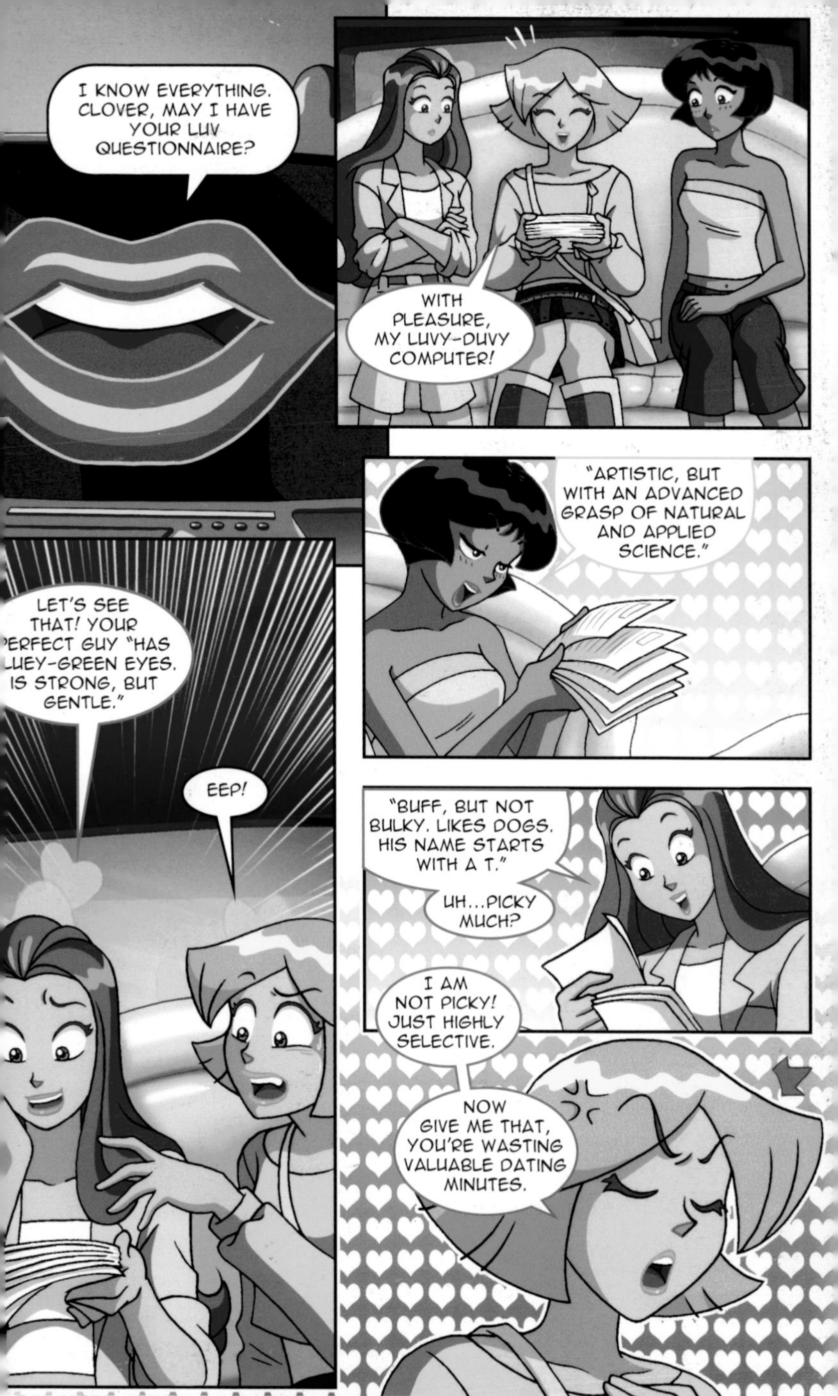
I KNOW EVERYTHING. CLOVER, MAY I HAVE YOUR LUV QUESTIONNAIRE?
WITH PLEASURE, MY LUVY-DUVY COMPUTER!
LET'S SEE THAT! YOUR ERFECT GUY "HAS LUEY-GREEN EYES. IS STRONG, BUT GENTLE."
EEP!
"ARTISTIC, BUT WITH AN ADVANCED GRASP OF NATURAL AND APPLIED SCIENCE."
"BUFF, BUT NOT BULKY. LIKES DOGS. HIS NAME STARTS WITH A T."
UH…PICKY MUCH?
I AM NOT PICKY! JUST HIGHLY SELECTIVE.
NOW GIVE ME THAT, YOU'RE WASTING VALUABLE DATING MINUTES.